slide

Also by Gerald A. Browne

Hazard
11 Harrowhouse
It's All Zoo

slide

Gerald A. Browne

ARBOR HOUSE
New York

Library of Congress Catalogue Card Number: 75–40510

ISBN: 0–87795–099–7

Manufactured in the United States of America

To Dr. Ruth Ochroch,
Dr. Marvin Belsky
and my dear daughter Cindy

slide

Forecast

He had a blue sweatband around his right wrist.

As though that would do any good.

The grip of his racquet was slimy, the way leather gets when wet. No matter how tightly he gripped, the racquet gave, turned some each time it met the ball. He couldn't get off a good, solid slam. It infuriated him, added to the feelings that had brought him there.

Man of forty-one with a thirty-two-inch waist. Wearing white sharkskin tennis shorts and a white cotton knit shirt, his lucky favorite. Thirty-five-dollar Tretorn shoes, the best, the kind that cushioned the arch, softly snugged the heel and made his reflexes feel improved. The shoes would be ruined after this; they'd probably dry stiff.

His shirt and shorts were so wet the outline of his jock strap showed, and his nipples. The hair on his head was thick black, dripping. Half of it was a weave job. Every once in a while he snapped his head to shake off the water, as animals do. The water was in his eyes, making them bloodshot. He clenched his eyes and tried to blink away the sting.

And there was the way he had to breathe. He could gasp with his mouth hardly open or breathe entirely through his nose, which was inadequate. If he panted normally with his mouth open, water got into his windpipe. That happened several times, causing him to double over and become red in the face with coughing.

Still, he did not quit, hadn't yet gotten enough of it out of him.

He hit a forehand, one of his strongest of the day. Some spin on it. The ball struck the dark green just above the horizontal white painted line that signified the height of an actual net. The ball ricocheted fast off to his left, his backhand. Leaping for it, he sacrificed form, made a wild stab and missed. It bounced by and across the slick blacktop, splashed through a couple of depressed patches where water had gathered and came to an abrupt stop. On a regular, fair day a new ball such as that would have easily gone all the way to and off the mesh fence.

The man swore aloud and went over to get another new ball. That morning he'd bought ten containers of the best Wilsons. By now he had used eighteen balls, nearly two-thirds his supply. He found that a fresh ball was good for about twenty hits, sometimes as few as ten. On its bounces and in flight a ball became soaked, got heavier and heavier, requiring that he put more and more muscle behind each stroke. Too soon a ball became impossible, like hitting an overripe orange.

Now, almost ritualistically, he snapped open the top of a container and peeled it. The dry hiss he heard was incongruous. He paused a moment to consider where he was.

4

In back of Beverly Hills High on a part of the school's wide, paved recreation area. Alone there.

And why.

Because he hadn't played in two weeks, not a swing. Two whole weeks of smashing was backed up inside him. Well, at least some of the wet on him now was his sweat.

He shielded the container with his body while he took out a new, dry ball. He put the container down among the others, covered it, and was again ready to serve to himself, as though this were any regular, nice day at the bangboard.

Also then, out in the Valley in the house the divorce had awarded her, was the woman who hoped she wouldn't overload again. What puzzled her was why it happened some times and not others, under the very same conditions, when she had everything going. Anyway, today she was prepared with eight extra fuses.

The room had been a marvelous idea, she thought. An example of how creatively her mind worked. No matter that she'd spent ten times more than she should have. It was a hell of a lot better than fading.

God, how fast a tan faded unless you kept at it.

After only four days of this bad spell she had stood before her full-length mirror and believed she'd already lost a lot of color, was several degrees closer to pasty. Before long she'd look sick.

She cringed at the thought, visualized herself — and fuck you very much you two-faced piece of reflecting glass — a thirty-four, really thirty-eight, -year-old woman, two-time loser, the white of dough, veins showing. Not very Acapulco or Palm Springs. Not a chance.

Maybe this bad spell wouldn't last much longer. She could always fake it for a while with makeup. She recalled those times she'd tried that tan-without-sun crap. She'd turned out looking more jaundiced than ideal bronze as advertised. Besides, anyone worth anything, people who counted, knew their tans. They could tell a phony at first sight.

What to do?

What to do came to her after one and a half sleepless nights.

The room, including floor and ceiling, was covered with mirrorlike silver Con-Tact paper. The windows were also covered over. Unless you'd known the room before you wouldn't know windows were there. To do the entire job had required fifteen rolls of Con-Tact. Regular kitchen foil would have been cheaper but more difficult to work with. Attached close up to the ceiling at a point where it could be aimed down at a typical angle was a two-thousand watt reflector floodlight. On the floor in opposite corners were a pair of General Electric portable heaters, the kind with built-in fans. Overhead, fixed to the middle of the ceiling was a sunlamp. The largest, most powerful ultraviolet sunlamp made for home use. Identical lamps were situated midway up each wall, so altogether there were five of those.

Centered on the floor was a plump, full-length lounging cushion of yellow sailcloth. Spread on that was an oversize blue towel with not a wrinkle, waiting. Electric cords dangled down, joining extensions that snaked around to consolidate into a single control switch located within reach of the cushion.

Now the woman was just outside the room. The door was closed. She snapped a switch that turned on the floodlamp in there, and the heater fans and a stereo tape that played surf and other seaside sounds.

She was nude. Except for a pair of purple wedgie espadrilles. A woven straw bag held things she might normally carry, including a recent issue of *Town & Country* intention-

6

ally folded cover out. She was ready, but she allowed a warm-up period, proving her patience by using the time to polish her dark glasses, the ones with special protective lenses. She didn't put them on.

She went in. She lay on the cushion, went down upon it with a self-conscious grace, as though she were being observed. She got settled, took two deep breaths and thought how nice and bright and warm it was. If she opened her eyes she'd be looking right up at the sun. Her eyelids were a blood-red background for the aerobatics of tiny squiggles.

It was hot.

There was a breeze, but not enough to prevent her perspiring.

Such a lovely day for the beach. Glad she'd come. She lay absolutely still, baking, browning in God's great oven.

Within a half hour she could hardly get her breath. A familiar penalty. She sat up and removed a vitamin-E lotion from her bag. She applied it to her skin, concentrating, doing it leisurely with a gentle self-respect. Until she had touched and covered every part of her. She lay back again and put on the sunglasses.

Her right hand moved, slowly. She hardly realized it was moving. It reached the switch. She hoped she didn't fumble. Once she had fumbled and it had taken almost an hour for her imagination to recover. This time couldn't have been better. Her contact with the switch was brief as possible, while the rest of her senses refused to acknowledge it at all—the hard, intrusive reality of it.

What did give her a problem, however, was the ultraviolet. Its odor. Such an exceptional smell that nothing she conjured up could appropriately excuse it. She was most successful when she dabbed Arpege below her nostrils and told herself that that, combined with the rather unpleasant, sterile vaporous quality of ultraviolet, was the original odor of air, before contamination. Pure as could be, she was being blessed with it. But really getting used to it would take some time.

Four hundred twenty-one suicides since it began.

The tally was not made public, nor was the fact that four out of five of the suicides occurred in the southern part of the state—that is, from Bakersfield on down.

Four hundred twenty-one was nearly ten times the state average and, although an accurate count, it was considered incomplete. Many people in Southern California were old and living alone. No doubt a number of those had taken their lives but had not yet been discovered. Four hundred twenty-one figured out to about thirty a day. But that wasn't how it went. During the first few days there were fewer cases. Then each day brought an increase. The official projection for tomorrow was another one hundred ninety-five.

Five hundred ten murders to now.

Four hundred seventy took place in the Southern California area. Some were everyday murders with motives. More were incredibly senseless.

In San Bernardino a businessman on a morning bus used a ten-pound rock from his garden to crush in the head of the female stranger seated in front of him. In Anaheim a likeable young nurse hypodermically injected cyanide into a dozen Sunkist oranges. Holding open the bag of oranges for whomever she happened to meet, she said, "Help yourself."

There were eight cases of mutual murder—people shooting one another point blank simultaneously upon a predetermined signal. One such pact involved three finely strung young men who fired as point blank as possible, each taking the muzzle of another's revolver into his mouth.

8

Business was suffering.

Nonfilter cigarette sales increased sharply, however.

So did booze, especially cheap wine.

Home haircoloring was up.

Many reducing salons and body-building gyms as much as quadrupled enrollments.

Legal person-from-person separations were up.

Rape was down, having dropped after an initial flourish.

The crime rate in general was above average. One category had an increase even greater than murder. It was arson. The rate for arson was up to seventy-five a day. There were some major fires at industrial plants, warehouses and oil storage facilities, but most of the cases involved private homes and small-business buildings. Police and Fire Department investigators were puzzled because all the fires, even some of the larger ones, were so obviously arson, lacking the finesse or clever subterfuge of the professional or the mentally disturbed arsonist. It was often as primary as a match being put to a crumple of newspapers with a sprinkle of backyard barbecue starter to help it catch.

In most cases the firebugs were caught. Only a few had ever been previously booked for arson. When interrogated, many of the offenders were confused, disbelieving their own behavior. Psychiatric probing revealed no common pathology. Of course, the psychiatrists agreed: the acts of arson were protests, combustions of tantrums, similar to the resentment expressed when children play with fire on a confining rainy day.

This was the fourteenth day.

The satellite weather map — a sheet of acetate flapped over a dark silhouette of North America—presented its view of conditions. A barometric high-pressure system existed from the Aleutian Islands diagonally across a corner of

Oregon and over to the Rockies. Another similar high extended from the Gulf up through Texas and Arizona. The two highs met and mixed, creating what professional weather people called an occluded front. A jam-up. Occluded fronts were not so rare, actually. They could be expected to cause some precipitation.

However, this combined high-pressure front was different. It didn't seem to have any top to it. It went up into the atmosphere as far as Earth weather can. Warmer air, moving in from the Pacific, hit against this wall. The warm air rose, tried to climb over, couldn't, and retreated, overlapping itself like a massive ocean breaker. The low-pressure area that formed had nowhere to go. It appeared on the satellite map as an opaque, cloudlike mass particularly concentrated over Southern California.

Ordinarily, Los Angeles and thereabouts got more cloudy days and more rainfall during the spring months. Nearly every morning the sky was gray, thick with haze, appearing as though it would surely rain. Then the sun would burn it clear away by noon. When rain came, it came in comparatively brief, benevolent showers that distributed in all only about two inches over the season.

But not this year, this May.

The area was now receiving its fourteenth consecutive day of rain—over three hundred hours of continuous drizzle.

The municipal drainage systems were not built for so much water. Gutters overflowed. In places the pressure, choked in the underground drains, blew off heavy steel street covers as though they were corks. Brackish geysers spewed up a hundred feet. Numerous intersections were so flooded they had to be closed and traffic rerouted.

Such inconveniences were relatively well tolerated. More

so the first week. Men wearing chest-high waterproof fishing outfits carried women across deep streets.

Chivalrous antics.

A kiss or he'd drop her.

Their picture in the next day's newspaper.

Fat women rode piggyback. It seemed that everyone was walking around barefoot, shoes in hand. And it was a lark to see men strip down right then and there to their undershorts so they could wade across, and women with their skirts held way up, often higher than necessary. After a few days some people went to and from work in bathing suits, toting their clothing in plastic bags.

Motorists went about at only slightly reduced speeds, sending up rooster-tail sprays in their wakes.

Throughout the day, every once in a while, nearly everyone glanced skyward. They held the faith that the sun would not forsake them, that it would come breaking brightly through at any moment, rewarding them for all the worship they had previously paid it.

Some said the Air Force was to blame. Because the Air Force had been conducting rain-making maneuvers above the Mojave and Death Valley. The United States had been the first to wage weather warfare, had chemically produced downpours to impede enemy troop and supply movements along the Ho Chi Minh Trail. Bombarding the sky with canisters of silver iodide. Well, this time the Air Force had given the atmosphere an overdose.

From Edwards Air Force Base and the China Lake Naval Weapons Center came official word denying any recent weather-warfare maneuvers or testing. That wasn't the truth, but the Pentagon thought it best to say that. Otherwise it would be in violation of the proposal made by the U.S. and the Soviet Union in June of 1975 to outlaw techniques for changing the weather for military purposes.

Then there was the old plaint: the problem was caused by messing around with nuclear weapons. Setting off all those bombs over the years had upset the weather. There had been many climatic fluctuations in recent years. Record-breaking colds in some northern regions, less rain than ever in India, where it was so badly needed, a drought in the Soviet Union that gave the Russians such a hunger scare they had manipulated the famous United States – Canada wheat deal. For six years in a row there had been droughts in Central Africa. International relief agencies hadn't been able to keep up with the starvation. More proof? Andrew Ransen, head of the climate project at the National Center for Atmosphere Research at Boulder, Colorado, stated publicly that it was his expert opinion that a benevolent climate could no longer be taken for granted. Climatologists agreed that over the next ten or so years the world could expect more frequent and drastic climatic changes — droughts, floods, temperature extremes. They didn't go so far as to blame any one thing, such as nuclear testing, but some hinted at it. Anyway, people said, certain people knew the score. London, for example, was not getting nearly as much rain as it once had. New York City was having milder winters and not much summer. Florida was generally colder but didn't want the fact publicized. Blast the world off position just a fraction and there could be igloos in Haiti.

One television network thought enough of it to schedule an hour-long science special called "Weather," co-sponsored by a coffee company and a tire maker, who were guaranteed an audience rating of no less than twenty-five.

Several prominent meteorologists appeared on the program as featured guests. In the most elementary and hopefully

12

entertaining ways they explained about lows and highs, how winds move counterclockwise toward the centers of low-pressure systems. They acted amused and a bit embarrassed when they admitted they didn't know why. All pressure systems normally moved eastward, they said.

What about that front currently dampening Southern Californian spirits?

Lightly, the meteorologists gave the front the name "High Boy" and said *he* was indeed a strange one, extraordinarily stubborn; *he* refused to move along and let the weather get back to being unpredictable.

For a closing the network's prime-time anchorman gave the weather report and forecast. He performed it with evident futility and with the camera in close, playing up to the resentful reaction his words would surely cause.

"Rain continuing tonight and throughout tomorrow."

It was initially intended that the program include three of the country's foremost geologists. Network executives decided against that after previewing the material those scientists wanted to present: a definition of the geological makeup of the Southern California region, graphically explaining it was a shallow mantle of calcareous soil with not enough natural subterranean troughs to handle the runoff of such a deluge. The geologists had wanted to warn that the ground was spongy wet, already saturated—to the danger point.

Hell, no use scaring anyone.

13

1

Frank Brydon felt the sheet slipping.

When the nurse, with her habitual efficient haste, had folded it down to just above his groin, she had left too much draped on one side. It was a fresh sheet, slick out of the hospital laundry. In a moment it would be on the floor and Brydon would be nude. His hands were free and he was about to reach for the sheet when a man's transmitted voice, as though a thought ahead of him, told him: "Try not to move, please."

The sheet slid off and Brydon didn't care.

He lay face up on a special high table that was cold and hard as a slab. For the moment the place was only partially lighted, which intensified or lessened its intimidation, depending on the patient's frame of mind. Brydon could make out the large, complicated apparatus above him, the heavy multi-elbowed arm of it that was controlled from an adjacent safe cubicle. On the end of the arm a conical, sort of beehive shaped, head. It was now slowly moved closer into position above Brydon.

"Breathe normally, please," said the transmitted voice.

Brydon watched the head of it divide into quarters, symmetrically, like a flower opening petals. But not silent as a flower; it made an ominous kaah-ploooomp sound and extended rather insolently from its center a tube that resembled an oversize lipstick.

The cobalt.

On Brydon's chest was painted a red fluorescent outline of a rectangle, a vertical rectangle four and a half inches wide by eight inches long with a red dot in its center. It was on the upper part of his chest, from the manubrium notch, that soft, somewhat indented spot below the Adam's apple, down to the tip of the sternum, where the rib cage comes together in front.

They referred to that outlined area as his anterior portal.

Meaning it was through that front door of his body that they could destroy certain undesirable cells, while hopefully killing or injuring a minimum of others.

Brydon heard a low hum and felt a slight fluttering in his ears as he was given 150 RADs. That part of it took only about a minute.

At once the tube of cobalt was retracted and enclosed within its conical-shaped housing. The arm of the apparatus was swung automatically away and aside. Brydon, as usual, was left lying there alone for several minutes. Longer than that, it seemed to him, a bit irritated. He suspected they were allowing time for any stray radioactivity to dissipate. Couldn't really blame them for not wanting to endanger themselves.

Finally they came for him, two nurses guiding a stretcher. Their eyes seemed focused upon something beyond the limits of this space, because of his nudity. The sheet was retrieved, shaken and used to neatly conceal most of him.

15

Then, at once, he noticed the change in their eyes, acknowledging him. Did they teach them that or was it something they naturally acquired? he wondered.

Making the sheet cooperate, he transferred himself awkwardly to the stretcher. "There we go," said one of the nurses. A small, fresh pillow went beneath this head. The sheet was again neatened, and he was rolled out and a short way down a corridor to one of the small private outpatient rooms. His clothes and other things were there. An electric signaling button was placed by his head. As the nurses left him they were discussing their next duty, something having to do with someone they called Number Twenty-one.

Brydon closed his eyes. But immediately changed his mind, preferring to look outside himself. There, a metal door and frame. Substantial, as were the walls, composed of steel extrusions and plaster, was Brydon's outside guess. Built to last. No windows. Of course not, two stories underground. Better planning to have the radiology department down there, less dangerous, easier to control.

Doctor Bruno came in.

He called Brydon Frank with his hello and asked how he felt.

"Generally or now?"

"At the moment."

"Okay, I think. Yesterday, though, I felt lousy afterward for quite a while."

Doctor Bruno explained that yesterday had been the first time they had treated Brydon via his posterior portal — through his back, where an identical rectangle was drawn in a corresponding position. "Posterior treatments usually have more side effects," Bruno said. "Nausea?"

"Mostly."

Bruno was a short chunk of a man. Almost totally bald, his skull skin freckled and tanned as his face. It exaggerated his stockiness. From a Neapolitan peasant line had emerged exceptional intelligence, insight and compassion.

16

The doctor placed his hand on Brydon's chest. "No pictures today," he said. "Monday or Tuesday." His hand remained palm down on Brydon's chest, perhaps consolingly, no pressure, just the weight of it. However, the longer it remained there the heavier it felt to Brydon and soon his impression of it changed. Were Bruno's fingers seeing into him, mystically diagnosing, estimating progress? Or perhaps they were healing with their touch, thought Brydon. He had been told of healers, particularly one in Taos, New Mexico, a part-Navajo, part-something else woman who had brought and could possibly again bring about miraculous cures through her touch. Power beyond all the powers of the American Medical Association. Often as few as three visits to her humble hut were all that was required, and no fee was expected, although a donation was appreciated, it was said. Brydon was not yet to the point of believing such a thing and he doubted he'd ever be.

A beeping sound took Bruno's hand away. He was being summoned. From the white coat pocket over his heart he took out the small electronic device to stop its call and signal that he was on his way. God, how much he disliked that device, the way it pulled and pushed him. From another pocket he brought out a small plastic vial. "Take a couple of these if you feel nauseous again."

Brydon's eyes must have questioned.

"Just Tigan," Bruno assured, smiling. "Same as we give for morning or sea sickness."

Brydon tried to think of something he hadn't asked that was important enough to ask now.

Bruno told him: "I'll try to get around to see you Monday when you're in. If not, then the day after. We should talk."

At least, thought Brydon, watching the blank door replace Bruno's back, he didn't mention the weather.

No good news or Bruno would have given it to him.

Patients must be patient.

He should have asked Bruno straight out how long at the

worst, but more of him hadn't wanted to know, hadn't wanted to hear expert Bruno verify his own research that said eight to eighteen months would likely be the rest of his life.

Brydon has known of his cancer for six weeks. Until this his ailments had been limited to normal brief battles with flus and viruses of various nationalities, and a complex fracture from skiing that was so stubborn to heal it stopped him from skiing forever at thirty.

Two months ago he felt a sort of gripping in his chest. He had shrugged it off as a touch of recurring bronchitis, a somatic toll he paid for living right on the ocean.

But it didn't go away with the shrug.

He had called his doctor, a general practitioner named Russell who rarely got to see him but this time managed to persuade him to come in for an office visit. Dr. Russell tapped, listened, felt, took a chest X ray and, with an explanation that was as understated as possible, recommended Brydon have a more thorough work-up.

First, a routine metastatic survey along with a thyroid scan. Then a tomogram—a barrage of X rays of the area section by section to determine more dimensionally where and how deep the problem might be.

At that point Dr. Bruno had come in on the case. He was an oncologist, a relatively new designation. His specialty: fighting the killer. By then everything that could be done to diagnose from the outside of Brydon had been done.

Bruno had zeroed in.

He knew the trouble was situated in the anterior compartment of the mediastinal area, the centermost area of Brydon's chest from lower throat to belly. There are several lymph nodes there at what is called the hilum of the lungs. Hopefully, what Brydon had was merely an inflammatory swelling of those nodes.

They had to go inside to see.

A far cry from bronchitis, thought Brydon, as he went under the anesthesia.

18

A small incision was made and a specially designed viewing device was inserted down through the soft tissued space behind Brydon's breast bone. That permitted visual examination of the nodes. They were enlarged. A tiny portion of them was cut away. For biopsy.

Positive.

Diagnosis: reticulum cell sarcoma, a form of lymphoma.

Chance of complete remission: slim, about 100 to 1.

Chance of survival beyond two years: not much better.

Treatment: radical cobalt therapy, tumoricidal doses and maintenance chemotherapy.

Since Brydon was told of his malignancy he had told no one. Actually there was no one to tell, and Brydon felt both fortunate and sad for that. No one close enough. No one he believed would honestly give a damn. The woman he had divorced eight years previously wouldn't want to hear about it. . . .

"I've got to get away."

"Why?"

"From you."

"I didn't realize you were so unhappy."

He had known.

She knew he'd known.

"It's me," she said, "not you, me."

A true lie.

"Where will you go?"

Eyes to eyes for a long moment.

"Maybe you'll stop me."

Swift amputating blade—from a proposed lifetime together to cut apart in less than half an afternoon. The familiar back of her head seen through the rear window of one of their cars, diminishing, going, last sight, out of sight down the road.

"Stop yourself. . . ."

Anyway, now she was far away with a new lease on everything. She wouldn't really want to know and he was almost sure he didn't want her to. Besides, Brydon reasoned, he had always equated strength with independence and it would have been weakness to cry out for help from anyone. Especially now when he was so helpless.

Over, done at forty-two. Christ.

His watch on the bedstand told him nine minutes to four. From that his attention went to the grayish green wall just beyond, and a single crack in the plaster there. Just a hairline crack, extremely fine, almost invisible, climbing erratically all the way up, zigzagging as though dodging something.

Symbolic of what?

Back before what seemed no more than a series of unrealistic flashes, that would have been merely a crack on a wall, another wall in a life involved with wall after wall and, of course, floors and ceilings. An oversimplified description of architect — but Brydon wasn't in the mood to argue with himself or get stuck on such a side issue.

More important was remembering how hot-shit confident he'd been. Particularly during the first ten professional years. So many offers from various firms he'd lost count — some from the largest, some from the best, some at salaries so ridiculously high it was obvious they were at least partially out to prove anyone was buyable. But Brydon managed, avoided attachments, gave his effort to maintaining his individuality rather than a position or office. He freelanced from his place on the beach near South Laguna, letting the work seek him out. And it did because he was dependable and talented.

Buildings.

How many had he done, nursed along, fought for, made do what they were intended to do in the most pleasing visual way? He could tell you. Exactly. Fifty-four.

His favorite was by no means the most imposing or the newest. It was an eight-room private residence completed in 1960. If anything, with some Mies Van Der Rohe in it. Clean, linear, framing itself, it was solidly situated, incorporated like a natural disparate outcropping of a huge granite boulder. In 1970 Brydon had driven to it, a few miles outside of Aspen, Colorado. Expecting it or himself or both to be considerably changed, he was delighted to find the house intact, still as he'd originally designed it, and for himself to still feel from every point of view it was fine. That supplied him with well-being enough to draw upon for he didn't know how many years.

He didn't know how many years.

He put on his watch, wound it a bit too tight.

From some time past came a fragment of conversation —with her, or her, whoever. Names, intimacies, most as forgotten as meals. No doubt because of the way he had his life arranged, she nearly always got around to saying:

"Let me be with you."

He would seem to be considering it.

"I mean for good," she'd say.

He often replied and silenced her at the same time with a kiss on her mouth that could as well have gone to her forehead. There was no mistaking it, and it was better than saying no, no matter how softly or gratefully he might say it.

They came, used, were used and went elsewhere to put in for their emotional security.

However, there were several pretty fine ones who had gone along with Brydon for years. On his terms. Overnight stays at his beach place were the rule, weekends the limit. Longer holidays were reserved for favorites. One especially, a woman named Anne, young but not a girl, a woman whose departures were always as pleasant as her arrivals, and in the time between at most only a hint of permanent possession in her eyes. There had never been a moment of sadness between himself and Anne, so he decided no, he wouldn't tell even her.

He wondered, however, when it would become impossible for him to conceal it. He was naturally lean, had a tall, tight, well-kept body. His leanness had served, helped him appear

21

younger, quicker, more desirable — although he'd always known it would eventually turn on him — in his old years when he went to jowls. But what about now? If he was due to waste away, there wasn't much to waste. Would his hazel eyes that were still so clear and alert become filmy dull and sunken? He had heard that people undergoing chemotherapy lost their hair, completely. He still had all his; thick, healthy, dark brown with a touch of interesting gray at the temples. He found it difficult to imagine himself slick bald. A different man.

That was something to ask Bruno. When would it start showing? When it did he would shut himself off, away from everyone. And was there any way he could finally avoid a hospital bed?

He snapped his thoughts out of it, not liking the way he had so easily slipped into hopelessness. Not proud of that. To prove he was far from done he stood quickly, practically jumped up, stretched, took in a deep painless breath. But then he glanced down at where he'd lain, noticing the impression the weight of him had made on the sheet. He imagined he was still there, invisible, passed over to another dimension. It made him consider all the spaces his body had occupied. When he moved from one place to another, one space to another, did he cause a disturbance in the atmosphere? Didn't the air rush in after him to fill and collide and eliminate any trace of his having been there no matter what he'd done?

He dressed, slung his raincoat by a finger over his left shoulder and went out to a desk where a black woman in baby blue with a silly kind of cap bobby-pinned perilously on her springy hair confirmed his next Monday-afternoon appointment. No one bothers with good-byes anymore, he thought, after saying it and pausing a moment to deliberately watch it go right through the woman, too busy. He had the urge to put his face down close, right at her, and say it again. She would probably have thought he was one of those angry advanced cases.

Up he went to the main floor and, approaching one of the exit doors, at the last second he decided to hell with the raincoat, just kept on going out and down the steps, not hurrying despite the rain. He experienced the rain, the drops striking his face. He enjoyed it so much he was laughing. Also, he was unusually aware of his stride, the sensation of it, his feet, his knees and hip sockets working. Ordinary and amazing, he thought all the way to the parking lot and his car, a last year's Jaguar XKE that he hadn't locked because he no longer feared having anything stolen.

Ten minutes later he turned onto the San Diego Freeway and soon had the Jag going twenty above the law. He'd always been a fast driver, good, not reckless, and he was almost always only one moving violation from having his license revoked. Once they had taken it away. For a year. But that hadn't stopped him. For six months he'd driven on luck and for the other six he'd managed to get a license from Nevada.

Now, doing an easy eighty, he frequently had to increase his grip on the steering wheel to offset the gusts of wind that splashed the car broadside. He came up behind a new Lincoln, its rear wheels spinning a lot of water up in under its fenders and throwing some arrogantly back at him. To make up for it Brydon floored the Jag, pulled out to the right and passed on the forbidden side. The sibilant sound of tires on wet pavement, the windshield wipers slaving.

Shitty weather.

Why not go someplace where there was surely sun, Brydon thought, some far-off new place? Splurge on some first-class comfort.

He had already considered doing that and a part of him was for it. But another part of him put up a good argument contending it was senseless for him to make discoveries now. Better not to experience or react too much. No need to increase the desire to live.

The Laguna exit was up ahead. He took it and continued over the San Joaquin Hills via Laguna Canyon for nine miles to the Pacific Coast Highway, famous California 1. After going south a couple of miles, there on the right was the Seaside Supermarket. It reminded Brydon that he had no beer at home, and he was sure this big place carried Carta Blanca, the Mexican brand he liked. He drove in to get some.

At 2:35 that morning the Steinway grand piano started rolling — across the bleached, hardwood floor that had a polyurethane finish, glossy, slick. The house it was in was built to jut as far out as possible, as high up as possible, on the hillside. Supporting the house were steel beams of an adequate gauge sunk deep enough into the ground to satisfy the Los Angeles County building codes.

Actually, there wasn't much of a change. If anyone had been up at that hour they could have walked across the living room and never noticed the difference. The tilt was that slight. For that reason it took over four hours for the piano to move from its normal position across the length of the room to the wide floor-to-ceiling windows, to press and break through, shatter out and fall upon the muddy steep, smashing into rocks as it tumbled over and over, an awkward, lopsided, self-destroying plunge because of its shape and the steepness of the hill. All the way down a quarter mile or more to stop and sink in there where it was now. The grand. Even through the diffusing drizzle the black finish of it, blacker wet, was easily pointed out by the people up on the ridge road, and pieces of it that had broken loose, especially its keyboard, could also be seen.

At four o'clock that afternoon Judith Ward and Marion Mercer were in 43, an upper room of the Holiday Inn at Corona Del Mar.

They had never stayed there before. They had never stayed together anyplace more than once. Once in San Juan Capistrano they'd had an awfully close call—at the Mission Bell Inn, a comparatively small Spanishlike place, peaceful, with porticos and wisteria-covered walls and walkways. It would have been good for them there, except Floyd Jensen also happened to be staying there that day. Never mind that the short, brittle-looking blonde with thin legs and a prominent bottom, looking so passively legitimate, was not Floyd's wife —he was well enough acquainted with Marion's husband, Len, to be a threat. It had been only a matter of luck and mere seconds that Marion and Judith hadn't run right into him. Too close for comfort and too bad because the Mission Bell was so conducive.

26

Of course, another thing about such places was the people who managed them. No doubt they had excellent memories and were not naive. To return and register at the same place for another afternoon in a room would be outright admission, embarrassing, Judith and Marion agreed. Fortunately, there were enough motels up and down the Coast Highway and all around Disneyland to last them for years. Although at the rate they'd been going, they had already used up the more convenient, better, predictably clean places.

Their relationship, as they alone referred to it, had been going on for nearly seven months. They had known one another longer than that—two years come next July Fourth. They met at a celebration and found a lot in common. Their husbands were the same sort of engineers employed by the same sort of electronics firms in Anaheim. They lived in homes of similar style and value at Dana Point, only about ten blocks apart. Each had a child, a daughter age six (eight now), attending the same school and some of the same classes.

From then on, gradually, Judith and Marion saw less of their previous friends. Quite early they both felt possessive, which seemed natural. They didn't recognize anything romantic in it at the time.

Judith and Marion. They believed they physically complemented one another. They enjoyed sharing mirrors.

Judith's straight dark hair was kept so it barely brushed her shoulders and it was cut with bangs that just hid her brows while helping her large brown eyes appear even larger. She had fine features, was fine boned, diminutive. It would have been perfect had she been graceful; however, although she was twenty-nine, there was a kind of adolescent gangliness about her, at times charming. And contradicting that was her voice, which didn't match her at all. Instead of the frail or sweet wispy voice her appearance led one to anticipate, she had a constant huskiness, as though she had been talking or shouting too much. Whenever the moment wanted, Judith could round out the sound of it into a mellifluousness that was, as she knew, as attractive as it was surprising.

Marion was just as pretty in her way. She was taller, almost five nine, and fuller but not unpleasingly heavy. That she was more mature than Judith was the first impression (she was six months younger). It had much to do with Marion's height and her ample breasts and the way she carried herself and moved about, always at an easy pace that implied patience, experience. She had a lovely honest laugh. Her hair, styled semi-short and wavy, was Miss Clairol light ash blonde shade number 28. However, she didn't get it from Clairol. It was hers naturally and her pubic hair proved it.

There was nothing masculine about either of these women. Quite the contrary, it was each other's total femininity that they found so desirable.

From the time they began experimenting with tenderness they knew they were taking a step out of step. But then neither considered it really infidelity. It was contemporary derring-do more than anything. Whispering:

"You like that?"

"Mmmm." (Conveying more than yes.)

"Does this feel nice?"

"Strange."

"Oh?"

"I mean different, better, without even trying."

"How about there?"

"You know."

"I know."

Fingertips, as light as possible, the very tips of nails barely touching, tracing the outline of arm from shoulder slowly all the way slowly to finger crotches. Their advantage was having confidence in delicacy, to run the sensitive surfaces of sides with conscientious touch, down the dips of waists, up the rises of hips, circling aureoles, appreciatively, and no doubt about it. Giving attention to neglected places that often showed relief by changing texture.

"There must be a better word for it."

"What?"

"Goose bumps."

Exploring, laying hands on with feathery slight contact. Spending an entire hour not moving, just holding, being gently pressed. Taking nothing for granted, not even taking giving for granted, but gradually over the stolen hours discovering one another's preferences and mentally tucking them away for future unselfish and selfish use.

So this was what they had heard and wondered about; this was what some women had done, were doing now? It wan't bad. It was certainly more than they had expected. They hadn't expected to unleash such insatiability, being able to achieve and cause again and again. It amazed them. They thought of it as the blessing of being female. A man could cope with it, perhaps, but hardly match or share it.

They were two months into it before they kissed; long, open mouth to mouth. For some reason of conscience they considered *that* the beginning of marital deception. For a while guilt intruded, tried to wedge seriously between them. They shut it out by getting even closer. They increased the flow of reliance. Fought guilt with affection.

Recently, however, they had been brought to face a truly practical crisis.

Judith's husband, Fred, was considering changing jobs. He had received an offer from a firm in Springfield, Massachusetts. It meant a substantial increase in salary and another rung up the executive climb. When he told Judith about it he thought she'd be delighted, all for it. She managed to act that way, despite the shock.

If it came about, for Judith and Marion it meant the end of the double standard they were enjoying. They'd be forced to choose: be separated by a whole continent, or bring it all out into the open, declare themselves.

They were in favor of standing up and out. However, the consequences of such a decision were numbing. Gone would be the financial security they now almost unconsciously counted on. They would have to fend for themselves. Neither

29

ever had. And that might not be the worst of it. No court in the country would grant them custody of their daughters. What court would ever decide in favor of a lesbian mother?

What to do?

The most logical and likely thing, Marion suggested, was for Judith to talk Fred out of taking the new job. Then everything could remain as was.

The dissuading campaign began.

Judith and Marion collaborated on strategies. Judith peppered husband Fred with uncertainty regarding the Massachusetts move. For believability she acted ambivalent. Sometimes she seemed pleased with the idea, contentedly made plans in that direction — next she nourished small doubts into full-grown, adamant opposition, which was, she hoped, more impressive. Damn California, anyway! If only the weather were better she could have used that for ammunition. She did anyway, forecasted horrid slush and below-zero days in the family's future.

Such tactics had not brought about as much progress as hoped for. Nothing definite. Fred no longer expressed enthusiasm for the change, but Judith could tell he still wanted it. It could still go either way.

Now in number 43 of the Holiday Inn there was Judith in the supersanitized bathroom close up to the mirror. Using a tiny, sharp-pointed brush she outlined her mouth with lipstick and then filled in straight from the tube. She blotted with a tissue that she discarded into the toilet bowl, giving attention, for some reason, to the way the tissue became nearly invisible as it became wet, while the imprint of her mouth on it became more pronounced.

She appraised herself in the mirror. Her eyes seemed vague, she thought, a little glazed, perhaps a result of having come so many times. She doubted the look would give her away, but she blinked rapidly, trying to eliminate it. Then she gathered her makeup into its small, overcrowded, zippered cloth bag and went out to the bedroom. She expected Marion to also be dressed and ready to leave, but Marion was still nude and on the bed.

Judith told her: "It's after four."

No comment from Marion. She was front up with her legs angled over the bed's edge. Judith understood.

"We'll be late as it is."

Marion's gaze continued upward and Judith recognized the soft covered quality of it, the want behind it. Confirmed when Marion slowly tightened in her stomach and clenched her buttocks, causing her pelvic mound to rise, requesting.

"Come on," Judith urged, not wholeheartedly.

Marion did it again.

Less than an hour later they were six miles from Dana Point. Marion was driving. She turned off the Coast Highway to where Judith, as usual, had left her car—in the parking area of the Seaside Supermarket. They entered the market together, ran in from the rain to buy convenient, fancy frozen things that would make it seem as though they had spent quite a lot of time and imagination preparing the evening's dinners.

31

Warren Stevens was cleaning one of his rifles.

The rifle his father had given him on his sixteenth birthday two years ago. It was a Champlain and Haskins 458 Magnum with the distinctive tapered octagonal barrel. Anyone who knew firearms knew right off it cost fifteen hundred.

Warren liked this rifle best because it had brought him recognition. He had gotten a grizzly with it—a six-hundred-fifty-pound bald-face grizzly, more scientifically known as an *Ursus horribilis.* Warren had looked that up and always said it because he thought it sounded monstrous.

He had gotten the bear with a single shot in the throat. His father had never been so proud. Imagine, a boy standing up to a charging bear, and not just an ordinary bear, but the kind big-game hunters said was as dangerous as a lion or tiger. Boy, talk about courage!

No one had witnessed Warren's kill of the bear, but there

was no reason to doubt his version of it. When Stevens senior and the guide came running, Warren was trembling with excitement and too modest to say anything, and there was the bear dead on its side with its right front paw up, as though taking a deadly swipe at heaven—and with its mouth wide open, corners pulled way back exposing its teeth. The taxidermist in Missoula who did the head was grateful for the final, ferocious expression the bear had given him to work with. The skin, with its reddish mane and black dorsal stripe, was made into a rug that was the first and last thing Warren stepped on each day. The claws and teeth were polished and strung into a necklace Warren put on sometimes.

Stevens senior told the story of that hunt and exhibited the head every chance he got. He always elaborated on how the bear looked as it charged, how it bristled hatefully and growled its killing growl when it attacked; in only a second or two it would have ripped Warren to shreds. Stevens senior added more detail each time he told it, not stealing thunder but heaping praise.

Warren had become tired of hearing it. He wished he could do something else that would be considered more courageous. All he wanted was the chance.

Such were his thoughts now as he applied lemon oil to the Circassian walnut stock of the rifle and buffed it vigorously. He snapped the Zeiss Diavari D telescopic sight onto its mount, brought the rifle up and sighted through it. Out through his bedroom window. He fixed the cross hairs on a figure moving among wet foliage on the hillside about three hundred yards away. One of the ranch hands. Warren took up the slack of the familiar trigger and began the careful squeeze that he'd first learned when he was five.

Rain drove against the pane, diffusing.

Damn, goddamn rain, Warren thought, it was ruining everything. Yesterday he had overheard his father saying how much damage was being done to the avocado groves. The roots of the trees would rot if the rain kept on. There'd be no crop this year or maybe never again from the Rancho Stevens.

Besides, this was supposed to have been the week for maneuvers at Camp Pendleton. Colonel Owens, a family friend, had invited Warren to watch from the command post vantage. Warren had been looking forward to it for over a month. He'd been told it would be the next best thing to an actual amphibious assault, with live ammo being used and everything. Guys always got hurt, even killed sometimes.

But the maneuvers had been called off.

Because of the rain.

Freaking rain, Warren thought, having nothing to do. He couldn't even go bird shooting. He leaned the rifle against the chair and stood gazing out, hating the rain, personally hating it.

He wasn't a handsome young man. His eyes that weren't large enough also lacked adequate space between them. His upper lip was sparse, while the lower was quite full, which made his natural expression seem grouchy, obstinate. It often surprised people when Warren smiled. His hair was sandy, cut short. It had an uncontrollable cowlick. He was medium height, still had some to grow. His chest and neck muscles were overdeveloped from lifting weights.

Call Leland, he thought. Leland was his buddy. Leland might want to drive down to T (Tijuana), have some beers and take in some dirty shows. Last time they'd gone they had seen a girl with a goat, and Leland had thrown up outside the place, blaming the enchiladas they'd eaten earlier.

Warren was about to make the call when his attention caught on movement outside, below on the wide drive. It was Lois, his only sister. She was two years younger, a pretty blonde, mature for her age, typically Californian in that respect. Warren watched her get into her new blue Mustang convertible. Going where? Warren believed he knew, according to the rumors that had been ricocheting around. He'd gotten it from several directions over the past few weeks, but

34

it hadn't occurred to him until now that he ought to be showing some responsibility, protecting his baby sister. At least it was a good day for that.

He wrapped his most successful, precious rifle in chamois and then clear plastic. From a built-in drawer he got out a Colt .45 service automatic and a shoulder holster. The automatic was new to his collection. He hadn't had a chance to use it or even practice much. He harnessed on the holster, then made sure the Colt had a full clip of seven. He put two extra clips in his pocket. He got a poncho from a closet, regular war surplus poncho, rubberized with camouflage markings. Loose as it was, it easily concealed the Colt. At his dresser he used some Visine eye drops. Three drops for each eye, so his vision would be sharp. He also doused on some aftershave that had the word "Man" in its proper name. Then he took up the rifle and went out.

Minutes later he passed through the large iron gateway of Rancho Stevens. Driving down the devious canyon road, Warren felt good about what he intended to do. High on it. He didn't mind the rain now. In a way it had given him the idea. The more he thought about it the higher he got. This could be even better than the bear, he thought. A lot better.

Where the canyon road met the Coast Highway, Warren headed north until he came to the Seaside Supermarket. As he had expected, there was Lois's blue Mustang parked around the side. Lois wasn't in it. He parked far enough away, planning to wait and watch, like a good hunter stalking. But after only ten minutes impatience got to him. He endured another five before deciding not to just sit there. Anyway, it wouldn't hurt to go in and reconnoiter his target.

All at once they started going up on the third straight day of rain—perhaps reacting to an instinctual alarm.

Up to higher ground.

The largest of the rattlesnakes were three feet long and about six inches around at the neck. Some were only a week or two old, no longer than worms. There had always been rattlers in that canyon and most of the other canyons of the Santa Monica Mountains that ran all the way from the ocean to Hollywood. Although most of the areas, such as Benedict and Beverly Glen and Coldwater, were fairly built up and considered choice, much of the terrain remained dry, scrubby-brushed, rubbled with crumbly, stratified rocks the color of rust and glinting with mica. Good for snakes.

They lived in all kinds of animal holes or in naturally formed recesses.

They abandoned those.

They went up, sinuously wound their way, using the broad scales on their bellies and their long, flexible muscles. There were thousands of rattlers within that area. Many, the very old and very young, did not make it to the top. The rain got them. But those that did make it found dry sanctuary within the foundations of houses.

36

Acceptable enough places. Except for the nearly constant human and other sounds that were especially disturbing to the rattlers, who were all ears, so to speak. The entire length of their bodies was extremely sensitive to vibrations—their hearing mechanism.

Also, there wouldn't be enough to eat, only spiders and crickets and such, and any mice unfortunate enough to come sneaking along. Hunger was not a critical problem, however, for the rattlers were cold-blooded and with their low metabolic rate could get along on almost no food. Forty times better than man to be precise. And no wasted energy.

They remained absolutely still at night for warmth, coiled and tangled around one another into ball-like piles. In day-time, when the air was not so cold, they moved about, searched for possible warmer places.

Above them were the understructures of the houses, composed mainly of concrete, raw wood planking and exposed pipes. Around some of the pipes were openings. Space enough for some of the snakes to crawl up through and get between the floorboards. Then, perhaps hoping for food or more comfort or wanting to feel more secure, they explored and found openings that allowed them to slither further up inside.

In the corner of the master-bedroom closet of one house, where hung clothing concealed a vertical pressure pipe, some fifty rattlers lay in the dark.

In another house in the cabinet beneath the kitchen sink, among the containers of Tide and Ajax, Drano, ammonia and Windex, were another fifty or so. Waiting.

4

Elliot Janick tried to disregard the darker brown aging blotches on the back of his well-tanned hand. It helped to think that his watch was the positively accurate kind that had no moving parts—a Pulsar digital in a case of solid platinum from Tiffany's for three thousand. On its dark red face now flashed the blood-red numerals: four, zero, zero. Somehow it wasn't like time.

His Rolls-Royce limousine was on the Coast Highway, at that moment passing through San Clemente, of all places. The limo was a 1967 designated by Rolls-Royce as "The James Young Model," after its designer. Nineteen sixty-seven was the last year Rolls-Royce limos were imported regularly into the United States. The car had cost sixty-five thousand then. It was worth a hundred thousand now.

Driving it for Elliot was a man he referred to as "my man Ted." Up front on the seat next to Ted was a white Maltese terrier. The owner of the dog, Marsha Hilbert, was riding in the back with Elliot. The dog kept trying to get to her. It jumped and hit against the separating glass partition. The wet of its nose and mouth caused smears that had dried white and ugly on the glass.

Elliot grumbled, "Make her stop."

"She only wants some love," Marsha said.

"Dumb." Elliot tried to disregard the dog.

Marsha could let the dog have its way, lower the partition by simply pressing one of the electric buttons near her arm rest. She thought of doing that but clicked on the television.

She knew Elliot detested television, so she was not really surprised when he cut the sound of it by inserting an earphone plug into the set, handing the other end of it to her. She gave him a glance that said she wondered why she put up with him, as she placed the tiny button in her left ear. She changed channels several times and finally settled on a quiz program: contestants from such places as Bismarck, North Dakota, and Scranton, Pennsylvania, showing how fast they could be smart.

Marsha was thirty but could look younger whenever she wanted. She appeared beautifully well-bred. Publicity had her from a socially important Dallas family, and by now that was believed even in Dallas. Part of her style was to wear her hair always slightly mussed so it served as a sensually suggestive parenthesis for her face. Her complexion was not easily definable, somewhere between ivory and olive, different. Her eyes of china blue often said more than her voice. She would have been a sensation even in silent films. Extremely photogenic.

Marsha was a star. She had what people in the business called a motor—a special, natural, attention-getting quality, the ability to invade and be used in fantasies on a mass scale. Her fame span had already reached nearly eight years over twelve pictures. Her first six pictures were done under Elliot, as were her last two. During the three-year interim she had broken away to marry a wealthy land developer, who

39

loved her with such gentleness and constancy that she almost went insane. She divorced on the grounds of mental cruelty and returned contritely to Elliot.

Elliot, in his early sixties, admitted to early fifties. His squash and badminton games helped substantiate the lie. So did his tailor.

Elliot had produced forty-seven films since the first in 1938. Counting only those he actually personally worked on. Producers often took full screen and social credit although connected to a production by little more than a few phone calls. Counting that way, Elliot could have claimed at least another forty. Also not included were any of Elliot's *streamliners,* a term left over from the early days, meaning features shot as slickly and quickly as possible, usually in twelve to twenty days, with no retakes even if an actor's fly was found open.

The films Elliot had something to do with putting together had won seventy-four Oscars in all categories from Best Sound to The Best. That was probably a record. His write-up in the *Motion Picture Annual* occupied an entire page and overflowed onto another for three inches of a column. He'd been respectfully ridiculed by The Friars and sycophantically praised at an industry dinner for him at the Beverly Hills Hotel.

Elliot would never admit it, but the turning point in his life was the year of *Easy Rider.* That was when everyone in the filmmaking business lost the marble under the sofa and were down on their knees searching. All at once everyone was clutching and quoting an official audience study that showed that 75 percent of those who went out to the movies were under the age of twenty-five. Suddenly, long-haired youngsters with distant eyes and wearing clothes that looked worse than some old costume company's throwaways were brought in like saviors and given the dollar sign to go ahead. There had never been such organized confusion.

Elliot sidestepped it.

Elliot declined.

Since then, as close as he'd come to having another big one was within twenty thousand of making a deal on the property that eventually turned out to be *Love Story*. Just remembering that was enough to give him stabbing pains above and to the left of his navel. Psychosomatic hara-kiri. Last year he made only one picture. A medium budget PG starring Marsha. Her being in it was the reason it grossed double break even. It also won an Oscar for Best Wardrobe.

In almost any other profession a man of Elliot's years and accomplishments would retire. But he wasn't about to step down and out. He still had some winners in him, he said.

Actually, why he stuck in there was he was still paid respect, the respect of fear.

Janick would never be a lightweight, no matter what. Items in *Variety* and *The Hollywood Reporter* saying what Janick was into or maybe getting into made rival producers distrust their intuitions and their agents.

To be feared.

It was more precious than money. Elliot needed it. He didn't need money. Over the better years he had taken plenty of all kinds of money over the Alps. It made him feel secure but it also bothered the hell out of him. He might die without revealing to anyone his account number in Zurich. He could just picture those Swiss bankers gleefully absorbing his financial remains. A cringing thought—almost enough to make him tell the number to ... well, there was only Marsha.

Now, being driven up the Coast Highway, Elliot took another script from the stack below the seat. He skimmed it, read a line or two of dialogue from every tenth page or so, got only a vague idea of it and, with an intolerant sigh, tossed it to the floor amidst the pile he had already similarly rejected. He took off his genuine tortoise-shell reading glasses and inserted them into the outside breast pocket of his blazer.

How easily, how nicely the glasses slid in between the fine flannel material and the pure silk Sulka square. Dapper was a good word, Elliot thought, and repeated it to himself several times. Dapper. Still in use but fading, damn it. Marvelous word.

On a fold-down tray was a wedge of Brie, just ripe and runny enough, a crock of Fauchon mustard and some tiny cold water biscuits from Scotland. Another compartment held a bottle of Aalborg akvavit and a silver ice bucket, sweating.

Elliot reached forward to knife some cheese onto a biscuit, and then a smear of the mustard. It was on its way to his mouth when Marsha made a whiny sound, begging for it.

Elliot disregarded her, ate it.

"That cheese stinks," said Marsha. From her purse she took a vial of Guerlain's Vol de Nuit 1933, dabbed some on her wrists and throat. Her current look — hair, makeup, clothes — was a rendition of the thirties. Today she was wearing dove gray, a silk jersey dress by Halston. Gray was now her one and only favorite shade. It never fought her, she claimed, borrowing from the most famous New York fashion photographer who had said it while shooting two pages of her for last month's *Vogue*.

Elliot made another Brie and cracker for himself.

Marsha's eyes followed it all the way to his mouth. She watched him chew. She imagined the cheese was poison, pictured Elliot doubled over in anguish, making a horrible dying face. When she saw him swallow she told him: "I read about a woman who grows cultures and eats the slimy stuff."

"What?"

"Cultures, all kinds of germs. She believes it builds up immunity, so she eats it."

To erase his distaste Elliot glanced at the rain splattered window. The inside of the window was coated with steam from their breaths. His hand was mid-air when he decided it would be futile and probably unpleasant to wipe the window. He reached for another script, didn't put on his glasses as he paged apathetically through it. The typed words were blurred beyond comprehension and yet he seemed to be reading; at least he seemed thoughtful.

After a short while he tossed the script to the floor, leaned forward and got a chunk of ice from the bucket. He made a fist around the ice, held it that way long enough for his fingers to be dripping.

Marsha saw it coming.

The word in her mouth was *"please,"* but she didn't let it out. She didn't flinch or anything when Elliot placed the piece of ice on her bare skin above her left knee.

He held it there.

She managed to pretend her attention was entirely on the television.

Elliot ran the ice up and down, up and down a short way.

She shivered, not altogether a cold shiver.

He ran the ice up under her skirt, up her thigh, sliding it slowly up all the way, between. The ice was soaking her. And her dress beneath her.

Her eyes closed. Her mouth opened. Now she couldn't help but say it.

"Please."

Mercy wasn't what she wanted.

Elliot knew that. But he stopped using the ice. The piece was considerably reduced. He withdrew it and held it above and she had to stretch up like a feeding baby bird to take it into her mouth.

At that moment Elliot's stomach felt a burning. The cheese and especially the mustard came back on him. He searched for some Maalox tablets. He nearly always carried some Maalox with him, however none today. All right, maybe his stomach would settle for a bottle of Perrier. But there didn't seem to be any Perrier either.

Over the intercom Elliot told his man, Ted: "Goddamn, there's no Perrier."

Ted apologized.

43

Marsha was sitting the same as before, exactly the same, as though someone had instructed her not to move.

"Stop and get some," Elliot told Ted.

The Rolls limousine turned in at the Seaside Supermarket. As though privileged, it violated the yellow painted lane markings and went diagonally across the parking area to the entrance.

Ted would go in.

But while Ted was double-checking with Elliot whether Elliot wanted anything besides Perrier, Marsha opened the door on her side. She jumped out.

Elliot shouted "no" at her, ordered her back.

But she was already well away, laughing, hurrying in to avoid the rain.

"Stupid cunt," Elliot said aloud, with sibilance on the first word and a hard coughlike start on the second. She probably wants to sign autographs, he thought. He'd better go in and get her.

Gloria Rand was seated on a large, inflated plastic cushion outside the front door to her apartment. A white telephone on a long cord from inside was within easy reach. She always brought the phone out whenever she swam or sat by the pool. It was the only way when a phone rang for her to know for sure whether or not it was hers.

Along the covered walkway the doors to most of the other apartments were also open. It was that sort of place. Down the way a couple of hibachis were smouldering, and, as usual, at least a half-dozen stereos were competing to underscore the moment. One seemed to dominate with a piece of Lou Rawls' soul.

In a few minutes it would be four o'clock. Gloria was watching Stuart and a married fellow named Murph as they flipped a Day-Glo red regulation-size Frisbee back and forth. Swift, skimming throws, frequent remarkable catches against the backdrop of rain beyond the covered area.

45

Stuart had on a pair of shorts, jeans, actually, cut off into shorts. They were frayed and nicely faded and they hung precariously low on the studs of his hipbones. He was twenty-two, six feet exactly, with a taut, sinewy sort of swimmer's physique. Stuart didn't live there at the apartment complex. That is, he was not actually a tenant, although since meeting Gloria four months ago he had stayed over and been around about as much as those who did pay rent. Prior to Stuart another good-looking young man had enjoyed the same setup for several months. And before him, another.

Stuart leaped high.

He made an amazing fingertip grab of the red Frisbee. His smile congratulated himself. He glanced over to Gloria.

She responded with: "Dynamite!"

Gloria appeared older than Stuart. About thirty, perhaps, maybe another year or two.

She had auburn hair, straight falling, long, worn middleparted to form an arch that nicely contained her face. Her face could scarcely be improved. Narrow nose, ideally tipped, eyes wide set, deep and brown. Her complexion flawless and pale — creamy pale, not sickly. Perhaps it was the paleness that gave the impression that she was pampered, that she overcared for herself. She conveyed that no matter how casual her attitude or dress — such as now, sitting with her legs drawn up, hugging her legs, wearing pleated, straight-legged jeans, espadrilles and a light cotton shirt unbuttoned three down to show she wasn't wearing, didn't need to wear, a bra.

The telephone rang.

Gloria answered it, got up and carried the phone inside.

"Shall I come there? . . . If you need me I'll come . . . Are you sure? I could catch a plane tonight . . . I suppose you're right . . . I'm fine," she said, changing to sound as though that were so. "I'm just fine. If only we'd get some sun here . . . No, I don't, but still it's nice to have sunshine . . . Day before yesterday, it occurred to me that the sun is up there going across the sky same as always and all this rainy mess is just in between and it seemed such a ridiculous idea, something I'd never thought about before, that it seemed I'd made it up. But then I realized that's how it really is." She paused. "I'm babbling . . . No, it's not okay, I shouldn't babble. It's a giveaway."

Stuart appeared just outside the front door, having to retrieve a bad throw of the Frisbee. He asked Gloria whom she was talking to.

Gloria covered the mouthpiece while she told him it was long distance, her younger, married sister Pam from Richmond, Virginia. Pam's eight-year-old, Daniel, was in the hospital with a concussion, a fall from a bike.

Stuart didn't hear the last part. He disappeared from the doorway like a slide being ejected from a projector.

After the phone call Gloria felt heavy, fixed in place. A fragment of Stuart's laughter struck her. She brushed it off and went to the hall closet for a tan trenchcoat that she put on, stuffed some money into a pocket and went out the back way, avoiding.

Across the patio, through the rear gate, around to the road with the happy name: Bluebird Canyon.

It was a winding, downhill mile to the Coast Highway and the Seaside Supermarket, where Gloria usually shopped. Sometimes, when she didn't intend to buy too many things, she made the walk. Today it was welcome therapy.

The rain.

She raised her face to it, thought of it as a beneficial drink for her skin. She took to the rain for the opposite reason she shunned the sun. The sun was a robber that could steal years from a face.

She'd heard it said that English girls owed the lovely quality of their complexions to English weather. A pretty thought — girls absorbing, deriving from something so commonplace and natural. As for herself, the only drawback to such prolonged damp weather was that it made her nose ache where it had been purposely broken, and also it caused arthritic pains in both her knees.

Gloria would be fifty-one her next birthday.

Seven years ago last February, when she was battling awfully with menopause, her husband made it worse by leaving her for a woman of twenty. Ego depleted, depression pouring in, Gloria tried suicide. She was methodical about it, to the point of making a list of the various ways and then eliminating those she found impossible. Oddly enough, what she left herself with were extremes — the most violent and the most passive: in the car at top speed on a high road to not match a turn with a turn, or in bed with a double prescription of Tuinals, taking one and purposely not remembering she had, so to take another, pretend not to remember, and another.

Her housekeeper found her — too early. Gloria was pumped, had a twenty-eight-hour sleep and awoke saved.

Having gotten that out of her system, she took a more optimistic view. There were blessings to count: plenty of money from the generous settlement her ex-husband's conscience had provided, her good health, and, perhaps most important, she had a few ties but no strings.

Her only adversary was time. She decided to make a fight for it.

To start, she spent eight weeks at Elizabeth Arden's ranch in Arizona. Getting her breath, losing pounds and gaining courage for what lay ahead.

Then aesthetic surgery.

That was what they called it now instead of plastic, which had become almost everything else.

She had it done in New York City. By the best.

Her chin, which had always been a weak feature, was corrected by the addition of a small piece of properly shaped bonelike substance. Her brow line, too prominent, was precisely deridged. Her nose was fractured, reshaped, planed down, given a perfect bridge, tilt and tip. The loose flesh and circles beneath her eyes were removed and so was the puffiness of her lids.

The work was done in phases. Gloria called them projects. As soon as one project was healed she went in for the next.

Not allowing time for time to discourage or affect her in any way—fighting time. Often it seemed she was winning.

Silicone sponges were implanted in her breasts. She resisted the idea of having exceptionally large, firm breasts. Actually, that would have been easier for the surgeon. She chose to have more believable, average-size ones. It required repositioning her nipples and aureoles and entirely sacrificing their sensation. The silicone was not detectable, pliant to the touch, and her breasts had a nice natural jounce to them.

Stretch marks and cellulite on her buttocks and upper thighs. That went. They pared her down. It was fortunate that she had abundant rather than too little flesh to work with, the surgeon told her. It seemed they could accomplish almost anything, if she would permit and pay.

Final project: her face was given a lift. By no means was it an ordinary superficial lift. Gloria willing, the surgeon did a more thorough, lasting job by working on the underlying facial and neck muscles.

Excellent results. The surgeon was very pleased.

Gloria was glad to hear that now it would be impossible for her to ever have a frown line.

After a year and three months there was nothing more the aesthetic surgeons could do.

Still, no time to waste.

Looking younger wasn't enough.

She flew to Geneva, and went on to the famous Niehans clinic for cellular therapy.

There she was first given the Abderholden Test, a urine enzyme test that in some secret way revealed any dysfunctioning of her body's internal organs. It turned out Gloria had a pituitary imbalance, probably a result of menopause, she was told. She also had a normal degree of cell and tissue deterioration for her age. A slight hyperfunctioning of some organs, a hypofunctioning of others. She was assured that the Niehans approach could revitalize her. It would cost ten thousand dollars. In advance.

49

Gloria paid.

The following day a pregnant ewe was selected from a special flock. It was slaughtered to obtain its unborn lamb. It was all done in the Niehans laboratory under the most antiseptic conditions and as swiftly as possible to maintain freshness. The various internal organs of the fetus, including its sexual ones, were separately cut into tiny morsels and placed in sterile dishes containing 20 cc. of normal saline solution. Each portion of tissue was minced, then forced through an extremely fine sieve and drawn up into individual 5-cc. syringes.

They were rushed to Gloria's bedside. With what seemed to her a flourish, the doctor removed the white towel that covered the tray. Gloria gasped when she saw the twelve syringes tipped with huge 14-gauge hypodermic needles. She glanced at the nurse, who wasn't at all pretty, and she wondered if behind that professional expression was the thought that this American woman was a gullible fool. She glanced at the rubber gloves the doctor was wearing, transparent blue, increasing the unreality.

For a moment Gloria felt helplessly a captive, like a passenger on a jumbo jet that was roaring down a runway for takeoff. She refocused her mind on the possible rewards, rolled over on her stomach, buried her face in the pillow, bit the pillow, clenched and counted. Six in one cheek, six in the other.

For a few days she had a reaction. Vertigo, nausea, diarrhea and a sense of depersonalization. Symptoms of mild shock from the foreign matter invading her system. It was frightening. She'd heard such injections had caused death in a few cases. No, she protested, not after all she'd been through.

The bad effects disappeared.

She waited for the good ones.

It was several weeks before she noticed the first major change. Her nervousness disappeared, a calm set in. She had the sensation that she was being refilled, made capable again in every sense. Her eyes as well as her urges seemed to verify it. Her eyes seemed more dimensional, deeper, brighter brown, definitely quicker. The change in her skin was amazing. It regained a youthful clarity—the skin of her face and all over.

Her menstrual cycle returned.

Gloria thought of those months as her renaissance. Could she live to be a hundred? Not just live but be active and enjoyably responsive? Her mirror and the way she felt replied by suggesting a hundred and fifty. Perhaps (she only allowed the point of the idea to barely prick her) she had found forever.

Every year she had cellular therapy, some years twice. Through arrangement with the Niehans people, a doctor in Beverly Hills gave her the injections using lyophilized fetal cells, freeze-dried like coffee. It was illegal. Against the FDA and the AMA. The substances had to be brought into the country *en contrebande* via Mexico. For Gloria it was more convenient, though more expensive, than going to Switzerland. . . .

Now, walking in the rain down Bluebird Canyon, her hair was soaked, matted to her head; the bottom of her jeans were heavy with wetness and her sandals squished with every step. Her mind was still on the phone call. She told herself it was an emotional waste to let a call from Pam get her down. She should be accustomed to it by now.

Exile.

She would never forget her last visit to Richmond over two years ago, when Pam had finally come straight out with it, said she was embarrassed because Gloria looked too young and, well, everything. Pam's inflection on the word everything made it quite specific. Son-in-law Cliff expressed what he called his gut reaction, said it was freaky, Gloria ought to act her age. And grandson Daniel — he had adored Gloria until then, always looked forward to her visits, had always run to her for arms around, snuggled and returned hug for hug. But they had set Daniel against her, intentionally or not, made him hold back, afraid, as though she were unclean or contagious.

She made fists in her coat pockets.

Not fair, she thought.

Why should she be penalized for not being a frump—made to feel guilty for prolonging, improving her sexual pleasure? There was no harm in fibbing about her age. She wasn't really tired of pretending.

For support she drew a mental picture of Stuart. How she would arouse him that night. And nourish herself.

She crossed over the highway and the parking area to the entrance of the Seaside Supermarket.

The market's electronic door swung sharply open as she approached it.

That unconsciously pleased her.

It was impartial, unjudging, dependable, somehow much better than a personal welcome.

Emory Swanson's undershorts were cutting him.

New kind of undershorts his wife Eleanor had bought for him at one of those swishy shops on La Cienega. She'd bought six pairs, made in France.

That morning, out of curiosity and against his masculine judgment, Emory had put on a pair. Powder blue, slick and skimpy as panties, they bunched and held his privates in a different, pleasant way — although being in a hurry was Emory's reason to himself for leaving them on.

Within a couple hours they started getting to his crotch creases. Especially when he sat, which, as usual, was most of the day.

Now he was tempted to pull over and get relief. It would require taking his trousers off first, and for a while he'd have to be bare-assed. That would be something, getting pinched for indecent exposure on the Coast Highway, Emory thought.

He kept driving, one hand, using the other to undo his belt and trousers. He lifted himself to reach in and find a leg-hole hem of the undershorts. He pulled, tugged hard, but the material wouldn't give. What the hell were they made of, glass? Furious, he yanked sharply, hoping to rip them, but he only hurt himself more where he was already rubbed raw. To hell with it—he zipped, buttoned and buckled up—he'd be in El Niguel in half an hour.

El Niguel was where the Swansons had one of their places. A twelve-room Spanish-style house, with swimming pool, built-in water-swirling massager, cabana, sauna, lighted tennis court. It was set amidst the eucalyptus on the edge of the sixth hole of the El Niguel Country Club. The Swansons called it their play house. Where they lived officially was in Beverly Hills, up Coldwater. Also, they had another sort of place at Lake Arrowhead.

At one time Emory had lived in one rented room around where Franklin Avenue intersects with Sunset. In those days Monogram Studios was near there. Most of the "Dead End Kids" movies were shot at Monogram—and so many cheap monster pictures that the studio got to be called Monstergram, the same as Republic Studios became known around as Repulsive.

Back then, Emory had owned only two suits. Bought at the annual sale at the London Shop. A dark gray and a navy gabardine. Always either one or the other was being pressed or cleaned at the neighborhood same-day-service cleaner's. That way Emory always appeared too neat to be poor. Another part of it was the shoes he bought, always top-grade Florsheims that he kept in shape by conscientiously treeing and polishing them.

To this day Emory still took pride in the way he could read a man by his shoes. Shoes revealed how much walking a man had to do. Scuffs and scars told where, and the condition of the heels said why. Style and quality were also considerations. Were the man's shoes cheap but stylish or more conventional, of better leather? Either told a lot, the way Emory saw it. He didn't believe he had ever misjudged a man by his shoes, and he was amused that, by the same means, so many people had been wrong about him during those early, crucial times.

Then.

How many policies ago had that been? Millions since those eighteen-hour door-to-door days.

Now, thank our land, there was a twenty-four-story earthquake-proof building on Wilshire Boulevard with his name chiseled on it. Home office of his People's Fidelity Insurance Company. Branches in San Francisco, Seattle and soon San Diego. Agents in almost every West Coast city.

Emory had become secure from people being afraid. Not only afraid of dying but of almost every aspect of living. The most benign and pleasurable things held hazards. Only someone dumb and asking for it would swim, walk his dog or even sleep entirely at his own risk. Mind's ease came with coverage. Snug it was under the vast, invisible money blanket. No need to shiver at the thought of cold poverty, that, of course, could result from nearly anything imaginable happening.

It had come to the point where people were now afraid of being afraid. And what they were most afraid of was one another: those thieving, beating, crashing, irresponsible, grubbing *other* people.

Emory kept that in mind like a personal secret. He believed knowing it gave him a man-over-man edge. He could always act braver.

Besides, when it came down to it, really the bottom-line fear of all was the fear of being moneyless, and Emory and his would never have to worry about that. All those policies. His actuarians fixed the odds and the fine print made it a sure thing.

Worth a million for each of his years.

He was forty-nine. Slightly shorter than average. His

weight fluctuated from fifteen to twenty-five over. He was going to jowls, despite the ten minutes of facial isometric exercises he did each night and morning — making faces at himself in the mirror under flattering fluorescence. He had two kids, girls, at Stanford, getting good enough grades and in with their own kind. And a wife who matched him Scotch for Scotch any time of day.

The way Emory counted, he also had many friends. A large circle of them. Quality people. When meeting someone new, after assessing the person's footwear, Emory would put it to them—same test question every time:

"Do you consider yourself an honest person?"

"Yes."

"Absolutely honest?"

"Yes, sure."

"Okay, then, let's say you're making a call from a pay phone. You don't get your number. Your dime drops into the coin return and along with it comes a bunch of quarters. Do you put those quarters back into the box or what?"

Emory figured anyone who said he'd give back the quarters was a liar and not to be trusted. Definitely not anyone he wanted to know. The most ridiculous reply Emory ever got was from a young man who said he'd walk away, leave the quarters and the problem for the next guy. A real do-nothing bullshitter, was Emory's opinion.

As for himself, Emory would pocket the quarters, damn right. Despite all he had, he still got a charge from such unexpected windfalls, and whenever he needed to think good thoughts he recalled little extras he'd gotten away with over the years. Once at a hotel cigar counter in San Francisco he'd been given change for a twenty instead of a five. He'd felt positively blessed. Usually, however, Emory didn't leave such things to fate. He created his own godsends.

Newspapers, for example. Whenever it was convenient or even a little out of his way Emory bought his newspaper from a vending machine on the street. When he put in his coin and the machine unlocked there was nothing to prevent him from taking two papers. He'd been doing it for years. An edge. Insurance.

Now, there he was, driving south on the Coast Highway in his 1976 Lincoln Continental Mark IV with the waving United States flag decal on the rear window. Humming and da-dee-da-ing along with a Mantovani on the triple-stack cartridge-playing stereo. To pass time he decided to call ahead.

He took the phone from its cradle, the operator came on and within seconds Emory was talking with wife Eleanor. She sounded a few degrees too cheery, slurry, and Emory knew she was already several stiff Scotches up on him.

"Coconut chips," she said.

"What?"

"Toasted coconut chips — you know the kind, the special kind. You know."

"Look in the cabana pantry."

"I looked, looked every goddamn place."

"Okay, I'll stop somewhere and get some."

"I've got a craving. You know me when I get a craving."

He sure did.

"I can be meaner than shit."

"I said I'd stop and get some."

"Toasted coconut chips like I like."

"Say please."

"Fuck you." She hung up.

A few miles further on Emory noticed the Seaside Supermarket. He went past, thinking it was raining too hard and to hell with her and her chips. But then he had a second thought that made him let up on the accelerator pedal. He found a spot to turn around and went back to the market. The excuse he gave himself was a temporary escape from his underwear.

The trip was another try for Peter and Amy Javakian.

Another try at making a go of it.

During the year and a half they'd been married they'd been separated twice seriously, twice briefly. The main reason, at least the admitted one, for this new try was Amy's sixth-month condition.

When she first learned she was pregnant, she definitely wanted an abortion. But there had been so much discussion with Peter, with his family, with her mother, that she became ambivalent. She let months pass and then it was too late.

Her body had trapped her.

She resented that, showed she did by resisting the pressure put upon her by everyone, including herself, urging her to reconcile with Peter. For the baby's sake, some said, their exact words.

For two months she lived alone in one room in Fresno,

58

worked there for an unmarried older woman, a lawyer who was very sympathetic.

In her fifth month Amy telephoned Peter and pretended the real reason for her call was not to share with him how active the baby inside her had become. Hearing his voice, she realized how much her resolve had weakened. In a roundabout, pride-saving way she let him know she might be receptive to another try.

And this was it.

Starting, restarting, with a trip.

So far it hadn't been promising. Several times Peter had almost been exasperated enough to turn the car around and head back home to Hollister. Just as often Amy'd had the urge to jump out and escape to anywhere.

"I didn't need any help," she said.

"You sawed the boards and everything?"

"Everything." A small smug smile, chin up.

"You liked doing it?"

She nodded, definitely.

"Even the sanding?"

"Sure," she fibbed. She had hated the sanding, had thought she'd never be done with it. It had made her arms and shoulders tired, sore.

"But you wouldn't ever want to do it for a living — be a carpenter, I mean. Not really."

"Maybe. Anyway, it's good to know I could if I wanted."

"There's a union."

"So?"

"They wouldn't let you in."

"They'd have to."

"Never."

"Women are working in steel mills."

"Where?"

"Someplace in Michigan."

"Paperwork."

"Uh uh. At the furnaces, rolling out extrusions. I saw it in a film."

Peter was surprised and a little annoyed that she used and seemed to know the word extrusion. He considered silence, letting her have the final say. He almost did. "Pepper wouldn't stay in it," he said, getting back on the original subject that was the doghouse Amy had built. Pepper was the pup they had chosen together at the city pound in San Francisco shortly before they were married. A mongrel that had consistently loved them both.

Regarding the doghouse, Amy could have said honestly that building it had given her a new sense of appreciation for any man who did such work.

Peter could have praised her for how well she had done. He told her, "It wasn't square."

"It was."

"The floor slanted."

"It did not."

"Not even a dog wants to sleep on a slant."

Amy kept her look straight ahead, clenched her teeth, kept in the string of words that came up from her anger. Her complexion felt flushed, but if she had looked in the mirror then she would have seen her face drained, pale. That was partly because she didn't wear any makeup, hadn't for the past few months — except those times when for no reason outside herself she'd given in to feeling inconsequential. Then she used all the usual devices to exaggerate the size and perhaps the power of her large blue eyes. But only her eyes.

Plain pretty without makeup, the most impressive kind of prettiness, really. More intelligent looking, Amy thought, and, as well, another shucking-off step toward independence, naturally facing things.

She was an only child and considered herself fortunate for that. Seldom having to share attention, getting spoiled with one sort of love almost made up completely for not having had a father since she was ten—half her life.

As she understood it then, and still, father had become

unbearably discontent. Father had left everything but one suitcase. Father had divorced her mother and, without ever being asked, had sent postal money orders for various amounts from various Eastern cities. He never visited, and only during her fourteenth and fifteenth years had she especially felt the need to know him.

But she never went to him and only remembered vaguely what he looked like. He disliked having his photograph taken, her mother recalled.

Amy's maiden name was Stone. By no means an eponym.

Even in pregnancy there was a lanky sort of immaturity about her, her movements and postures, which seemed to convey an indifferent attitude. The opposite was true. She was vital, extremely suggestible, and almost always too quick to respond. Whenever she spoke or listened, her eyes widened and fixed on the other person, as though that allowed her to say or hear more.

That was one of the many things Peter liked about her.

Peter was twenty-two. The second eldest son of an Armenian farmer, whose crops were mainly celery and children. Typical of his extraction, Peter had an abundance of dark, deep brown hair, speckled black eyes, thickly lashed. A sensual look. His mouth also contributed to the impression. The bridge of his nose was prominent enough to make him appear all the more interesting. He was not a large man. Solidly boned, though. Strong.

Being second eldest in his family had its advantages. Peter didn't have to be totally concerned with the farm; perhaps he could look forward to something else. As a boy he'd always been intrigued by color and drawing. Later at San Jose State College he had concentrated on what seemed a polarity of subjects: concerned with what he might have to do and what he hoped to do. He majored in agriculture and minored in art.

Did passing well, dutifully, in modern farming.

Better at putting color to canvas, huge stretches of canvas

61

for furious slashes of color, adamant, virile, the abstract shapes of his emotions — sometimes — and at other times, more diminutive but equally powerful work: bright, joyful landscapes of his feelings. Like that in life too, he was extremes. Brooding and gypsy melancholy one moment, affable and laughing the next.

Amy frequently called him a purebred manic-depressive.

For her benefit she once used a Magic Marker pen to label the lids of his eyes "glad" and "cry."

It was not Peter's galvanic moods that irritated Amy. She believed his spontaneity, up or down, showed how unusually sensitive he was. It was one of the many things about him that she admired.

What she could not tolerate was what she called his Armenian macho. Ironically, that also had been one of her original reasons for loving him. She had enjoyed being necessary to him in an abiding way. It had made her feel in place, secure.

That was before she saw the liberated-female light, before she was brought to realize that she was another victim of gender. How blind she'd been, how much she'd been used, limited, how grateful she was to know better and how sorry for every woman who didn't. Amy became so fanatical about the feminist cause it got to the point where it seemed Peter couldn't say or do anything without committing an offense.

He was often guilty. But it was difficult for him to admit or even recognize that. An Armenian male naturally assumed the controlling role in his family. It was also expected that he would worship his wife.

When Peter explained that to Amy, she'd told him she'd gladly forfeit worship for equality.

Side by side, they were now on the Coast Highway, headed for Mexico. The first day of two weeks of stopping anytime and anywhere they wanted, and maybe, if their money held out, they might make it all the way to Puerto Vallarta, or even Acapulco.

62

One of Amy's sometime wishes was to be on the beach at Acapulco. She had always pictured herself there in a skimpy bikini, a turn-on. Now she would have to settled for sitting swollen in the sand in a smock.

"Hungry?" she asked.

"No. You?"

"No."

Their stomachs grumbled. They laughed.

"Pick a place and we'll stop."

She rolled the window down a bit to see better. She noticed two, three likely restaurants but let them go by.

"I could fix us something to eat on the way."

He preferred that. It would be less expensive. But this was supposed to be a vacation. Besides, he knew what friction it would have caused if he had suggested it.

Amy read his thoughts. She glanced down at his free hand, imagined it touching her as it had and would. She felt herself anticipating it.

Stop, she thought, and the word came out. "Stop . . . here."

He shifted down, pulled in and parked in a space close as possible to the Seaside Supermarket. They went in together to buy the makings for sandwiches and some soft drinks.

In the rainy afternoon light that made everything seem older the woman lay on her side of the bed with the crocheted afghan over her. She was in her fall-to-sleep position, with her legs drawn up, hands pressed flat together between her thighs. She felt tired, had been dragging around all day. Also irritable. The way she usually got just before her period, although that couldn't be because she'd finished her last only a week ago.

She tried to put everything out of mind.

Three sounds were predominant.

The beat of drops on the roof. The shrieks and laughter of her children, son, four, and daughter, six, playing in the backyard. And the monotonous tumbling of the automatic clothes dryer. The dryer had been going practically nonstop since she'd decided to hell with the rain and for her sanity's sake let the children go outside to play. Each time they came in soaked to the skin she stripped them and threw sneakers and all into the dryer. As many as four changes a day. Not a bad mother, she told herself.

Smart too, she thought. If not for her they might be in real trouble now, like those families whose houses were in danger of sliding down. She'd been against getting that house up on

Mulholland, no matter how good a buy it was. She had stood her ground and they had stayed where they were: on a street off Beverly Boulevard north of Whittier. The last house on a cul-de-sac. She preferred calling it a cul-de-sac rather than a dead end.

For one reason "dead end" was too close to the truth. The rear of their lot bordered on the slope of a cemetery. Rose Hills Memorial Park, second in size, statuary and grave sites only to famous Forest Lawn. Fortunately, that part of the so-called park was higher than their house, and the rest of it lay beyond out of view. Anyway, they had become so accustomed to it, even the many bouquets and growing flowers at the graves on the hillside no longer reminded them.

The clothes dryer began buzzing to let her know it had completed its cycle. At the same time she realized the children were inside, shouting for her. They came into the bedroom, and she was about to scold them for tracking when her daughter said she'd brought a surprise, presented it in her open hand.

"Where did you get this?"

"From the lady."

It was a ring. It appeared to be authentic, a round-cut diamond of about five carats flanked by two baguettes.

"What lady?"

They would show her, were eager to show her. They'd had lots more fun playing outside today.

At the back of the backyard was a coffin.

An expensive coffin of brushed bronze. Sitting there in the rain. It was open. Tufted white satin inside and what remained of a woman who had been dead ten years. In a white silk crepe dress. The rain had made the material almost transparent. Another ring, this one with a large emerald stone, had fallen down a fingerbone to the tip where it and the tip lay loose.

Two, three more coffins were partially exposed, slipping out of the saturated earth at the foot of the hill.

65

8

Lonnie "Spider" Leaks was in automatic, doing with his body but not with his mind. That way, like a machine, he couldn't feel low, get bad or anything—just work. Something he had learned to do while in slam.

His job at the supermarket was lugging boxes of groceries out to people's cars. It was the second job since he'd been let out of San Quentin three months ago, a year early for ordinary behavior. His parole officer had made him quit the other job at the Bim Bam Car Wash in Balboa. At the car wash Spider had started as a wheel and bumper scrubber inside the conveyor, and because some guys kept not showing up for work he got to be one of the finishing crew that wiped and shined with chamois in the sun and had a chance for tips.

Then someone at the Bim Bam got busted for booking numbers and horses. Not one of the brothers, either. The white manager.

Spider's parole officer, a sixty-some-year-old named Mrs. Graham, wouldn't stand for Spider being even close to trouble such as that. No matter that Spider had stayed mainly straight, caused no hassles, even passed up some easy chances—she had to lose that job for him and tell him he was better off being a box boy.

BOX BOY.

That was what it said after his name on his time card.

As for things going on, practically everyone there at the supermarket was into some kind of ripoff. A couple of guys in the meat department left every day with five or six pounds of top sirloin or filet mignon wrapped in plastic and taped to their lower legs under their trousers. In the receiving department, some of the clerks intercepted and put whole cases of imported stuff into the trunks of their cars. Like olives and cheese and chocolate. And the check-out girls had ways of cashing in for themselves, especially whenever it was really busy. There was no way, however, for Spider to get away with anything much more than a dime Hostess cupcake or a box of crackers.

Once when he had a toothache because a big filling that had been done by a San Quentin dentist came out, Spider asked around for aspirin and no one had any, so he went to the store's Health and Beauty Aids section. He found bottles of Bufferin there but only in the 100-tablet economy size. His tooth was aching so much he opened a bottle and took a couple. The aisle captain, Lyle Stratford, saw him do it and told him he'd have to pay for the Bufferin. Spider turned his head away so as not to be heard when he mumbled, "Fuck you." Then he had to act compliant, a price to be paid along with the ninety-five cents. Spider was sure the ninety-five cents went into Stratford's pocket. Anyway, no way was Spider going to get himself back into slam for any Bufferin.

Spider was twenty-seven. He had spent eight years, or nearly one of every three of his days, in a penitentiary. According to the black average that ratio would double when he got older. Spider's last stretch in Quentin was his longest.

67

Five years. For armed robbery. He'd taken part in hijacking a truckload of what was supposed to have been furs that turned out to be cheap wool coats.

At times Spider had carried a gun, but he'd only shot at *things*, practicing, never at a person. He figured if everyone was as afraid of a gun as he was, a gun was good to just have. He got his ominous name from having arms longer than they should have been and, as a kid, being best at climbing fences and other such vertical structures.

Chances were Spider would never have gotten into trouble with the law if he'd had any of the stereotypical black abilities. But he wasn't at all musical, for example, didn't have the head, hands, feet or voice for it. One thing he always wanted to be was a disc jockey, but he wasn't really glib enough. And he wasn't outstanding at any sports.

The only sort of so-called typical thing was he looked fine in clothes. Lean and mean, it was said. Unfortunately. Because for Spider to dude himself up right required more money than he could make being anything he could just naturally, legally, be.

At the moment Spider was being strong, carrying out over a hundred pounds of groceries, including sacks of charcoal briquettes, for a frizzy red-headed fat lady and her chalky-skinned husband, who got into the car and made Spider wait in the rain while he tried three pockets before coming up with a thirty-five-cent tip, counting five pennies.

It was then that Spider noticed the blue Mustang drive in. He recognized it as the one that belonged to the rich white chick Lois Stevens, the friend of Felicia. Felicia Artez was one of the check-out girls, a comfortably built Mexican. Earlier that day Felicia had mentioned to Spider that she had connected for some methamphetamine. As usual Lois had supplied the money for it. She and Felicia and Spider would go to Felicia's apartment later, drop some of the speed and ball maybe, probably. They'd done it before.

Spider watched Lois get out of her car and go into the

market. She saw Spider but didn't acknowledge him, which he thought was cool of her.

Spider was glad to see Lois for another reason. After work he had to go down to San Diego to report to his parole officer. Now at least he wouldn't have to ride the effin' bus.

For thirty years that piece of coastal property had two houses on it, located as far as possible off the highway so as to be directly overlooking the beach and water.

One of the houses was large, twenty-some rooms, the other less than a third that size. There had also been a restaurant on the highway there. A small seafood place. It was an eyesore, had changed hands often and no owner had ever made enough from it or cared enough to want to help the wooden building fight the quicker deterioration that came with being near the ocean.

In 1967 the larger house was sold to an anonymous buyer, who never moved in. A year later the smaller house was purchased by someone and left vacant. The restaurant went shortly thereafter, its owner glad to make a little more on it than he'd ever expected from a buyer who, represented by a real estate broker acting on behalf of another broker, remained unknown.

All three transactions complete, titles cleared and transferred, it came out then, and the former owners bit themselves for not having held on for more, at least twice as much or more.

Lots 10938, 10939, 10939A of Orange County tract 673 had been patiently, cleverly acquired by one large business.

Within six months the property was transformed and there stood the Seaside Supermarket.

On its own private bluff.

The coastline at that spot scalloped out as much as a thousand feet. All along the edge it was a sharp drop of nearly two hundred.

Between the market and highway was a blacktop parking area for five hundred cars. To help circulate customer traffic a double-lane drive ran around the rear of the market, but after business hours a heavy chain was strung across to prevent anyone from using it. Splendid view of the ocean, out of view from the highway, it had become a nighttime place for loving in cars. What spoiled the good thing was that too many people left evidence of their ardor.

The supermarket itself was mainly cinder blocks and glass, a rectangular-shaped structure 120 feet deep by 280 feet long, hoping to make up with size for what it lacked aesthetically. An impression of spaciousness, increased by height—a single story equal to two and a half.

Despite its ample dimensions, like so many buildings throughout Southern California it did not give a feeling of permanence. It seemed unsubstantial, as though put up hurriedly with little faith in the future, short-term prosperity in mind. A California habit, perhaps the remnant influence of gold rushes and earthquakes and certainly persuaded by the climate, usually so mild.

Royal palms. Groups of them helped soften the market's corners. Other landscaping was limited to semitropical spear-leafed shrubs, defiant full-grown growths set in beds covered with layers of wood chips, so they hardly ever needed tending.

71

The northern end of the building was solid, windowless. The southern end had a high, extra-wide opening for stock delivery. There were two doors in the rear, an emergency exit and a way in and out for employees only.

The front, the face of the place, made it appear light and open. It was almost entirely glass, large sections of heavy gauge plate glass that ran from ground to roof. Entrance–exits for customers were located extreme left and right. A special mesh gate was used to protect the glass front from outside. It was electrically controlled. From its housing along the edge of the roof it rolled out and down all the way and automatically locked itself in place. Once the gate was in down position it was impossible for anyone to enter or leave the market without switching on the automatic control mechanism. That required a unique magnetic key. Identical steel-mesh gates also made the side and rear doors impenetrable.

The mesh gates were not part of the market's original design. They had been installed a year after completion, because young men defying law and death at three in the morning included the parking area in their version of a Monaco-style race course. Twice cars had screeched around, fishtailed and crashed through the market's front panes.

Since the gates were put in, several times there had been trouble of another sort. Employees got locked in and had to call the manager at home to come let them out. Once a pair of muscular stock clerks and a good-looking blonde checker got left inside on a Saturday and had to spend the weekend in there because the manager was out of town. Considering what they could eat, drink and do, they made the best of it.

Across the front of the market at the roof line, individual lighted letters seven feet tall changed from all red, added some white and became bordered with blue as they rotated in unison:

SEASIDE

One of 538 stores in a chain. However, the only one where the chain name "FOODWAY" was given second billing. FOODWAY was a totally owned subsidiary of Horton Simpson, Incorporated, a conglomerate with such diverse holdings as Fiberglas speedboats, room deodorants, a reptile-skin processing plant and lipstick. At Horton Simpson board meetings on the seventy-third floor of the Horton Simpson building in New York City the agenda often included visual reassurance that the firm actually did own so many different things. A slide show of photographs accompanied by a pretaped spiel. The Seaside always represented the rest of the supermarket chain. Same slide everytime: the market shown from its most favorable angle with its palms set ideally against the Pacific and a true-blue California sky.

During the year 1974, the 40,960 supermarkets in this country rang up a record ninety-eight-billion, two-hundred-sixty-five-million dollars.

The Seaside did its bit, much better than average. Two hundred and ten thousand a week.

Over ten million for the year.

On the inside the Seaside had some features that made it extraordinary. Several supermarkets in its area were just as large, but they didn't appear to be, didn't give the feeling of nearly as much space. That was as planned: the Seaside's ceiling was exceptionally high, twenty-three feet with no supporting interior columns. The effect was openness, room to breathe, conducive to shopping.

Another attraction was the advanced method of checking out at Seaside. It had what the trade called a completely computerized front end. All eleven of its check-out stands were equipped with IBM 3660 scanning systems. Each purchase was exposed for merely a moment to a four-inch-by-eight-inch glass-covered slot in the counter surface. Just long enough for the scanner within the slot to read the Universal Product Code that appeared on each item. The Universal Product Code was a symbol made up of numbers and an arrangement of lines of various lengths and thicknesses. The scanner translated it into price, category, brand and other information. No need for a checker to punch her fingers numb. The scanner did everthing—except make mistakes and steal.

The Seaside's fully electronic front-end system fed data into a central processor. A touch on a console key and instantly there came a readout, a positively accurate count on how much a certain check stand had in its till or how much to the penny was the total take of the market at that moment. The system also kept inventory, showed what products were moving well, which brands were shelf warmers. It advised when to stock, what to push, even gave an early warning signal against overstocking. As one old-time grocer said: "It did everything but wipe the store manager's ass and maybe would have done that if its roll of paper had been softer."

In other ways the Seaside was similar to other supermarkets of the 30,000- to 35,000-square-foot category. It had twelve gondolas of tiered shelves (islands) for merchandise, each seventy feet long, six feet high. The islands were constructed and arranged according to the recommendations of marketing experts who made a science of such seemingly obvious things. There were no cross aisles, for example. Once a customer entered the store and headed down the first long, sleek, polished terrazzo aisle, it was practically impossible for him not to shop the entire market. It was like being caught in a very well planned maze — down and around, down and around, the shopping cart somehow getting fuller than intended.

To buy a staple such as milk or butter, a shopper had to go all the way to the deepest corner of the store. There was method to the inconvenience. Only the most single-minded or extremely hurried persons could make the long trip there and back without being attracted or reminded to buy other things.

On the perimeter of the store, going clockwise from its southern end, were: frozen foods, produce, dairy products, meats (with special polarized lighting so the meat looked a fresher, fleshier red), liquor (high-profit item set apart within a carpeted alcove), gourmet foods, delicatessen, bakery, housewares, toys and school supplies, photo shop and a pet-supply center. The entire western side of the building, a 7,000-square-foot area, was partitioned out of sight for receiving, storage and stock preparation.

The management office and the computer system's processing center were situated within a wide overhang above the south end of the store. A spiraling metal stairway led up to it. The office had a long window for an overall view.

By no means unseen were the large styrofoam letters displayed across the flat of that dominating overhang. Letters in red. Again that same attention-demanding red. Customers saw it without realizing, the motivational researchers claimed. It splashed the shopper's unconscious with:

BUY THE SEASIDE

The play on words was punctuated before and after by an identical pair of suns. Brilliant orangy yellow styrofoam cutouts with irregular flaming circumferences and smiling, happy-eyed painted faces.

Opposite the supermarket, on the inland side of the Coast Highway, stood the office of Grove Realty. A nice white ideal country house with banistered porch, peaked roof and an eave.

It was a real illusion. Californian, like one of those forty-foot rotating doughnuts, except the house was under- rather than overscale. Only two small rooms.

Less than a hundred feet away on that same side was a Gulf service station, a six pumper.

Both these businesses had literally carved places for themselves—out of the hill that came down right to the edge of the highway.

The hill was one of those called the Sheep Hills.

Part of the San Joaquins.

It went up for almost eleven hundred feet. Poor soil, crumbly in some places, sticky, claylike elsewhere, ranging in color from pale beige to ochre. Sparsely covered by scrubby, shallow-rooted plants that didn't look alive.

Nevertheless, it was rich ground.

Propped and nestled on it here and there were homes of the hundred-fifty-thousand to two-hundred-fifty-thousand class.

Twenty-seven altogether had taken advantage of any slight crease on the steep, dug in and spread out. Most had private gates and drives, reflecting name plates, full-grown trees brought in. Got their good green atmosphere from as many hibiscus and gardenia bushes as their expensively hauled topsoil could hold.

All said it was well worth the effort. Especially those situated at the top said that.

What a fantastic ocean view. And practically perfect television reception.

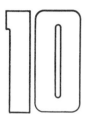

"Like another asshole," Kemp said.

"I didn't mean you need it." Dan shrugged, palms up, and smiled, easing the sales pressure.

"Know how many items I already carry?" Kemp made it sound as though it were a personal burden, the market and everything in it. He was the manager. It was his usual way to answer himself. "Ten thousand three hundred and some."

"You do a hell of a job, Phil. Everybody says."

Kemp agreed. Dan walked with him down Aisle Two toward the front of the store. When they reached the end of the aisle Kemp paused to tidy up bottles of a national brand of salad dressings that were abundantly displayed. He did it only to get to Dan. "Besides," Kemp told him, "the committee didn't approve it."

That sounded like a turn-down. Dan knew better, interpreted it correctly that Kemp was inviting a deal. Generally,

Kemp had to go along with the buying committee, same as all the other markets in the chain, had to stock whatever brands the committee decided. But the fringes were left for him. It was something upper management undoubtedly knew about, accepted practice as long as it didn't cause any trouble or major losses.

Dan Mandel was one of those fringe benefits. District retail man for a San Francisco company called Future Foods, a division of Western Americana Chemical. Its products were nonfood foods, such as canned puddings that had the most convincing flavors, appearance and consistency. Fifteen ingredients listed in very small print on the label. Fourteen out of the fifteen were chemicals and preservatives. Kids ate them, as suggested, right out of the can, because they came with easy, peel-off lids.

"Our puddings taste even better than real," Dan earnestly claimed.

The Future Foods line also featured a whipped topping in the skinniest, tallest can. It squirted out fluffier and could be piled up higher than actual whipped cream. There was also a dietetic ice cream-like food that couldn't possibly make anyone fat because it didn't offer nourishment of any sort, 100 percent artificial and mostly air.

At the moment Dan hoped to persuade store manager Kemp not merely to stock his company's brand-newest product but make it a push item.

Morning Squares.

They were sweet, brownie sort of cakes that were said to contain the chemical nutritional equivalent of a juice, bacon, eggs and buttered-toast breakfast. Meant to be nibbled on the way to work or dropped into the stomach of anyone in too much of a hurry.

"They don't spoil," Dan said, selling.

Kemp acted dubious. There was nothing he disliked more than a product spoiling on the shelf.

"No shit," Dan assured. And it was the truth. There wasn't

anything in Morning Squares that could spoil. To make triple sure, they were loaded with three different kinds of preservatives.

Kemp remained unreadable.

Dan went into his act. Magic was a pastime that suited him. He was a short, quick man in his late thirties. Practically everything about him was quick — his speech, movements, smile. He liked surprises, puzzled reactions. Sleight of hand seemed natural for him.

He had come prepared. He palmed a slip of paper and seemed to pluck it out of Kemp's breast pocket. He handed the slip to Kemp, who unfolded it and glimpsed the name Rita and a Long Beach phone number. He stuffed the slip casually into his pocket.

Dan took that as a sign of agreement.

Kemp continued his indifference, added to it by aiming his attention at Check-out Stand Four. The checker there was a dull-haired blonde, a Phyllis something. Kemp suspected her. He hadn't caught her yet but he was certain she was raking back. A number of times he had noticed the same customers waiting in her line with large orders, waiting even though other lines were shorter.

The one way a checker could beat the electronic scanning system was to appear to be exposing an item to the scanner while actually bypassing it. A checker had to be fast to get away with it. Usually the items bypassed were higher-priced ones, such as meat. So an order that should have totaled, say, fifty dollars came out only thirty. By prearrangement, Phyllis would meet her *steady* customers somewhere to split the difference. Kemp believed she could be raking back as much as two hundred a week, maybe more.

He watched her now, running through a big two-cart order, her hands a blurr of efficiency. Kemp was near-sighted. Squinting, he tried to detect any bypassing of the scanner by Phyllis. He thought of putting on his glasses but decided to hell with it, he'd catch her someday—soon.

Dan asked: "Did you see her?"

"Huh?" Kemp had the feeling his mind was being read.

"She walked right by, just now, right here." Dan directed Kemp's view down the aisle to a nice figure in gray. "Marsha Hilbert."

"Probably just somebody who looks like her."

"No way. I've seen all her pictures. That's her. Christ, I wish she'd turn around."

A moment of silent appreciation for the legs and buttocks of a star. She went from sight. Dan rushed over to the next aisle for another glimpse of her in profile passing across the opposite end.

"Sweet-eating stuff," he muttered.

"Get her autograph," Kemp said.

"On my face."

A scoff from Kemp. "Dream about it."

"I have, plenty of times."

They shared brief, knowing laughs.

Back to business. Dan had a brand-new fifty-dollar bill. He had it folded a certain way as tight as possible so it was only a thin half-inch square that showed the face of President Ulysses S. Grant. He flashed it discreetly so only Kemp saw it. Then he made it disappear.

Dan was really good at it, so quick with his hands that Kemp, though watching every move, didn't see him do it. Dan grinned his most winning grin. Kemp wasn't surprised when he fingered inside his breast pocket and felt the fifty there with the slip of paper. They belonged together.

Kemp had decided on it, just in case, from the start. He told Dan, "End of Island Five." Displayed there now were some private-label cake mixes. They had been there a week, about as much time as the cake-mix salesman had paid for, according to Kemp's way of figuring.

"Front end?" Dan hoped.

"Rear."

Front would have been better but Dan didn't press. He'd

80

gotten what every peddler wanted: his product displayed at one of the ends of the islands, apart from the common, crowded shelves. Featured in abundance, important looking, announced by the big red words "NEW" and "SPECIAL," Morning Squares wouldn't be overlooked. Even if they didn't sell big it was worth the fifty for an end-of-island location at the Seaside. Dan would take color Polaroids of it and use them as leverage with other markets. Also, his reputation with Future Foods would get a nice boost.

"I'll have product here by Monday," he told Kemp.

The manager was already walking away.

Dan did some mental arithmetic on Kemp's back. Twelve islands. Twenty-four ends. At fifty each, a thousand extra every week for Kemp. Minimum. Cash. Jesus. He doubted that Kemp would use the Rita number, but if Kemp did, he, Dan, owed Rita another twenty-five for her promise to be especially good and not show her impatience. He wondered where Kemp kept all that grease.

Kemp also had his mind on money as he climbed the metal spiral stairs to the office. Not his own money but the next thing to it. He hesitated on the landing and glanced at the safe. Safe enough, he told himself.

The safe was built solidly into the wall, up out of reach, accessible only by a narrow metal ramp off to the left of the office. In plain view of everyone during the day, kept brightly spotlighted so it was easily seen from without all night.

Bothering Kemp was the fact that the Brinks armored car had not made its regular pickup earlier in the week. They'd had to skip the stop, were running behind on all clients because of the rain. Next pickup at the Seaside was scheduled for tomorrow, Saturday. Brinks had told Kemp when he called. They'd be there Saturday for sure.

They'd damn well better. He'd be more than uneasy if he had to leave that much cash in the safe over the weekend.

A hundred seventy-eight thousand.

81

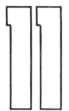

The crack.

It began at the northern edge of the bluff about twenty feet out from the shoulder of the highway. Not zigzagging but almost perfectly straight, it ran parallel with the highway for the entire length of the supermarket parking area.

The crack occurred on the blacktopped surface around noon of that day. It was only a quarter-inch wide, not noticed by any of the people in the hundreds of cars that passed over it, coming and going. Perhaps if there hadn't been the rain someone would have noticed. Perhaps someone walking along in the sun would have seen it, but even then the crack probably would not have caused concern, certainly not alarm. Nothing extraordinary about such a defect. Things, especially, so it seemed, in California, became faulty too soon: sleekest buildings, smoothest sidewalks, freeways after only a week's traffic.

The same indifference prevailed even when at four-thirty the crack on the parking area spread to nearly three inches, and the people in the cars experienced a faint jolt as they rolled over it.

If someone had stopped, gotten out, taken a look, had the knowledge to appraise what was happening, there still would have been time enough to evacuate everyone.

At five minutes to five the first shudder was felt inside the supermarket.

It wasn't much, just a slight back-and-forth motion that lasted five seconds. A shake that instantly brought the same fear to the front of everyone's mind.

Earthquake.

There were two hundred thirty-eight people in the market, including thirty-two employees.

Some grabbed on to anything, expecting worse to come, some laughed for courage, a few traded appropriate blasé exclamations such as "Oops!" Many wanted out. They rushed to the front of the market, creating a jam-up at the lane openings. Panic was contagious. People climbed up and over counters.

Then a lot of things happened at once.

The crack on the parking lot suddenly widened, became an eight-foot-wide chasm. All along, the entire bluff separated by that much from the mainland. A couple of parked cars tumbled into it. So did Mrs. Mary Berrigan with her carload of groceries and three young children. Her car, an American Motors Gremlin, was right over the crack when it opened up.

The supermarket wrenched in place, twisted one way and the other.

The long, large structure shook and bucked a bit, though not too violently.

It settled at a fourteen-degree pitch, front lower.

At a spot six feet up on the north wall a water pipe burst, broke apart at a joint. It was the eight-inch pipe that carried the market's main supply for fire protection. Seventy-five-pound pressure, as required. Water gushed through the wall and quickly flooded the front of the market, the lower part, end to end.

Sixty-six people were in water up to mid-calf.

The terrazzo floor split. A slab of it crunched, ground against itself and buckled upward. Jagged hunks of it formed an opening.

Immediately, from that opening, like a cannon from a turret, emerged a section of six-inch steel pipe, the conduit for the market's high-voltage cable. And there it was — the cable, one inch thick, black vinyl insulated, containing thirteen thousand volts. It seemed too substantial to stretch and snap easily as it did, like a string of licorice.

The concrete-encased transformer vault exploded at the rear of the store.

There was the ominous odor of electricity scorching plastic.

The cable whipped the air, performed wild contortions for a few seconds before it reared its crackling hot head and plunged into the water.

Sixty-five out of sixty-six persons experienced the silent, slamming death of electrocution — thirteen thousand volts seizing the legs, at a stroke invading every extreme, overpowering the capacity of the heart, the brain. Done in little more than a flash.

The sixty-sixth person standing in the water was Spider Leaks. He saw the people around him go rigid, saw their mouths open for screams that never came out, eyes bulging as though to pop from sockets. Spider didn't know then why it happened to everyone except him. Not until they had all collapsed did he realize that his rubber boots had saved him. Damn good old knee-high boots that he'd needed on his previous job at the car wash. Because they made walking heavy he hadn't worn the boots yesterday or the day before and he almost hadn't today. His regular working shoes, his only pair, had dried hard and too stiff to put on.

84

More explosions now. Sputtering bursts in a back room. Circuits shorting out. Forty-two twenty-amp fuses blowing, the main distribution panel spitting sparks.

Then nothing, not a watt of power.

Lights off, refrigeration off, everything.

The electrically controlled steel gates released and fell, covering the entire face of the market, as well as the side and rear exits.

For a long moment everything was still, everyone remained absolutely in place, breaths held as though movement even that slight might set something off or cause imbalance.

Rumbling in the ground beneath the market, like peristalsis in a huge bowel.

The market itself, with its more than ten thousand items, had suffered relatively little damage until now. Some gallon containers of milk had fallen and split open, causing a slick mess. Here and there a few cartons and cans had tumbled from the most precarious stacks, such as cans of Bumble Bee chunk white tuna that had plunked to the floor, some landing so they rolled down the inclined aisle.

But for the moment, stillness. And in it, surely amplified, disbelief and terror.

A glass jar fell. Bing cherries in thick syrup made a blood-red splash. Which seemed to cue the start.

Outside, the bluff separated further from the mainland, forming an abyss forty feet wide and three times that deep. At the same moment the body of the bluff gave way, sank a hundred feet, the height of a nine story building.

For those within the supermarket it was as though they had been flown into a deep air pocket. But that helpless dropping sensation was completely out of context here. The market by its proportions defied such treatment. It seemed to tear at itself, lurched, heaved every which way, gyrating laterally as it plunged. . . .

An eleven-year-old boy who nearly always had to be

bribed to eat any kind of vegetable was killed by broccoli. The one-pound package of it, frozen hard as a brick, was flung out of the freezer case. It struck the boy in the back of the head.

A thin woman was pierced through, back to front, by a broken spearlike bottle of diet cola. Almost deliberately, it seemed.

A man wearing prescribed dark glasses was smashed to death between the eyes by an aerosol can of window cleaner. The container, if purposely aimed, could not have been more dead center on target.

One brand of soups that had always dominated its section by occupying all three tiers of shelves took off and, at incredible speed, momentarily swarmed about an older woman before attacking her like red-and-white bees. The woman never knew what hit her.

Another woman, younger and shapely, was struck by a twelve-pound frozen turkey, the sort considered more desirable, with artificially induced larger breasts. The cold, dead bird, thrown hard like a fleshy stone, caught the woman mid-chest, crushing her.

In the specially appointed alcove where liquor was sold hundreds of bottles buffeted and flew about, smashing against one another. The carpet in the alcove was immediately sodden. Three customers and a clerk were badly wounded by glass, but they died from inhaling such a concentration of alcohol fumes.

In the fresh meat department two knives honed razor sharp jumped from their brackets and cut across the air to sever the main arteries in the forearm and thigh of a butcher. Accustomed as he was to the sight of blood, he could only scream while his own quickly spurted the life out of him.

Shelves were left bare. Everything shot or tumbled or slid off. Some people were buried beneath tons of canned goods. The bakery and delicatessen counters overturned. The entire contents of the meat, dairy and other open cases bolted up and out.

Shopping carts became angry, lethal vehicles that rammed mid-air into people or mowed them down at high speed.

For those few moments in the Seaside Supermarket life and death played turnabout. More than ten thousand items were animated into what seemed a retributive frenzy, as though they took this opportunity to spend their wrath on creatures who normally swallowed them and used them and took them for granted.

At the end of the drop, on impact, all the floor-to-ceiling windows along the front of the store shattered. Hunks of heavy-gauge glass burst out. Shards of it shot through the air like shrapnel.

The drop and its consequences killed sixty-two.

One was the check-out girl Felicia Artez, who had taken a break and was in the employees' toilet with Warren Stevens' younger sister, Lois. In that privacy Felicia has passed over the speed to Lois — twenty Ambars, yellow-coated ten-milligram tablets. Sixty dollars' worth. That much because they were, as Felicia explained, long-ball hitters. Meaning they took her up, leveled off after a while and then came on strong again, distributing their effect over six to eight hours.

Lois transferred the Ambars from the plastic vial into a small cotton pouch. She undid her jeans and placed the pouch inside her bikini panties. She patted, flattened it so it didn't show.

Meanwhile, Felicia had gone into the toilet booth and was using a foot to work the flushing lever when it happened.

Water belched up six feet from the bowl. Felicia had no chance to grab on to anything. She slid against the smooth inside wall of the booth, went up and hit the low ceiling.

Lois, who had been using the wash basin, clutched its under edge. She was shaken but unhurt. She called to Felicia. No reply. The booth door was bolted from inside. Lois retrieved an overturned paper towel receptacle. She stood on it to look over the top of the booth.

Felicia was bent front up over the toilet bowl, legs and arms at awkward angles, like a tossed rag doll. Her head hung limp by its own deadweight in an impossible position, twisted completely around.

Frank Brydon, who had stopped in at the market only for some Mexican beer, was reaching into an upright beverage cooler when it happened. He used the cooler, with both hands got a good grip on one of its permanent wire shelves, managed to shove his legs with pressure against the thick frame of its opening and hunched his head as much as possible. Bottles banged around inside the cooler, striking his arms and shoulders and grazing the top of his head. The full-length cooler door slammed at his back and side. But he managed to hang on.

For a moment Marsha Hilbert was weightless and then let down hard. The beautiful motion picture star slid unbecomingly about thirty feet to the facade of a check-out stand, probably would have been hurt but for some packaged loaves of spongy white bread that cushioned the impact.

Elliot Janick was flipped end-over-end into a refrigerated case. Inelegantly, the famous filmmaker replaced ham, bologna and other cold cuts. The uncomfortable frosty confines of the case protected him.

When Warren Stevens, the bear killer, was thrown down, he doubled up, knees tight to chest, making as small a target as possible. He was pelted by, among other things, jars of baby food.

Gloria Rand, the fifty year old who looked thirty, was in the fresh produce section. She put her hands tight over her face. Heads of cabbage and cauliflower, eggplant and honeydews whirled around her like taunting satellites. She ended up wedged against the base of a large bin that had contained a special on early, tasteless strawberries.

Ex-convict, box boy, Spider Leaks was almost killed for the second time in less than three minutes when the front windows shattered. A chunk of glass came down like a guillotine within inches of his head, and another smaller piece sliced some skin from the round of his shoulder.

Judith Ward and Marion Mercer had just chosen identical

things they might claim they had cooked from scratch. Packages of frozen noodles Romanoff, asparagus soufflés, and an assortment of homemade tasting cupcakes. Judith and Marion wouldn't be seeing one another again until Monday, because Marion had to drive up to Bakersfield for an overnight visit with her sister-in-law. It would be another long, lonely weekend. Marion would phone, she promised. They headed for the express check-out. Suddenly, they were clutching one another. Their arms were wrapped and their legs overlapped. They took the shock together.

Amy Javakian got a bloody nose from a hit, like a punch, from an airborne potato. It knocked her down but not out. Her first thought was to somehow protect her unborn child. She remembered from something she'd read that to relax was best. She ended up among some cartons of macaroni, noodles and dried beans.

Amy's husband, Peter, took some painful knocks but was not badly injured. He found himself jammed against a magazine rack beneath a pile of paperback books and egg-shaped containers of panty hose. Some of the hose had popped out right before Peter's eyes and looked like bunched up patches of shriveled skin.

Emory Swanson, the insurance man, could have gotten out in plenty of time—if he had left the market as soon as he was told it didn't carry the brand of toasted coconut chips his wife, Eleanor, wanted. However, Emory, in his fashion, had to get away with something. He helped himself to a bag of Pennsylvania pretzels that had been baked in Glendale, and he nibbled those as he strolled the aisles. On the lookout for something likely. Capers? Anchovies? Tobler chocolate? He settled on Ultra-Brite toothpaste. He had a way with toothpaste. He opened the flaps of one end, inverted the carton and let the tube slide into his jacket pocket. He then put the empty carton back into place on the shelf, and that was that.

When it happened, Emory survived because he got sandwiched in, surrounded tightly by three other people, who absorbed the danger. Two of the three were killed by well-known nationally advertised flying objects.

People wanted to see it.

Traffic was barely moving on the Coast Highway. A number of drivers had pulled over to park so they could get more than a passing look. Cars were backed up for miles in both directions.

The state highway patrol got things moving. They promptly cleared and closed that section of highway, a six-mile stretch. Northbound traffic was rerouted via the Crown Valley Parkway. Those headed south had to use Laguna Canyon. Only residents of the area with proof of that fact were allowed through the police blockades.

The rain was persistent as ever. Actually it seemed to be coming down harder, streaking, and the wind made conditions worse. It had started getting stronger earlier that afternoon and by now it was almost up to gale force. It was the sort of deceitful wind that alternately lulled and gusted,

90

blowing from seaward or down coast from the north or frequently, as though to demonstrate its perversity, from both directions at once.

The rain tatooed on the yellow raingear of the highway patrolmen.

The time was five-fifteen.

The rain rat-a-tat-tatted a slightly different sound on the beige-colored waterproof "turnouts" of the firemen. Four firetrucks — pumpers — had come from Laguna Beach. The Orange County Fire Protection Department had dispatched an aerial unit, more commonly known as a hook and ladder. Because the bluff was partly within the limits of Laguna Beach, that city's fire chief was in charge of the operation.

Fire Chief Croy.

His white helmet stood out. Only a chief could wear a white one. Other fire officers had red helmets and ordinary firemen wore black.

Chief Croy and his officer assistant, a man named Pinkett, stood on the shoulder of the highway, apart from their men, who had hurried and now had to wait for orders.

The chief was a thick-trunked man around five eight. He appeared strong, body and face. The butt of a filter-tipped cigarette, extinguished by the rain, was in the left side of his mouth—not forgotten, a comfort. He was a no-hands smoker.

He walked along the roadside and tried his best to conceal his incredulity. The whole goddamn bluff had broken away and dropped. Now it was like an isolated mesa a thousand feet long by a thousand wide, and there on its far edge was the supermarket.

Chief Croy called for and got a pair of binoculars. He focused on the front of the market. Through the rain, through the market's steel gate he saw people inside, like prisoners, close up to the grillwork, gazing out, some waving frantically as though fearing they might be overlooked.

How to get to them?

"We got the aerial," Pinkett reminded.

91

"Yeah." Croy thought about it. "What's the lowest angle we can get on it, thirty or what?"

"About thirty."

Croy through more about it, grunting as he did. The aerial truck could be brought right to the edge. Its ladder could be extended sixty-five feet. At an upward thirty-degree angle that would just about put the tip of the ladder over the bluff. In this rain and especially with the wind that ladder would be swaying like a reed, and even if a man did manage to hang on all the way to the top, from there he'd still have to shinny down a hundred-fifty-foot line. Croy decided he sure as hell wouldn't want to try it. He also knew if he asked for volunteers he'd get them.

"Think of any other way?" Pinkett asked.

"Could be."

Croy went to his municipal car, a bright red Buick. He lighted a fresh cigarette and got on the radio phone. He called the Marine Corps air station at El Toro, ten miles away.

The flight officer told him, "We're grounded here, not putting anything up."

Croy explained the problem in detail.

The flight officer told him, "Hang on."

Croy assumed permission was being asked from higher up —anyway, advice.

In a couple of minutes the flight officer came back on. "What's the minimum you need?"

Croy told him.

At that moment Captain Dodd arrived on the scene. Dodd was area commander of the highway patrol, headquartered in Santa Ana. A tall man, about six four, he had just turned fifty. He could quit anytime he wanted, was already in five years over the twenty required for retirement.

When Dodd saw the situation he seemed more angry than anything else. He mumbled to himself. He wasn't wearing any boots. He was the only man there without boots. And when Chief Croy went over to him, Croy noticed a snag tear in the back shoulder of Dodd's raincoat. Evidently Dodd wasn't personally prepared for such an emergency, Croy thought.

The two men exchanged nods and each other's names for hellos.

Captain Dodd was told the plan.

He made no comment, glanced dubiously upward, then down to the market, then turned his back to the wind.

"Not much daylight left," remarked Chief Croy.

Twenty minutes later two helicopters came from inland, over Sheep Hills, low, noisy. They were HSL-1's with twin-bladed, tandem rotating propellers fore and aft. The sort of choppers that had been used in Vietnam to evacuate casualties. These two might very possibly have seen action in Nam the way they were camouflaged, splotched green, brown, yellow. They were piloted by Marine Corps officers and each carried a contingent of six Navy medical corpsmen.

The choppers swooped out over the ocean at an altitude of a thousand feet, made a wide banking turn, descended to five hundred and came back, flying south to north, for a look at their objective: the paved open area of the supermarket's parking lot.

"Those guys got balls," Chief Croy said.

Captain Dodd went closer to the edge of the breakaway to better examine it. He mentally bet it would still let go some. No telling how much or when. If the men in the choppers did what was expected of them, the rescue would take an hour, two at most. No more than two. Night was due at eight, and darkness would come even earlier because of the rain.

The choppers were coming in now. From seaward, one after the other. The closer they got, the more evident it was how little control the pilots had. The wind was fighting them, blasting from every which way.

The choppers gave up on two approaches before committing to a set-down. They hovered above the parking lot, reacting more like lightweight insects than heavy machines. They floundered, spun, bobbed.

Finally, one of the choppers managed to touch down.

The moment its landing gear came in contact with the blacktop a sheet of wind, more violent than any before, wrapped itself in under the chopper, and, at the same time, another powerful gust smacked it from starboard. The chopper was scooped up, flipped over on its side and for a moment was suspended mid-air.

The second chopper was about fifty feet higher and fifty away from the first, normally a safe distance. A tremendous gust caught it head on, forced its nose straight up.

Then, as though within the power of a pair of giant, invisible hands, the two choppers were slapped together. The explosion was instantaneous, a brilliant orange-and-red billow. Parts flew and fell and the fuselages of the two craft, melted together by the fiery impact, smouldered on the parking lot. No survivors.

Chief Croy went and sat in his red car.

After a few minutes he reported what had happened to El Toro.

The flight officer asked twice if there were any survivors. Out of habit he said, "Thank you, sir," when he clicked off.

Captain Dodd got into the chief's car.

"Fucking wind," Croy said.

Dodd agreed.

"Got any ideas, Dodd?"

"A possibility."

"We'd be over there by now if it wasn't for the wind." Croy's cigarette between his lips went up and down in cadence with his words.

Dodd didn't believe a man could enjoy having smoke in his eyes most of the time.

"What's your idea?" Croy asked.

Dodd was picturing it.

"We can't use the aerial. We already thought of that."

"I know."

94

"Well, let's have it."

Captain Dodd took out a note pad and a felt-tipped pen. He made a crude profile sketch of the breakaway, the chasm and the bluff. "We'll go man for man on it," he said. "One of yours and one of ours."

"Need the publicity?"

A bad joke, to relieve the tension, Dodd decided, giving Croy the benefit of the doubt. "Just that it's risky," Dodd told him, and continued outlining his plan.

The fireman chosen for it was Ed Larrabee, who had had special instruction in scaling the coastal cliffs.

The highway patrolman chosen was Jack Madsen. He had done quite a bit of mountain climbing on his own time.

Both men, in their mid-twenties, were in excellent physical condition. While things were being made ready they talked together amiably. It was by no means a contest. They genuinely wished one another luck as they were about to go over the side.

It had been decided that rather than be lowered in tension they would repel down — that is, with a line around their hips, they would control their own rate of descent. It gave them greater freedom. They were each equipped with two-way constant walkie-talkies strapped to their upper arms, so at any time they could easily communicate with those above and with one another.

Over the edge and down the line they went, spaced forty feet apart. With the repelling technique they used their legs to brace and push off from the face of the newly formed cliff. They went down virtually in leaps and bounds, yelling to let out what was part apprehension, part exhilaration.

At about the hundred-foot mark they were across from the level of the bluff. At that point they moved laterally, searching.

"Something, here," Larrabee said.

He kicked vigorously at the face of the cliff, causing considerable dirt to give way.

"No good," he reported.

95

That same sort of hope and letdown was repeated several times by both Larrabee and Madsen. Finally, Madsen came across what appeared to be a really substantial outcropping—some kind of stratified rock, three or four tightly packed layers.

Madsen kicked at it. It didn't give, seemed solid. He called to Larrabee, who swung over. Together they stomped hard as they could, testing the outcropping. Then they worked on the dirt above it, causing the dirt to fall away. What they created was a small ledge.

Madsen would try it.

He rotated to be facing out from the cliff. He placed his feet on the ledge and gradually transferred his weight from the line until all one hundred ninety pounds of him was being supported by the ledge.

Larrabee added his two hundred.

"Got it," he reported.

"Maybe," Madsen added.

Above, the ladder was ready. A fifty-foot ground ladder that weighed two hundred twenty-five pounds. Under regular hurry-up fire conditions four men were assigned to carry it. Now, two lines were attached to an end of it and it was eased over the edge of the cliff and lowered, slowly, to within reach of Madsen and Larrabee.

"Little more," Madsen told them.

"Another three feet."

"Give us a few inches."

"Keep tension until we give the word."

Would the ledge support that much more weight?

Madsen and Larrabee guided the ladder to them, to the surface of the ledge. It required all their strength to keep the ladder close in. When they were sure they had it, Madsen said "Now!" and Larrabee said "Let's have it!" and the men on the lines above released all the weight of the ladder.

The ledge took it. And held.

Larrabee and Madsen gripped the ends of the ladder's

rails, left and right, creating as much inward tension as they could, difficult with the ledge narrow as it was. When they agreed they were set, Larrabee shouted, "Let her down!"

The men above paid out their lines. The ladder came down diagonally. It quivered in the wind, rocked and was almost flipped over but finally it was there, horizontal. The outward end of it just did reach the bluff across the way by a foot or two.

Now came the tougher part.

Larrabee claimed, being a fireman, he was more accustomed to ladders.

Madsen stood on the end of the ladder to help balance it. Larrabee got down on all fours. He used the rails to crawl along, and at first he made good progress. However, when he was about halfway across the wind seemed to discover him. It hit him hard, swirled rain around him spitefully, rattled the ladder that was already bent some under his weight. To save himself, Larrabee had to go belly down on the rungs.

From there on he inched along. The closer he got to the other side, the more the wind seemed to resent him. It tried its hardest to rip him off, kept at it, and then, at the exact moment Larrabee reached the bluff, the wind gave up completely.

Madsen was hauled up.

Captain Dodd had laced black coffee and personal thanks ready for him.

Now rescue was imminent. A special line-throwing gun was put to use. It shot a projectile connected to a lightweight cord over to the bluff. Larrabee retrieved it. The cord, tied to a nylon line of five-thousand-pound test, was fed to Larrabee. He secured the line to the chassis of one of the cars on the parking lot.

By then numerous press people were at the site on the highway. Television dominated, of course. There were the familiar-faced reporters, many technicians, men with sixteen-milli-meter-film cameras and portable video cameras harnessed to them. Everyone wet, dripping, told to keep out of the way,

97

complying as much as their competitiveness allowed. Always nudging forward, not to miss anything. Some cameras, for vantage, were placed atop remote transmission vans.

From a distance, from out to sea looking coastward through the diffusing rain, this area of the highway glowed weirdly, near religiously.

In the banks of television lights Chief Croy's slick white helmet caused flaring blue aftertrails on the monitors each time he moved his head.

"Is there any doubt now about getting those people out?"

"I don't foresee any trouble."

"How long will it take?"

Croy thought, seemed about to reply but didn't, committing the most awful sin of television reportage: silence.

"What's your guess, Chief?"

"Two, three hours," Croy promised and hoped he looked confident. His eyes challenged all the cameras.

"Do you know yet if anyone down there is injured or dead?"

"No."

For heightened drama behind those words the director cut to another camera hand-held on the ambulances parked in an orderly, ominous line. Ten, and more on the way from the nearby hospitals: South Coast Community, Hoag Memorial, San Clemente General. Some resident doctors of those hospitals had come with the ambulances, some on their own. Also nurses.

The firemen had established several lines to and from the bluff. Going down would be a swift ride in a sling. Coming up would be slower and considerably safer via a powered pulley. A fireman took the first, the test, ride. He waited at the bottom along with Larrabee, while two young doctors made the trip, followed by a nurse, and another. Supplies and equipment were lashed to slings and sent down.

Seven-thirty. No letup by the rain. In another half hour it would be dark.

The rescue party hurried across the parking lot toward the supermarket. On the way it passed a Rolls-Royce limousine, overturned. There was a man inside it, dead. A chauffeur with his skull bashed in from having hit the separating glass partition.

When they reached the supermarket the doctors and nurses couldn't take time to indulge their amazement. They went right to work.

"My God. Oh, my God," was all Larrabee could say, while from above on the highway Chief Croy demanded a report. Larrabee finally described the situation.

"How many dead?"

"No way of telling exactly. Not yet."

"About how many? Fifty?"

"More."

Several more doctors and nurses went down. Also firemen with a pair of acetylene torches. There was no way into the market, no way to get anyone out. They would have to cut the gate. They chose a spot, set up the tanks and began burning through. The gate was of tempered cadmium steel. It would be slow going. The firemen requested an additional acetylene torch and tank that were sent down.

Meanwhile, inside the market the dead were placed off to one side. Some of the stock clerks did most of that work. Spider Leaks helped. So did Peter Javakian and Frank Brydon. First the front of the market was cleared of the dead and the glass. The dead were put into shroud bags supplied by the firemen. The kind of shiny black plastic bags with drawstrings used only for that morbid purpose. Best to get the dead from sight. The bodies took up a lot of room. They were placed side by side, but respectfully, not in any way atop or overlapping one another.

The injured were carried to the gate, as close up to it as possible, so the doctors and nurses could attend them through the grillwork. The more seriously injured received priority treatment. For some the most that could be done was take them out of pain with injections of Demerol and morphine. Inverted bottles were hung all along the gate, bottles with rubber tubes running from them, feeding plasma into veins to offset shock and loss of blood.

Now Larrabee reported: "First count, dead—one hundred twenty-two; injured—forty-one. Repeat. . . ."

There was the hissing of the acetylene torches, the crackling jumps of the sparks they made.

Night came.

The firetrucks directed their searchlights down onto the front of the market. A five-thousand-watt floodlight and an equally powerful spot. Other lights on the pumpers contributed five hundred watts each.

It was difficult enough for the doctors and nurses to do their work impeded by the gate, having to reach through its openings to reach wounds that often required swift and delicate attention. Now they also had to contend with shadows.

Flashlights were provided.

Some were handed to those inside the market. Brydon, Spider Leaks and Peter Javakian each got one. The flashlights were the type with a handle, powered by a seven-volt battery. They gave off strong beams but were unwieldy.

Having the flashlights was what brought the three men together. They quickly introduced themselves and went searching. It wasn't easy going, picking their way over broken glass, layers of cans, all sorts and shapes of products.

Partway up Aisle Eight Brydon's light lit upon something different. A small shoe. Peter and Spider tossed aside two shopping carts, removed debris. A boy. In his clutch was a box of breakfast cereal that featured an unbeatable hero. Brydon put his head to the boy's chest. No heartbeat. He lifted the boy tenderly, as though the boy were alive, and carried him over to the rest of the dead.

At another aisle they came upon an old woman, a thin old woman who appeared to be a Mexican. She was unconscious, a rivulet of blood from her nose. Peter and Spider got their arms beneath her, joined their arms and easily took her up and away. Brydon noticed her purse left behind, imitation patent leather. It was open. He was compelled to look into it: a handprinted unofficial identification card, creased and frayed, two dollars and some cents, twelve dollars' worth of federal food stamps.

When they saw to it that the old woman was being cared for, the three men continued searching. Up and down aisles, throughout the back rooms. Brydon and Peter got to know the market, even became familiar with its rubble.

In the vicinity of the shelves that had held gourmet foods, Brydon found one and then another jar of Romanoff caviar. He recognized the unusual-shaped containers immediately. Two-ounce size. As a souvenir, provisional one at that, he put the caviar in his pocket. What he was really looking for, wanted more than anything, had come there for in the first place, was a beer.

Peter Javakian uncovered a six-can pack of a local brew. It was so local it didn't even have snap-off, easy-opening tops.

"Anybody got an opener?"

Spider borrowed one from a stock clerk. Each time the opener punched a triangular hole in the top of the can the agitated beer spewed out fast and high, so nearly half of it was lost.

Brydon, Peter and Spider sat on the bottom shelf of Island Number One. The beer tasted fine. From there they could see the firemen cutting the gate. The blue hot beams of the torches.

"How much more they got to go?" Peter asked.

"Somebody said they're half done," Brydon told him.

Peter asked Spider: "You from around here?"

"Most of the time. You?"

"Hollister," Peter said — then to Brydon: "How about you?"

"I live down the beach." Right away Brydon thought, that

101

word, "live." Wasn't there anything that didn't remind him? He gulped the rest of the beer, opened another, and, with his mind elsewhere, got squirted in the face.

He lowered his head, shook it slowly and laughed aloud at himself.

The supermarket manager, Phil Kemp, was up on the ramp, which had come unbolted from the wall, was wobbly, giving. Kemp hoped to Christ it held long enough for him. He had waited until the firemen were close to through the gate before he came up to the safe. Kemp was disturbed anyway — with the cash registers. When the electricity shorted, for some reason the cash drawer of every register sprung open and couldn't be shut. Before Kemp could get around to them someone had taken the money from four of the registers. He thought he knew who. He had noticed, or at least he was almost sure he had noticed that Negro box boy, the one who had been a convict, close by one of the registers that had been rifled. Sure as he was or not, Kemp believed that boy was the sort low enough to take advantage of such a moment.

Kemp opened the safe.

He had two large canvas money bags with "Brinks" stenciled on them.

The safe was a double safe. Kemp opened the inner one. He didn't bother with the rolls of coins, took only the paper money that was bound by sturdy rubber bands into five-thousand-dollar units. He put equal amounts, by estimate, into each of the bags, belted and buckled the bags closed. Double-checked them, used some heavy twine to hitch the bags together in such a way that he had a halterlike arrangement. He put on the money halter, and finally felt secure enough about it.

As he went down the metal spiral stairs that swayed precariously, Kemp decided that from then on he would stay close to the gate, close to where the opening was being cut. He would tell the firemen who he was and why he should be first out.

Captain Royden Dodd was in Car Thirty-one with the front seat pushed back as far as it would go. Even then, when he slumped down, his legs were too long for comfort, pressed up on the hard underedge of the instrument panel. It wasn't the car as much as it was the way Dodd was built. He was more than half legs, Gary Cooper style.

He tried to relax his head, to let the top of the seat take all the weight of it from his neck and shoulders. But his neck especially hung on tight.

It had been one more long day—worse than routine, which was usually bad enough—and it wasn't over yet.

First thing that morning they had found two more sun lovers at the State Beach in Balboa. A fellow and his girl, both about eighteen, parked head out to sea in a blue Oldsmobile Starfire with a pair of surfboards racked on it. His and hers.

The car's muffler was stuffed with their bathing suits and the end of it was tightly taped over.

The couple were in the act of love, arms wrapped around, tight together in rigor mortis.

There had been twelve almost identical cases since Friday last week. Eight of them had been in Highway Patrol Zone Six, which covered the entire southern section from Los Angeles to the border.

Dodd took two deep breaths, used his second finger and thumb to squeeze the bridge of his nose, as though that slight pressure might help ease the pressure. It was something he usually did when he was discouraged.

He closed his eyes.

Instead of relief, that brought a busy blackness. Among his thoughts: Helen, his wife. She had broken her wrist ten days ago, had fallen on a sidewalk while shopping in Costa Mesa. Sidewalk slippery when wet. Costa Mesa's fault. An attorney neighbor had advised Dodd to sue. Dodd examined the shoes his wife had had on the day of the accident. Slick leather soles. Besides, an area captain could, but shouldn't, sue a city in his area. And his backyard roses. They were goners. Roots soaked soft, rotting, stalks and stems unable, for some reason, to stop guzzling it up. All their leaves turned pale yellow.

The metallic drumming of rain on the car roof, not soothing, a lethal reminder by now. No more wind, though.

Dodd opened his eyes, adjusted them to the refracting drops on the window. God, he was tired. Couldn't recall when he'd been more so. Tired all the way in to his bones and down to his wet toes. Old bones, he thought, and tensed his legs and shoulders simultaneously, trying to squeeze the cramps out, the tiredness. Hell, he wasn't even sixty yet, had nine and some to go before sixty.

Executive Lieutenant Porter was rapping on the window. Dodd didn't sit up, just lowered the window.

Porter leaned in. "The latest count is a hundred thirty-one," he said.

Dodd gazed past Porter, at nothing. Only numbers so far,

he thought, no names. "How long before they can start bringing the others up?"

"Croy says an hour, maybe less."

"Madsen leave?"

"No."

"I told him to go home."

Porter shrugged. "Eager."

"For what?"

"Motorcycle assignment."

"Remind me."

"A couple of the television guys had a pretty good go at each other."

"When?"

"Just now, over who was going to get to interview the first survivors brought up. One got an eye. They're trying to cover it with makeup."

"Crazy bastards."

"Everybody's edgy."

The radio had been on. Highway Patrol Center in Santa Ana and the units in the field transmitting back and forth. Sibilant volleys peppered with static, words so clipped they were practically indecipherable by the ordinary ear. Out of habit, whenever he was in the field, Dodd half-heard them, enough for him to picture what was going on throughout his area.

Now the voice coming over said, "Code eleven-seventy-nine. . . ."

That got Dodd's entire attention. Code eleven-seventy-nine was an accident with injuries requiring an ambulance. There had been some bad ones lately.

Dodd called in to ask how bad. He started the car and the light rack on top. Until he returned, Executive Lieutenant Porter would be in charge. Dodd hit the siren briefly to make some of the television crowd jump aside.

When he reached the freeway, he went full out along the shoulder, passed thousands of cars standing absolutely still in the rain, belligerent. Finally, a red glow was in the atmosphere ahead and then there were the emergency flares on the pavement. Dodd pulled up and got out. One of his senior officers came over to meet him. Five units were on the scene, two patrol cars and three motorcycles. All lanes of the freeway, southbound and northbound, were closed.

No one knew exactly what had happened except those who had been in it and most of those were dead.

A Jaguar, going too fast for the law and the weather, had spun into a Cougar, sending the Cougar out of control, so a Mustang couldn't stop from slamming into it from behind. Swerving to avoid, a Hornet hit the curb of the median, flew up and clipped the top of the dividing fence, came down across the oncoming lanes where it was smashed broadside by a Pinto and then head on by a Skyhawk, followed by a Colt and another Mustang.

It sounded like a mad menagerie. Eight of them were totaled, six were afire.

Blame?

The rain?

Who?

The young man in the Jaguar that was now smouldering on its side with him pinned in and burned to a black crisp?

Captain Dodd kneeled to a girl who had been a passenger in the Hornet. She lay face up on the wet roadbed, partially covered by a highway patrolman's bright yellow raincoat. She kept biting her lower lip. Dodd recognized death in her eyes. The girl was not aware that her right arm had been torn off. Dodd wanted to say something — not something consoling; he wanted to tell her good-bye. But he didn't and she stopped biting her lip.

How many faces had he seen go slack, set and be gone like that, young and old? He hated it. Certainly it had always been unpleasant to witness but he had come to really hate it. There had been so much of it in his life, on his job. Fuck the so-called blessed relief. Fuck death, fuck it, *fuck* it, his senses were satiated with it, rubbed the wrong way raw by it.

He pulled the raincoat up over the girl's face. He thought he should have said good-bye. He stood and, like a ministering priest, went to someone else who lay nearby, dying.

There were twelve dead.

Nine others might live.

Altogether ninety cars had suffered some damage, mostly to front and rear ends.

The time was nine straight up.

It would be hours before all lanes both ways were clear and flowing. The patrolmen had the situation under control, Dodd decided. No need for him to be there any longer. Nor was there any need for him to feel guilty for wanting to get away from that place of death. After all, he thought, he was going back to another.

He got into his car.

The radio was calling him.

Ten minutes before nine.

The people who lived up on Sheep Hill had a perfect view of the rescue. Like front-row seats in the loges. The activity on the Coast Highway was just below, and the supermarket was lighted like a distant stage. It was all the talk in every household. Children watched it out their bedroom windows; housekeepers kept an eye on it on television while preparing dinner.

"What's happening now?"

"The man just said they'll be getting the people out momentarily."

"Momentarily?" Seldom-used word, television word.

"That's what the man said."

The Lufkin household was typical in many ways. Vern and Nadine Lufkin and their two boys, twelve and fifteen. The

Lufkin house was situated on two and a quarter acres halfway up the slope. It was more or less French regency style, had that sort of roof and lines, thirteen rooms including servants' quarters but not counting the utility room.

The house was done by a professional decorator. A western attempt to achieve eastern taste — expensive copies of French, English and Italian period pieces, violated but not entirely spoiled by dashes of lucite and garish modern things. These accessories and ornaments were purchased and put in place by the owners when the more subtle, pervasive European effect had become boring.

Vern Lufkin was at times called "The Candy Man." By everyone except wife Nadine, who had originally dubbed him that. The reason for "The Candy Man" was Lufkin Candy, thirty-three shops throughout the southland, twenty-two company-owned, the others solidly franchised. The business had been started and left by Vern's late father on a much smaller scale. Recently Vern had gone national, made distribution deals with several major eastern department stores such as Bloomingdale's. No matter that the country was in the pinch of a recession, even the unemployed could not deny its sweet tooth. The Lufkin candy business had never been better.

Tonight the Lufkins had the Barnetts over, their nearest and newest neighbors, Alan and Marcy. For the past four months, since the Barnetts had purchased the place next over on the hill, the two couples had seen a lot of each other. They had become chummy enough to just drop over either way practically anytime. In the row of cypresses that bordered their adjoining properties, there was a space that allowed easy passage.

Alan Barnett was thirty-five. On first impression he seemed quite good looking, but the more one saw of him the less attractive he became. He was reticent, not in a shy or ordinary self-conscious way, but as though he were observing the world from some superior perch and didn't really want to be bothered with it. He was one of three sons of a highly ranked social family. He did nothing for money, just had it. He owned an art gallery in Laguna Beach that was run at a loss for him, and at the Newport Beach Yacht Club he kept a boat that slept ten.

Marcy was twenty-two, a lovely, tall girl who retired from fashion modeling as soon as she struck it rich.

Vern and Nadine Lufkin were the same age: forty-six. Actually, Nadine was four months older. Vern was prematurely gray. He secretly darkened his hair.

Tonight the four were in the Lufkins' den. The plan was to go out to dinner. Reservations had been made at a place called The Bird and Bun.

Alan was sitting in the far corner. He was drinking wine, a vintage white as usual.

Nadine was on the suede-covered couch. She had taken too long a sauna at eight, so she was feeling limp.

Marcy was on a huge Missoni knit-covered cushion on the floor, nicely posed.

Vern had a glass of Glendullan malt whisky in one hand and the television remote-control switch in the other.

Nadine told him: "See what's on seven."

Vern clicked from two to seven.

"Same thing," Nadine complained impatiently. "The hell with it, let's go to dinner."

"Don't you want to see them bring them out?"

"Not if it's going to take all goddamn night."

"Hungry?" Vern asked Marcy.

"Yes, but I want to see this." She indicated the television with her chin.

"What about you, Alan?" Nadine asked.

Alan shrugged.

Vern tossed the remote-control switch to Nadine. From a cabinet he got a pair of powerful binoculars and went to the

110

sliding glass door. He focused on the supermarket. "Puts you right there," he said.

"So does channel seven," Nadine remarked.

Vern offered Marcy a look through the binoculars, and when she got up, had them in hand, Vern suggested they go out by the pool for perhaps a better view.

Marcy didn't say it was raining—Nadine did.

Vern got an umbrella from the foyer closet, said he was going to turn off the pool lights to eliminate glare. He and Marcy went out.

When they were on the extreme end of the pool deck around the side of the cabana, for a moment, a concession to appearances, they did use the binoculars on the supermarket.

He was standing directly behind her.

She took a small step back to be able to press her buttocks against him.

He got hard, quickly.

He reached around with his free hand, raised her skirt and found her exactly when she helped by taking a slightly more open stance.

No woman he had ever known, at least no woman he'd known in the past twenty-five years, had responded to him so spontaneously. Which was the reason for his own easier capability.

For her he was the first older man. It amazed her that she had such passion. Now, for example, with only a little more play with his fingers like that, his authoritative, forbidden fingers, she would come.

She did.

And again after a moment, just as intensely.

He felt vital, strong except for his legs, which were suggesting he should be prone or at least sitting.

Through the compelling distraction of what they were about, Vern and Marcy heard a fragment of a scream.

Nadine's scream.

111

It was the last thing they heard before the tremendous, rolling roar as the mud poured over them.

The forward searchlight on Pumper Truck Number Three was manned by Fireman Collins, an old-timer. The rain was beating hard on his helmet, so his reaction wasn't to something he heard. He sensed it, out of intuition swung the searchlight around to beam it up Sheep Hill. He did it at the last second and there was only time to shout one word.

"Slide!"

When Captain Dodd reached the slide area a county firetruck had just arrived and taken position a safe distance away.

Dodd drove around the firetruck. He didn't stop until he was at the edge of the slide, the front wheels of the patrol car up to the hub caps in the mud.

The five-thousand-watt searchlights on the firetruck swept slowly up and down the slide, raking the slope from top to bottom for a sign of life, of anything.

Dodd got out and for a long while followed the searching of the light, not really hopeful. He felt changed, as though something invisible but substantial had come between himself and existence. The rain did not seem the same. Neither did the car beside him, the night, the place. His senses were altered. He could see and hear just as well as before but now it was as though he were seeing and hearing from a different

113

dimension. His sense of smell was more acute. The odor of the mud was dank, offensive.

He brought his hand to his face, both hands to his cheeks, and his hands and cheeks seemed slightly anesthetized. When he swallowed there was a bitterness to his saliva.

Moving, but with a reduced sensation of movement, he got back into the car.

He sat there all night.

Frequently his mind offered him the thought of all the lives the slide had taken.

He refused it—until dawn.

Then he got out again, cramped, stiff. He found a path down to the beach. From there, for the first time, he could see the scope of what had happened.

The slide was from the crest of Sheep Hill, thirteen hundred feet, all the way down to the ocean. The entire side of the hill, at least a thousand feet wide, had shed a deep layer of itself, gathered its tremendous wet mass to crush and bury everyone, everything on its way.

Everyone, everything, everyone.

With the surf lapping at his ankles, Dodd slowly scanned the muddy steep. He noticed it was still running down and shifting here and there.

Against his usually realistic disposition, Dodd gazed at where the highway was covered under and he imagined Lieutenant Porter popping up out of the mud there, Porter waving and shouting, floundering but savable. And Madsen, too, and Chief Croy, the television people. All of them.

Coming back from the fantasy, he came all the way back. The sense of being outside himself left. He was exhausted, hungry, thirsty, soaked.

And angry. Clear through.

114

It was like being buried in a gigantic box.

Alive.

The atmosphere was heavy, cool as underground, and the thought that *this* was likely to be his coffin made Brydon feel, among other things, miniature.

With him atop Island Eight were Gloria Rand, the time fighter, and the young blonde girl, Lois Stevens.

All twelve islands were still intact and in place because their framework had been built as part of the supermarket's foundation. Seventy feet long, eight feet wide, the islands now served as individual wooden platforms.

Spider Leaks and Emory Swanson—box boy and wealthy insurance executive together on Island Seven.

Elliot Janick, the movie producer, was up on Six.

His star and emotional dependent, Marsha Hilbert, was

atop Island Five. Also there on Five was Dan Mandel, the nonfood food salesman.

Island Four: Marion Mercer and Peter Javakian.

Judith Ward had gotten separated from Marion, as had Amy Javakian from Peter. Judith and Amy occupied Island Two.

The market manager, Phil Kemp, was alone on Island Five.

At the other end of the market on Island Twelve, as far as possible from everyone, was the young man wearing an army poncho over a shoulder holster that contained a .45 Colt service automatic. Warren Stevens, brother of Lois, big game hunter.

The slide had occurred nine minutes ago.

The rescue party and those trapped in the market had had warning. A slick, licking sound along with a sound like a roll of far-off thunder, just before all the lights from the highway went out.

In complete darkness the mountain of mud came sliding down at them. They didn't realize what it was until it was upon them, thousands and thousands of tons.

The medical teams and the firemen were mashed against the steel gate. The mud gushed through the grillwork of the gate like cold lava, instantly covering those who were already injured. Others inside were not swift enough. As they retreated, the mud caught them by the feet, the knees, pulled them down and covered them.

Only those fourteen were left alive: They alone had managed to get to the top surface of the islands. They climbed by instinct, as most creatures would have, going for the highest possible points.

Brydon expected the island would be at best a momentary refuge, offering no more than a brief delay of death. The mud invaded everywhere. When it reached a depth of four feet, however, it leveled off, settled like brown batter.

Brydon aimed his flashlight at the gate thirty feet away. He tried to reason why the mud had not continued to fill the place. For one thing the gate had become jam-packed with

116

debris — shrubs, trees, whole sections of houses, various kinds of building materials, even furniture. There, for example, the beam of his flashlight found something hard white that might be a refrigerator or a bathtub.

At another place twelve feet up on the gate his beam hit upon the face of a young woman. Framed by one of the spaces of the grillwork. She was staring in death. Her mouth was open as though she would cry out.

Elsewhere, more grisly evidence. A man's arm stuck through the gate, arm limp but hand made into a fist.

Gloria Rand was repulsed by the sight of it. Brydon had forgotten she was beside him. To spare her he clicked off the flashlight.

"Better save the battery," he said, knowing that expressed hope. There were two flashlights, because Peter Javakian had also held on to his and now had it placed so it reflected off the acoustical panels of the ceiling, providing dim but adequate light.

Another reason why the mud had stopped rising, Brydon thought, might be the position of the market. Originally it had squarely faced the highway and hill. After the bluff broke away the market was turned about twenty degrees. So the slide had not hit it flush. The mud had come at an angle, a tremendous glancing force that might have rotated the structure so it was now facing the opposite direction.

Did anyone recall such a turning sensation when the slide hit? Brydon asked.

Amy Javakian thought she had. So did Marsha Hilbert. They weren't sure, though.

Brydon tried to remember what he'd felt. He had been way off balance and thrown about, but his memory of it was vague. His will to survive had been foremost at that moment, adrenergic, overpowering all other reality.

Anyway, if the market was turned around that would explain the mud level. The main flow of the mud would be down the slope rather than in through the gate, where it was now only seeping in. But could a structure this size be spun about like a plaything? Perhaps, when the ground beneath was so mushy and undermined.

Brydon tried not to buy the theory. He didn't like it. It went against the grain of something he would prefer to die retaining—a faith in architecture, if not its everlastingness at least its endurance. He felt all the more insignificant.

The voices of the survivors.

A vitreous quality to them, faintly ringing, carrying as in a cavern. The inclination was to whisper.

"Are you sure you're okay?" Peter asked Amy, who was two islands from him.

"Judith, how about you?" Marion wanted to know.

"I'm all right, really," Amy assured Peter.

"So am I," Judith said.

But I want to be over there, Amy thought, with you, I need you. And she thought how absurd it was now to feel self-conscious about such intimate admissions. She came right out with them.

Judith could only hope Marion got her identical, silent message.

"I need you to hold me," Amy said, close to crying. She didn't want to cry, didn't want to be the first to cry.

The islands were spaced seven feet apart.

Peter would try to jump across if he had to.

He still had the beer can opener. He used it on the metal stripping around the edge of the island's top shelf, pryed a length of the stripping loose and away. That allowed him to get at the one-by-twelve planks that were joined to form the shelf.

Peter gripped the end of a plank and pulled up. It didn't give, not at all. Another try with all his might, grabbing, trying so hard the slivery edge tore at his hands. The plank was too well nailed.

The next?

Peter went at it even more determinedly, met the same resistance. He fought and finally the plank surrendered, its long nails creaking in protest as it gave up. He got his fingers

118

in under the sides of the plank, worked along, maintaining upward pressure until the plank came free.

It was eight feet, would just do.

As a bridge to Island Three, it bowed beneath Peter's weight. When he was across he took up the plank and extended it from Three to Island Two. He made doubly sure it was in place, held it steady.

Amy hesitated. Never, even in her childhood, had she found fun in the dare of walking any narrow, slightly higher thing, such as the top of the garden wall. Now in the dim light she could hardly see the plank. It would be like stepping off into space.

Understanding, Peter told her, "Put your arms out for balance."

Instead, Amy placed her hands on the curve of her pregnant belly, her elbows out evenly. Without looking down she felt for the plank with her right foot, found it and told herself it would be merely four or five ordinary steps. She would be more likely to fall if she tried to inch along. She disliked being afraid.

Actually, there was good reason for her fear. Brydon had warned them about it. Although the mud was only four feet deep, anyone who fell into it would probably be lost. Being in mud was not the same as being in water. When you fell off balance into water of that depth you could easily bring yourself upright. But with mud you sank in and immediately its consistency prevented you from recovering. Try as you might for a standing position, the mud would have its way. Unless, of course, you just happened to be lucky enough to go in exactly feet first, and even then, getting out would be no easy matter.

Amy put all that from her mind, replaced it with the reward of being with Peter. The baby gave her an inside kick that got her started.

She stepped one, two, three, four, across to him, to the safety of the strength of his hands, the cave of his arms. Body against body, hers unable to fit. Their kiss was brief but grateful. They said one another's names.

119

Judith also came across. Marion received her and led her a ways down the island where the light was much dimmer, before holding her for a moment. An exchange of covert whispers: "Love you."

To be together was important for them all. As Peter had done, they all had pried up planks and used them to connect the islands. Placing two, three planks side to side they created wider, safer bridges. It was a lot of work but worth it — a relief to be able to go freely from island to island, to overcome insularity at least to that extent. They got acquainted with one another and became better accustomed to their increased confines. It lifted their spirits.

All except Warren Stevens'.

He took no part in the bridge building. He sat cross-legged on Twelve — three islands and four aisles from the others. Just sat there observing them as though they were performers whom he did not appreciate.

Lois called out to her brother several times. He didn't reply. She was concerned that he might be injured.

Brydon put a plank in place and went over to Island Nine. Then to Ten and to Eleven. From there, from across the aisle, he asked Warren if anything was wrong.

Warren stood up. He mumbled something.

"What?" Brydon had the plank in hand, was about to extend it to Island Twelve.

"Leave me alone."

Brydon tried to make out the young man's face, to read his expression. "Don't you want to be with us?"

"Why should I?"

"Just thought you would."

"Fuck off." Warren snapped it like a command.

They'd all heard it, there was no need for Brydon to explain when he returned to the others.

"That's how he gets sometimes," Lois said, half-heartedly apologizing.

Brydon was rankled. The back of his neck was hot and his throat full. He swallowed, rubbed his neck and took his gaze from Warren's direction. Placing his hand on Lois's shoulder, he told her: "He's okay. Anyway, he's not hurt."

"He'll get sick of being over there alone," insurance man Emory Swanson predicted.

"Uptight mother," Spider Leaks commented. Spider didn't really care one way or the other about Warren, but he used the situation to make known his alliance with Brydon. His convict's intuition told him Brydon was the head man.

Brydon got that, and he realized then that the majority of the group seemed to be directing its hopes at him. Was that why they had chosen to gather on Island Eight? Hell, he thought, he was more of a loner than a leader, didn't want the responsibility. Besides, there was no reason anyone should be in charge. Considering the apparently hopeless circumstances, they might all do just as well on their own.

As though picking up the thought, Emory Swanson said, "We haven't got a chance." He blamed, hated more than anything he'd ever hated, the tube of toothpaste his hand felt in his jacket pocket.

Phil Kemp tugged uncomfortably at the money bags he still had haltered about him. Their weight was causing the twine to cut into his shoulders. "Only possible way out is the back," he said.

"Why?" Peter asked.

"Can't be as much mud there."

"Probably just as deep," Spider said.

"I mean overhead. Maybe the slide didn't even cover the back of the building."

"So what? Here, there — we'll still be locked in," Peter said.

Manager Kemp, as usual, resented having his opinion questioned. "Could be the wall is broken through or the roof caved in," he said. "Anyway, if we're going to get ourselves out or if someone's going to rescue us it'll be the back room."

"Makes sense," Dan Mandel said, still agreeing like a salesman.

Brydon had remained silent. Now he explained his theory

121

about the slide, how it might have altered the position of the market.

"Bull!" was Kemp's reaction.

Emory Swanson agreed. "Kemp knows the place."

Brydon didn't argue that. He couldn't be absolutely certain he was right. It was as much hunch as it was logic. "The back is the wrong way."

"What do you think?" Elliot Janick asked Marsha Hilbert. He hardly ever asked her opinion, never about anything important. As much as possible, a star was to be seen and not heard.

"You tell me," she said.

"I don't know." He lowered his head. "I don't know."

"Some help you are," she said, a bit cutting, wondering how he'd take it.

He just took it.

Kemp grabbed one of the flashlights and went to the end of the island. Swanson and Dan Mandel went with him. Kemp played the light on the rear wall. The permanent freezer cases were under mud. But not the fixture shelf above the cases. It ran the entire length of the wall to where a doorway with double swinging doors gave access to the receiving and storage area. From the end of the island to that shelf was a good fifteen feet. So close, and so far. The temptation was to jump off and wade to it.

"Rip up a couple of planks," Kemp said.

They did.

Two eight-foot planks would be just long enough if there was some way of joining them. Kemp decided the best possibility was to overlap and nail them. Mandel used one of Swanson's shoes, the hard leather heel of it, to drive the nails that were bent and difficult. The shoe wasn't really heavy enough to hammer with, and after hundreds of hits three nails were in place through both planks.

"That's good enough," Kemp said. He tested the planks by lifting and shaking them.

Never hold, was Brydon's opinion, and although he wanted to say it he held back, knowing it was useless because it wasn't what Kemp, Swanson, or Mandel wanted to hear. Also, Brydon realized once again that he might be wrong. He watched them extend the plank from the island to the shelf. Only inches to spare at both ends.

Because it was Kemp's idea and he seemed so sure of it, it was assumed he would be first to go across. However, Kemp used the excuse of having to retie the money bags, so first was up to Swanson or Mandel.

Swanson was convinced. No doubt in his mind that when he reached the back of the market, he would be safely out of it. Let the others wait until too late—screw them—he'd be out and home tonight—warm bath, straight drink. He'd brush his teeth with that toothpaste. Damn right.

He stepped out onto the plank.

Brydon told him not to, told him, "It won't hold you."

Swanson disregarded that. He committed himself with three cautious half-steps, paused, took three more. Then he was at the most critical place, where the planks were joined, and he was hit with the realization that he was gambling his life on the cooperation of three ordinary nails. Unequitable. Poor insurance. Not fair, he thought, not fair. His legs went numb, incapable. He didn't dare move.

"Go on," Kemp urged.

Swanson couldn't.

"Keep going, for God's sake."

Swanson felt the planks give some and that suddenly turned his legs on, all of him becoming electric with fear. He took six short, quick steps and reached the shelf, could hardly believe he was standing safely on the solid metal shelf.

He didn't wait for anyone, went along the shelf to the doorway. He leaned out to peek through the slight space. Nothing. Pitch black in there. Perhaps when he opened one of the doors. He grabbed hold of the top of the nearest. The door looked easy—but it was impossible. Off to the side as he was he couldn't get much leverage. It wouldn't have made any difference anyway. The pressure of the mud four feet deep on his side, and the other side of the door held it like a vice.

Swanson gave up.

"Keep trying," Kemp shouted.

Swanson told him to shut up. He retreated along the shelf to the planks. Stood there. The planks seemed narrower now, not to be trusted. Swanson glanced across.

"Stay there," Brydon advised.

Swanson hated all of them. He had been used. The bastards had tricked him into the risk, and now he was over here alone. He had to get back at them. He didn't want to be alone. He had to get back. No matter what. He stepped out onto the plank, took six short steps to be halfway across.

On the seventh step the planks came apart.

Swanson dropped ass first into the mud. His head, arms and feet were above the surface. He struggled, slapped at the mud, screamed for help, but there was nothing anyone could do but watch. His head and hands sank from sight, and his feet, encased in expensive shoes, went under last.

For the other survivors, Swanson's gruesome death was a demonstration of what they could expect. They sat huddled on Island Eight. No talk of what they had witnessed or any discussion about trying to get out. They sat silent, in touch with one another for consolation. Brydon had Gloria Rand pressed close to one side, Lois Stevens to the other. Marion Mercer and Judith Ward were together, using his back for support.

For a long while closeness eased them, but gradually it turned on them, became uncomfortable. It reminded them how futile any attempt was they might make to share truly and thereby lessen their plight.

One by one or in pairs they dispersed, went without a word to other islands, where they were as far apart as possible.

Brydon was the last to move. He was relieved to be alone. He stood, stretched, rotated his head, trying to get rid of neck tension. There was whispering from several directions, the same sort of sibilance he had heard once in a cathedral in Spain — people praying. He hadn't gone there to pray, he remembered, had sat in a pew to study the cathedral's architectural merits. That had been back in his free-and-easy time. He grunted at the memory, and his next thought was how sorry he was for the others, sorrier for them than for himself. They had more to lose, more months, years of sensations.

Nevertheless, he wanted his time, all he had coming. What a no-good Indian giver God was — had promised him a regular lifetime, taken it back, giving him only a year or two and now was even reneging on that. Now death could come with the mud pouring in any moment.

No, Brydon protested, and no, it wasn't like him to give up. He went from Island Eight, found Kemp sitting on Three. Kemp started to rise. Brydon yanked him up roughly by his shirt front and told him, "That was stupid."

Kemp tried to break Brydon's hold. "I still say the back way is our best bet."

"Don't say!"

"I'll do whatever the hell I want."

Brydon was almost angry enough to shove him off. He let go of him. "Next time *you'll* walk the goddamn plank."

Eleven A.M., Saturday, the day after the slide.

Still raining, no wind, the rain coming straight down.

Sightseers were gathered at the police barricade on the highway north of the slide. Some had come as far as a hundred miles for a look. They couldn't see much from there and they resented not being allowed nearer. The fascination, of course, was death, and binoculars were used to scan the distant muddy slope for any sign of it.

Sirens and motorcycle growls.

The crowd parted, the barricade was lifted aside for a pair of highway patrolmen on Harley Davidsons, escorting two Cadillac limousines, an Army-colored Chrysler and two highway patrol cars. The limousines had government insignias, eagles, attached to their bumpers front and back. Also decals of orange Day-Glo that said:

126

The vehicles stopped a short distance beyond the barricade. Senator and Mrs. Hugh Tyler got out of the lead limousine. Both had on clear plastic raincoats. She wore a clear plastic bonnet that tied beneath her chin and his hat was identically covered. Large black umbrellas were held over them. A man from the second limousine hand-held a sixteen-millimeter motion picture camera that he aimed at the senator and shot in spurts from various angles. Another man took stills with a Nikon. The senator glanced at the crowd, acknowledged them with a quick smile and a single wave, but he didn't wait to see that no one waved back. Changing his expression to grim, he turned his attention to the slide.

The rest of the inspecting party consisted of Brigadier General Schyler and Major L.C. Babb of the Army Corps of Engineers, James McCrary, former television network news analyst and now the senator's campaign adviser, Bill Everett, commander of Zone Six of the highway patrol, along with his immediate assistant, Supervising Inspector Hal Chapin.

From the last highway patrol car, last to get out, Captain Royden Dodd. He hadn't been home at all, had only changed his socks, put on the fresh pair he kept in a desk drawer at headquarters.

The group proceeded along the highway in the direction of the slide. Senator Tyler held his chin forthrightly up and out, an affectation he believed in, although it often gave people the impression he was looking down his nose at them. Dodd walked slightly behind, in range of Zone Commander Everett in case he had any questions but definitely away from the senator and his entourage. Dodd hadn't voted for the man in the last election, wouldn't in the next.

A hundred yards from the edge of the slide the senator stopped so abruptly General Schyler stepped on his heel. The senator had decided he was near enough. He was skeptical of the hillside on the left, camouflaged his apprehension by pointing to the top of the slide for General Schyler's benefit. That also inspired the cameraman, who hastily switched to a longer lens that would optically make the senator appear close up to the slide. Campaign adviser McCrary clipped a microphone to the Senator's lapel.

"Is it on?" the senator asked.

"Not yet."

"Tell me when."

"Okay, when."

McCrary, on camera, introduced himself and announced where he was and who he was with. The camera angle widened to include the senator.

"My schedule called for me to speak at a National Association of Manufacturers breakfast this morning, but as soon as I learned about this terrible tragedy I hurried here."

"You have a special personal reason for involvement, Senator."

"Oh, yes," the Senator remembered the leading statement. On the way down from Los Angeles he and McCrary had gone over what they would say. "Yes, I most certainly do. I was born and raised right here in Orange County. In Fountain Valley to be exact, where my father ran a grocery store. So, these are my people."

"Yesterday the President designated Southern California a disaster area. How do you feel about that?"

A thoughtful pause. "I most certainly agree the situation calls for emergency measures."

The interview continued.

Zone Commander Everett signaled Inspector Chapin with a glance and they went further down the highway. Captain Dodd followed along. All the way to within a few feet of the slide. They stood in silence for quite a while, then Everett asked Dodd, "How many did we lose?" Meaning highway patrolmen.

"Twelve."

Everett lowered his head and shook it slowly. It was worse than 1970, when four officers had been killed in a shootout in Newhall. "Families been notified?"

"All but two."

"Sure?"

Dodd was sure because he'd seen to it himself, had spent all morning on the phone. He'd always made it a point to know the personal lives of his men, got acquainted with their wives and families whenever possible.

"You were real lucky, Dodd," Inspector Chapin said as he appraised the slide.

No comment from Dodd. Being the only survivor wasn't a distinction. He should have been dead and buried with the others. He didn't give a damn how it looked to anyone. That wasn't it. It was how he felt. Every breath he took now was borrowed.

Everett told him, "Lucky for us." The commander seemed to realize the weight of the guilt that had been turning over and over in Dodd's mind.

Dodd thanked him.

"I'll send you up a replacement for Porter," Everett said. "Unless you have someone you especially want."

The man Dodd would have wanted was with Porter, dead.

They returned to the others. Senator Tyler was concluding his film interview.

McCrary was asking, "Have you ever seen anything so horrible as this mud slide?"

"No, and I hope I never do," the senator replied, aiming sincerity right into the lens. He was campaigning for a second term. Thus the slogan on the bumper stickers: TYLER 2

The senator, his wife, McCrary and the cameramen retreated to the limousines. Everett, Chapin and Dodd remained there with General Schyler and Major Babb.

"The army will do all it can," Schyler promised.

"How long will it take?"

129

"I'd say we could have the highway open in three weeks, maybe a month."

"What about down below, the supermarket?"

"That could take another couple of months, at least. Anyway, there's no reason to hurry, is there?"

They looked to the slide.

"Not really."

"We'll bring in the equipment and get to it soon as the weather clears." Rain was pouring from the beak of Schyler's gold-braided cap.

"Nothing you can do now?" Dodd asked.

"Nobody can handle that mud," Schyler said.

They went their separate ways then, Dodd back to headquarters on East Santa Clara Avenue in Santa Ana. There he drew a mug of coffee, put his feet up, and phoned the two victims' wives he hadn't been able to reach earlier. One, the second, was Rita Porter. Dodd knew her well, so breaking the news to her was all the more painful. Rita absorbed the first shock and, still sobbing, asked Dodd how he thought she could best tell her two sons.

"They're good strong boys. Tell them straight out." Thirteen and fifteen, they would supply the support she needed, Dodd believed.

When he clicked off he had a bad taste in his mouth. He tried to wash it away with coffee but that made it worse. He sat there staring past a lot of paperwork and decided he needed to go home, to see Helen.

He used his own car rather than an official one, hoping thereby to avoid any chance of being pressed into duty along the way. Heading north on Harbor Boulevard he was passed by two speeding souped-up cars, a young couple in each. For their amusement they were causing splashes left and right, all the way up onto the sidewalk. Dodd's automatic reaction was to hurry and stop them, but his fatigue let them go. Nothing short of a holdup would get to him, he promised himself.

On 17th Avenue he noticed an outdoor advertising billboard for a suntan lotion that had originally shown a girl displaying most of her skin ideally bronzed, along with the words, "DON'T BURN! NEVER PEEL!" Now the advertisement itself was peeling, panels of it soaked and coming down in places, so that it read "BURN!" and the girl's good looks were splotched and she was possibly topless.

Further on in a residential district Dodd saw that a house with a large lawn had its sprinkler system on despite the downpour. Perhaps the sprinkler control mechanism was out of order, or, just as likely, the owners had reached the point of denying reality.

When he arrived home, before going in, he took a look around the backyard. All the roses were definitely drowned. And the fruit-bearing lemon tree he'd planted ten years ago was losing its leaves, which had turned pale yellow. He reached up to pick a lemon, disturbed a branch and caused more leaves to fall. Losing his temper, he grabbed the branch, shook it hard. When he let go it was practically bare.

Not feeling any better from that, he turned, saw Helen's face at a kitchen window. His first sight of her in two days. A smile. He went in to her, to a welcoming kiss and another, and he held her longer than usual.

She was forty-five, a warm, attractive woman of few words. Short-cut salt-and-pepper hair, eyes the color of chestnuts, very little makeup on her exceptionally fine, clear complexion.

"I made soup," she said.

He sniffed, a wonderful hearty smell. Vegetable soup the way she made it from scratch was one of his all-time favorites, and this was the time for it, she knew.

He had two large helpings that truly helped and nearly a half a loaf of toasted French bread.

"Pretty good one-handed soup," he said, lightly referring to her right arm in a cast.

"Left-handed soup." She laughed, and then, after some eyes-to-eyes silence, fondly, "You don't look tired."

131

That was her special way of telling him he did.

He went into the living room, intending to stretch out on the sofa, but Helen wouldn't have it. She urged and tugged him into the bedroom, insisted that he take off his clothes, take a relaxing shower. By the time he came out, drying, she had the bed turned down. Fresh sheets.

"In with you," she ordered, contradicting her severity with a kiss.

He grumbled and that was the extent of his resistance, although, really, he didn't feel the least bit deserving.

132

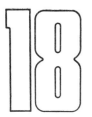

Brydon's sense of time was off.

Minutes — five, fifteen, an hour of them — swept swiftly around the face of his watch. But that same time, when he concentrated on it, also seemed compressed in keeping with what his existence had come down to. Each moment exaggerated itself, went inevitably by, but slowly, very slowly, as though somehow restrained.

The rise of the mud was as regular as clockwork. Brydon used a nail to scratch his estimate of inches and feet on the length of a plank that he stuck in and down until it reached bottom. Fixed in place with metal shelf stripping, it could be read like a tide-level marker.

According to the marker, the mud was coming up steadily one-half inch an hour. At that rate there were thirty-six hours left before the mud would reach the tops of the islands.

During the night Brydon at times stretched out on the hard

wooden surface, his jacket balled up for a pillow. He didn't sleep, only napped for a minute or two. He spent most of the time pacing Island Eight, seventy feet from end to end, trying but unable to believe in rescue, so, instead, trying to figure some way out. Anything that came to mind was quickly vetoed as impossible. If only he had the most primitive sort of tools, even an ordinary rock for a hammer, some fibrous vines to bind and tie. But he had nothing. There was no way.

Eventually futility won out so many times that his ideas balked, refused to be presented, and all that got through were the irking messages of hunger and thirst.

He went to Spider Leaks on Island Seven. Spider had been observing Brydon, whose pacing looked familiar to him. He had seen men pace their cells when they were about to flip.

Spider stood as Brydon approached.

Brydon kneeled.

So did Spider.

"Hungry?" Brydon asked.

"My stomach thinks my throat's cut."

Brydon remembered the little jars of caviar he had in his pocket. He wasn't in the mood for anything so delicate and, he decided, neither was Spider.

"Crazy thing, man," Spider said, "us being in here with nothing to eat."

The shelves were bare. Everything was under the mud.

"Think we're being punished?"

"I didn't do anything."

Peter Javakian overheard and joined them. Amy was extremely hungry and he had been considering ways of getting at the food. His best idea, he thought, was to make a net. "We could weave it with strips of clothing," he said, and went on to describe something of the sort used to catch butterflies.

"What would you do for a pole?"

"Use a plank."

134

Possible but difficult and unwieldy. Another problem would be what to use for a hoop to form the mouth of the net.

Peter suggested metal shelf stripping. Doubled and twisted, it might be sturdy enough.

Brydon doubted that but he respected Peter's spirit, tactfully told him: "I don't know about you but I'm too hungry to fool with anything that complicated."

They crossed over and went to the forward end of Island Five. Judith Ward and Marion Mercer were there. The two women parted quickly and got up. Brydon apologized for the disturbance.

"Going fishing," he said, "and I seem to remember this was a good spot."

He took off his clothes, everything. Removed his belt and looped it around his right wrist. "Just in case. It'll give you something to pull on."

Peter Javakian took off his belt and tightened it around Brydon's left wrist.

By then the others had come to Island Three. Brydon felt their attention on him. He stepped to the edge, sat, hesitated a moment to look down at the dark mass. It seemed placid, almost inviting. Putting his weight on his hands he turned and lowered himself, feet first, into the mud.

It was colder than he'd anticipated and had it been water he would have plunged in, taken the shock all at once. But it was necessary that he go in slowly, and as nearly straight as possible. To his knees, to his crotch, to his waist. If he should lose balance he would be in very serious trouble. Like Emory Swanson.

His feet touched bottom.

The mud, its thick, clammy consistency, was up to midchest. He experienced the weight of it now, the encompassing pressure. The top surface of the island was just above his eye level. He glanced up. They were all looking down at him — quizzical, dismayed. Phil Kemp's mouth, his eyes showed a trace of amused contempt. Gloria Rand was offering concern and hopefulness. And there were Spider and Peter directly above, ready to help if he needed them.

He tried to move his feet, to feel and search with them. It took a lot of strength to move them even an inch at a time.

There. His right foot had found something. He couldn't make out the shape as a clue to what it was. He hoped for a can of beer.

He took three deep, filling breaths and held the third, clenched his eyes and mouth shut just before going under. Rather than bend and reach to one side, he went down in a well-balanced squat, both feet planted evenly. The sensation of being completely submerged in mud was strange, eerie, especially on his face and hands. The mud prevented any normal pace or motion — he had to push to bring his arms down. That alone took so much time he was sure he would run out of breath. He groped on the bottom with his right hand. His fingers went around something cylindrical, slippery. He got as good a grip as he could on it.

How long had he been under? His lungs were already beginning to burn. His throat felt as though it were being inflated. He had the urge to open his eyes. Was that instinctive — the impulse to see death and thereby somehow prevent it?

He concentrated his strength in his legs and shoulders. He pushed upward. The mud resisted, gave but only very gradually. A fact flashed like an alarm from his memory: one cubic yard of ordinary dirt weighs one ton. Mud at least double that.

His lungs were on fire now, worse each second. His throat seemed about to burst. At the deepest his head had been under twelve inches, perhaps sixteen. Where the hell was the surface, air? Under pressure of the mud he lost the ability to determine position, couldn't make out how much his legs were bent, so he couldn't tell how much progress he'd made.

136

He had never held his breath this long. His legs were trembling, demanding that he give up.

He opened his eyes.

He was surprised to see the island. But only half his head was above the surface. The mud level was across the bridge of his nose. He still couldn't breath. Excruciating, the polarity: life within easy view, death with a heavy hold on him. Both life and death inspired him to keep shoving upward, and when his nose finally emerged, he snorted out loudly and drew in through his nostrils. Revitalized, before long he was standing, handing up what he had found. A can of something.

He felt wonderfully exhilarated, like laughing, a victorious feeling.

Peter shined the light on the can.

Spider wiped the mud from it, exposing some of its metallic red and yellow and the words:

OVEN CLEANER

It seemed to Brydon that everyone moaned at once. He felt the focus of their disappointment; his own was converted into anger. Again he pumped his lungs full and went under.

He had learned from before, knew what to expect, didn't waste energy. He went under with his arms already down at his sides. That saved time. He grabbled along the bottom, found something. He pushed upward but this time didn't try so hard, gauged the limit of ascent the mud would permit and kept to it, and although he didn't have breath to spare when he reached the surface he also didn't have to endure the agonies of near suffocation.

What he brought up this time was a plastic container of margarine, the newer, more convenient kind of semiliquified margarine that could be squirted. At least it was an improvement, something edible.

Spider Leaks had now taken his clothes off. Some of them tried not to look at him. He was a middleweight with a tight, sinewy body, hard from work. Lean waisted, stomach muscles defined.

Covered with mud, Brydon was darker than Spider. Brydon's eyes and teeth, set in contrast, now flashed whiter. He told Spider how best to go under, what the dangers were.

Spider nodded. He didn't appear frightened, although at that moment his pulse rate was up to one hundred twenty from a normal seventy-two. When he lowered himself in he uttered a string of swear words, as though to counter the offensiveness of the mud.

Brydon took hold of the edge of the island, tried to pull himself up and out. He struggled, was stuck. Peter and Dan Mandel grabbed the belts to haul Brydon up. He never would have made it alone.

Sitting on the edge for a breather, Brydon watched Spider sink from sight, and he hoped for the black man. The mud showed no sign where Spider had gone under. Brydon watched the spot. For a moment, in his imagination, the mud was animate, a malicious creature that had swallowed Spider and was now digesting him. It seemed Spider had been under a long time — too long. The worst had happened, Brydon thought, and he wondered if there was something important that he hadn't told Spider. But then, Spider's head broke the surface of the mud and slowly became totally visible.

Spider handed up what he'd found. **"PUREE DE MAR-RONS NATURE"** the fancy decorated can said. Mashed chestnuts imported from France.

Brydon grimaced inside. Chestnuts in any form were one of the few things he truly disliked. He stood and went down the island a ways, like a trout fisherman hoping a new location would bring better luck.

There, and at other places, he and Spider continued to search for food until they were exhausted. Hauled out, they lay face up on the island. Every inch of their bodies coated with mud, their backs and buttocks and legs slippery against the island's surface.

After a while, when they were not so exhausted, they wiped off the mud. Brydon tore the tail from his shirt, used that, first on his face. Just then he would have given anything, except a day of his life, for a shower. The mud couldn't be completely wiped away. It didn't show as much on Spider's skin, but he felt it as much, the dirtiness of it. Spider wiped himself off with his socks and a nearly clean handkerchief. Brydon eventually had to use his entire shirt. They waited until the remaining thin coat of mud dried. Then they slapped and rubbed their skin and shook their hair, causing a dusty cloud around them. When they put on their clothes, they felt an all-over uncomfortable grittiness.

Peter and the others cleaned most of the mud from the items that had been salvaged:

2 bottles clam juice
1 can white hulless popcorn
1 bottle Tabasco sauce
1 can vanilla frosting
1 staple gun
1 container plastic toothpicks
2 yellow twelve-inch candles
24 beef bouillon cubes
1 can Irish oatmeal
1 self-applicating shoe polish
1 container flavored bread crumbs
1 can olive oil
1 can frozen lemonade concentrate
1 half-gallon can liquid floor wax
1 gardening claw
1 box wild rice
1 box No-Doz keep-awake tablets
4 cans evaporated milk
2 boxes plastic trash bags
1 container dog food
5 cans 7Up
2 bottles Coca-Cola

9 cans diet soda, cherry, club and creme
Also the oven cleaner, the puréed chestnuts
and the squeeze margarine.

Brydon examined the lot. The dog food appeared to be the most appetizing thing. Of course, the milk, the oatmeal, the frosting and such would do in a hunger pinch—and the soft drinks were good — but he had hoped to do better. Somewhere on the bottom there were thousands of better things to eat. Considering the abundance, it seemed ironic, almost vengeful: toothpicks, trash bags, a gardening claw—and what the hell could be done with a staple gun?

Brydon tossed a can of the milk to Peter, who jabbed it with the beer opener and gave it to Amy.

"Anybody for clam juice?" Brydon asked.

No takers.

He wondered if the time would come when there would be.

He rationed the soft drinks, one for every two persons.

Phil Kemp griped about that. Brydon told him if he was so thirsty he could dive for more. Kemp called Brydon a shithead, but he mumbled it low so Brydon didn't hear.

"I'd like some of that," Lois said, indicating the vanilla frosting.

Too sweet for an empty stomach, Brydon thought, but he opened it for her. She took it to Island Five. While she sat gazing at nothing she frequently dipped her fingers into the frosting, childlike.

Back on Island Eight, Brydon lighted one of the candles. Less light than the flashlight but enough. He realized then, as he put the book of matches back in his pocket, that someone had taken the caviar. Both jars. While he was risking his life in the mud, someone had rifled his jacket pocket. What especially bothered Brydon was when the caviar was stolen — when. Anyone could have had it for the asking. Who had taken it? Brydon thought Kemp. That was why Kemp had such a big thirst, from gobbling salty caviar.

140

To put out some of his anger Brydon gulped on his half of a Coke, trying to pretend it was a Carta Blanca. Even before yesterday, before all this, he had begun to do a lot of pretending.

Marsha Hilbert and Elliot Janick.

"You're acting creepy," said Marsha.

"I'm not."

"Creepy," she said.

"I'm sorry."

The only time she'd heard the word "sorry" from him was when a rival didn't have bad luck.

"I don't like it," she said.

He looked directly at her, and then, as though submitting to the power of her gaze, he looked away.

His eyes appeared watery, she thought. Perhaps because he hadn't slept.

"I wonder what happened to Ted," he said. His concern for his chauffeur was also a first.

"Probably home in Beverly Hills ordering from Jurgensen's and wearing your silk shirts."

"I doubt that."

"Oh? Once I came back unannounced from Palm Springs and found him taking a bath in your big marble tub."

It wasn't true.

"With a glass of cognac and one of your genuine Havanas."

Elliot didn't seem to hear.

Marsha exaggerated a disgusted sigh. That alone would have ordinarily been enough to get to him.

They were seated on Island Two; nearest to them was Lois Stevens on Five.

"Do me a favor?" Elliot asked.

"What?"

"Hold me."

"You're kidding."

"Hold me."

She reached for his crotch.

141

He knocked her hand away. "Not that!"

"I thought . . ."

"The mentality of a part-time hooker."

" . . . you wanted to be held." She felt suddenly confused, then better because he had reverted.

"I do," he said softly.

He moved closer, leaned to her, led her arm over and around his shoulder to place his head on her breast.

She was uncomfortable.

After a while he said, "I've loved you, haven't I?"

"Sure."

"I showed you how much I loved you, lots of times, didn't I?"

"Yeah."

"It's a good thing to love."

"My tit is going to sleep."

He reduced his weight on her but held her hand so she couldn't take her arm from around him.

"If we get out of this I'll make some changes."

"Why?"

"No more fighting it," he said. "We'll buy a house in the south of France."

"Cap Ferrat."

"Far from it. A lazy little village and not too large a house, just room enough for us and once in a while a couple of friends."

"Friends?"

"Real ones for a change. We'll make them."

She was reminded that several of her friends had already been made by him. "You'd be bored shitless," she said.

"I might even marry you. Wouldn't you want a peaceful life like that? To settle down?"

Settling down sounded to her like going to the bottom. Dreary thought. Especially for one at the top. She quickly slipped her hand free, took her arm away, separated from him.

142

Aloud to himself he said: "We're going to die."

"No."

"I know we will. I can feel it."

"Speak for yourself."

She tried a brief down-scale laugh, meant to sound mocking but it came out sort of nervous.

He disregarded it, as though he were alone or deaf.

That made her furious. He was doing it purposely, she thought. He knew her, knew how to get to her. What she would do was think of some way to retaliate, snap him out of it.

Someone was coming across the bridge.

Dan Mandel.

He apologized for intruding.

Elliot seemed to welcome having someone else to talk to. He even said please when he invited Dan to sit.

Dan and Elliot discussed the chances of being rescued. They went on about it, repeating the possibilities, which revealed how little they believed in them. Dan talked to Elliot but his eyes kept going to Marsha. He mentally pinched himself to confirm her presence.

Marsha recognized the symptom. She thought little of it but then it occurred to her that she might put it to use. She raised her knees, an easy, natural movement. The slick jersey fabric of her dress slid down her thighs. She was in profile to Dan, whose view now was a tantalizing arch of bare movie-star legs. Marsh tensed her ankles to exaggerate the line. Tossed her hair twice as though bothered by it, and her eyes wandered left, down, right onto Dan.

He didn't believe what her eyes were saying to him. He attributed it to his wishful thinking, and, to offset being obvious, asked, by way of a diversion, "Did you eat anything?"

"No appetite," Elliot said.

"Have you ever had clam juice?" Marsha asked Dan.

"It's not bad," he said.

143

"I'll bet you love it," Marsha said.

Dan thought he knew what she meant. He grinned, a little embarassed, and told them, "I've got something you might go for." From his pocket he took out two white-capped jars of caviar. Romanoff imported beluga, two ounces each.

Marsha was delighted. She sat up, faced Dan, her dress carelessly high. Whenever she wore silk jersey, to avoid lines, she never wore anything underneath.

In the extremely low light Dan couldn't really see anything down there between her legs except a dark area, but because it was hers it had an intense effect on him. He stopped staring, forced his attention to opening one of the caviar jars by prying its lid with a coin.

Marsha accepted the jar. She made her left hand flat, emptied the caviar onto it. A mound of caviar on her palm that she brought to her mouth for a nibble.

Dan was about to open the other jar when Marsha offered her handful to him.

Dan glanced uncertainly at Elliot.

No sign from him.

Dan ate out of her hand.

She extended her hand to Elliot, intending to withdraw it quickly if he went for it.

He didn't.

Angrier, she brought it back to Dan. He tried to be delicate but she pressed her hand to his mouth and he lost control. He devoured the little gray-black eggs, lapped them up. She spread her hand for him to tongue her finger crotches. One, two of her fingers entered his mouth.

She glanced at Elliot. He was like stone. She got up abruptly, led Dan across to Island One. He was beyond discretion. Besides, they were obscure enough to anyone more than an island away.

She lay open. Dan went down, tried to get his head between. Did for a moment, but she outmaneuvered, got him on his back, made sure they were in Elliot's direct view from just across the way when she took Dan into her mouth.

Her eyes remained on Elliot, and his on her. It was something he had made her do for others several times over the years, once to a room-service waiter at the Carlton in Cannes. However, doing it on her own would surely be a violation. She expected Elliot would come over and slap the hell out of her.

Dan's entire body clutched, and constricted sound came from him, as though he were in pain, when he finished.

She left him there, went to face Elliot, waited for him to strike her.

After a long moment, he told her: "One, three, nine, eight, zero, nine."

"What?"

He repeated the numbers and added: "The identification code word is zephyr."

She understood then that he had just revealed all that anyone would need in order to withdraw his money in Switzerland.

"You're one cruel son of a bitch, you son of a bitch," she said, and started to cry.

"You were right," he said. "If anyone's going to get out of here, it'll be you. You've always been up to your ass in mud."

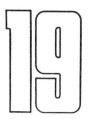

Captain Dodd awoke suddenly. He was at once so alert he thought he must have slept several hours. But daylight bordered the edges of the drapes that were drawn. He snapped on the bedside lamp. The clock said ten to two in the afternoon of the same day. All he'd gotten were two hours.

He closed his eyes, hoping to sink back to unconsciousness.

Helen entered as noiselessly as possible. She observed him for a moment, like a tending nurse, and was reaching for the lamp's switch when he told her, "Never mind."

"Did I wake you?"

"No."

"I was feeding my plants and I dropped the watering can."

"I didn't hear it." Even if he had he wouldn't have said so. He stretched.

"Go back to sleep."

146

He liked her suggestion but he got up for the bathroom to splash double handfuls of cold water on his face. From in there he asked how her indoor plants were doing.

"You won't believe it."

"Might."

"They're doing better on Berlioz than they did on Schubert. For some reason they're greener and they've grown more."

"How long now have they been on Berlioz?"

"Nearly a month."

He held back saying probably the reason the plants were flourishing was the increased moisture in the air over the past three weeks. The plants didn't miss sunshine because she had them under a special compensating light.

While he dressed she got him a coffee. He turned on the television to the channel that featured hourly news. He eliminated the sound and only every so often glanced at the picture:

Houses high on Mulholland that had slid down.

Others that were about to.

A Bel Air home worth over a million with mud oozing from its second-floor windows because a rear retaining wall had not lived up to its high cost.

Areas being evacuated.

Faces being interviewed.

Truck gardens swamped.

Farmers in financial pain.

The Los Angeles River flowing fast and high in its cement bed like a real river.

A flight of pelicans at Dodger Stadium, which they must have mistaken for a lake.

A strange kind of mold that was rapidly multiplying in the continual dampness, its spores causing an allergic reaction—human eyes swollen shut, tongues swollen and bulging.

An elderly woman in a wheelchair being rescued, chair and all hoisted up from a collapsed house.

Dodd appreciated that.

Helen buttoned his shirt cuffs for him. Fresh shirt. Somehow she managed to keep at least two complete changes ahead of him, even in this weather. "Can't you stay home?" she asked.

He shook his head.

"Be back for supper?"

"No."

"I meant a late one."

"Don't wait."

She turned away on the excuse of straightening the bed, and so he caught only a glimpse of her resentment. She had difficulty making the bed one-handed. Dodd took time, went around to the opposite side to help, and by then she was showing nothing but her love for him.

A thermos of the soup was on the kitchen table ready for him to take along, and some of the French bread. Evidently she hadn't really counted on supper with him at home.

As he backed the car out, he thought about her resentment, didn't blame her for it. Just that he hadn't seen it in her for many years. Maybe he hadn't noticed. No, he would have. Anyway, she didn't resent him but the job. Her antenna must have picked up how close to him death had come the night before. He wondered if she'd felt the same all the other times.

An image, like a photograph projected at nearly subliminal speed, wedged itself repeatedly amidst his thoughts of Helen. Not until he was parking the car in his space at headquarters did it definitely come to him.

The elderly woman being hoisted in the wheelchair he'd seen on television. . . .

Wishful thinking, Dodd thought, dismissing it.

He went in to his office. On top of all the papers on his desk was the daily summary, a neatly typed compilation of arrests in the area. Every major category was up, from forcible rape to speeding. He noticed a big jump in auto thefts. A month ago such figures would have been incredible. It was like an epidemic. It wouldn't subside until the rain stopped. The best they could do was try to keep up with it.

148

Dodd glanced at the floor where ordinarily at this time of day there would be an irregular rectangle of sunlight from the side window. Rain was hitting on the window glass. He had become so accustomed to the rain he would have been surprised not to hear its tattoo.

Again he pictured the elderly woman in the wheelchair.

He picked up the phone.

"Get me Zone."

A few moments later he was talking to Zone Commander Everett in San Diego. Everett sounded rushed but he heard Dodd out.

"Of course I've considered the possibility," Everett said.

"We might get General Schyler to change his mind."

"I doubt that. Especially not when he's right."

"I think he's wrong."

"Look, Roy, what you ought to do is back off, give yourself time to get some perspective on this thing."

"I'm not the problem."

"Seems you are, in a way."

"If there's even one person alive in there I want to get him out."

"No way anybody could live through a slide like that."

"I did."

Those two words hung in a pause.

"If conditions were normal I'd tell you to take a few days off."

"I don't need any time off."

"They're buried," Everett said emphatically. "All of them, dead and buried and—"

"I have to be sure."

"Back off, Dodd." An order. "I don't want any more losses in that goddamn slide."

Dodd let silence speak for him. Commander Everett accepted it as compliance. The two men exchanged quick but less official good-byes.

Dodd tried to give attention to some paperwork. Couldn't keep his mind on it. Rather than initial pages without reading them, he put the stack aside. He had a coffee brought in, took three tasteless gulps and let it get cold. There were still four to five hours of light left in the day. He called the Newport Beach Police. Chief Keeler was glad to do the favor and be owed one.

By three-thirty Dodd was in a Bell 47G1 helicopter that was painted black and white with "NEWPORT BEACH POLICE DEPARTMENT" lettered large in green. The helicopter pilot was Stan Hackley, one of the younger officers on the Newport Beach force.

Hackley handled the helicopter skillfully but with such nonchalance that, at first, Dodd was apprehensive. The chopper, given full throttle, practically sprang off the ground, climbed sharply and swooped out over the ocean. The exterior of its plastic-nosed cabin was splattered by rain, further limiting visibility. Below, the coastline was consistently trimmed by the reaches of the surf. The beach was deserted, not even a mark on it. Hackley put the chopper on a southward course just off the coast at an altitude of five hundred feet.

In seven minutes, there on the left, was the city of Laguna Beach. In less than another minute, there was the slide.

It appeared even more extensive, steeper from this vantage. A wide chute of raw, mucky-looking earth. Slick in the rain. Rivulets of rain running down it like a system of veins. All the way down to the water, where it caused a large, umber-colored semicircle.

Hackley made six slow passes, while Dodd studied the face of the slide, both with and without binoculars. On the fourth pass Dodd noticed what he thought might be an irregularity about a hundred and thirty feet up. He lost sight of it, tried to pick it up again on the fifth pass and did so on the sixth.

A horizontal projection like a mud-covered corner.

Dodd asked for a closer look.

Hackley answered by heading the chopper right at the

150

slide, so fast that Dodd flinched, didn't see how they could possibly miss crashing into it. Hackley, unruffled, nosed the chopper up just in time and leveled it off in a hover, mere feet from the face of the slide.

Any other time Dodd would have chewed out the young man, but today such daring seemed appropriate. He directed Hackley to that cornerlike spot.

Dodd pulled the hatch open for a better view. No way of telling exactly what it was, that protrusion. From the angles of it, it had to be some sort of structure. Possibly it was only a section that had broken away. Dodd had brought along a ten-foot pole with a brass hook on its end. He held it out and down, wanting to probe the mud. The pole wasn't long enough. Dodd climbed out onto one of the chopper's landing skids. Hackley obliged by maneuvering the chopper closer to the slide, so close now that its main rotor blade was nearly biting the slope.

Dodd jabbed at the mud. The pole struck something solid, about two feet below the surface. Exploring with the pole from there didn't satisfy Dodd. He signaled Hackley what he intended to do. Hackley's expression questioned Dodd's sanity. He held the chopper as steady as possible. Dodd threw the pole down and lowered himself via the landing skid. He let go of the skid, dropped to the mud, sank in. For a moment there was fear that he would continue to sink, but he went in only to just above his knees.

He retrieved the pole and began poking around. He found solid footing off to his right. The mud, though, made it almost impossible for him to move about. His feet felt as though they had powerful suction caps on them. He managed a couple of steps. Probing farther and farther until the pole was in up to its hilt, he determined more of the underlying solid surface. Encouraging, but it didn't prove anything. What he was on could still be merely a part of any building, perhaps one of those houses that had been carried down from Sheep Hills.

Where the mud was shallowest, Dodd jabbed sharply with the pole, several times. Signaling. He waited for a reply, signaled again, listened again. All he heard was the rain beating on his head and the roar of the chopper, whose blades were causing a turbulence that splashed about unpredictably.

Dodd gazed up the slope.

It was overwhelming, immense, so steep it appeared to be about to descend upon him. His automatic reaction was to take a step back. His legs, held by the mud, couldn't move that quickly, and he was suddenly off balance.

He fell backward.

Over the edge.

He grasped for something as he went over. Got nothing but mud. He saw the helicopter, way out of reach, and Hackley's face, Hackley alarmed for the first time.

Over and down at the mercy of the mud that absorbed his fall. He was sprawled in the slime. It threatened to engulf him, but its slickness and steep pitch actually helped. He was out of control now, in a writhing, flailing plunge—head first, then feet first. He saw sea, sky, mud, quickly over and over but not in order and he couldn't tell which way was up all the way down to the beach and into the slush of the surf.

He ended in a painful, contorted position, his right leg and arm twisted beneath him. He recovered, kneeled, stood up, stunned by what he'd just been through, amazed that he wasn't injured.

Twice in the last twenty-four hours he had been in the hand of death and escaped before it could make its fist.

Hackley was coming for him, setting the chopper down practically on top of him.

Dodd looked a mess head to toe, like a monster made of mud. He glanced up at the slide, to that spot where he'd just been. Something, probably his fall, had disturbed the mud there, caused it to give way. Now, partially exposed, was a huge, three-dimensional letter E.

152

Gloria Rand, the time fighter, thought she needed Brydon to kiss her. Needed him to come over, take her head in his hands and draw a kiss from her. Do it without a word, be helplessly attracted.

To herself she told him, *Do it.*

She fixed her gaze on him, thinking her feelings were so intense that perhaps if she concentrated he might be influenced. Mind over mind. She was skeptical but if it did work it would open up all sorts of possibilities.

She had asked Brydon about the chances of rescue and he had said they were excellent. Actually, the word he used was good. Gloria expected any moment now someone would come breaking through a wall or the ceiling. Then her life could return to normal—but not the same as before, she had decided. First thing, she was going to rid herself of that Frisbee-catching Stuart. He'd be the last of that sort. What a foolish phase. She'd expected more from it. Oh well, she'd make up for it. With Brydon.

She saw no reason to tell him her true age. Her guess about his was early forties—say, forty-one. To make it less of a fib, she would tell him she'd be thirty-five come August. Of course, he would remark that she didn't look it, looked younger. For substantiation she would arrange to have her birth certificate altered, something she'd been meaning to do, anyway. She'd pay someone to do it. That would allow her to have her birth date be August 12, 1941, on her passport. No one ever doubted a passport. She wondered whether or not the passport people would refer to her original application. If they did, she'd be caught in the lie. If. She refused to believe no woman had ever gotten away with younger than truth on a United States passport. She'd risk it, would have to. Because she foresaw a lot of happy, faraway traveling over the many years ahead. With Brydon.

She must have been attracted to him from the moment they were stranded together there on Island Eight. At the start terror must have numbed her. It had to subside before she could realize what she felt. From then on the attraction had steadily increased, nourished itself with the sight of him, his closeness. The courage he had shown when he was diving for food had inspired her to demonstrate a different kind of courage just a short while ago. She had taken his hand, and, thank heavens, he had responded and later, after her tentative questioning, told her, yes, he did want to see her when this was over. Something in the way he said it, and the seriousness she detected in his eyes, made her believe he meant more than a platonic or casual relationship.

A kiss.

Why didn't he come take it?

She gave up looking at him, trying to will it. Evidently he wasn't a man to be dominated, probably not in any way. Head up, she used the tips of her fingers to comb back her hair. She smiled faintly, unaware she was smiling, while she thought she had never been so optimistic.

154

Although it appeared that Brydon's eyes were on Gloria, they were aimed beyond her, trying to make out Warren on Island Twelve. Warren was still alone there. Brydon had expected that by now the young man would have had enough isolation. He had forgiven Warren's lashing obscenity long ago, chalked it up to panic, and periodically over the past hours he had looked in Warren's direction. All he'd been able to make out was the vague, dark mass of a figure some forty-five feet away.

He decided against shining the flashlight in that direction. Instead, he got up, walked toward Gloria, passed her and crossed over to Island Nine, Ten, Eleven.

Another attempt to communicate with Warren from directly across from him. Even that close it was too dark for details, such as facial expressions. Warren was stretched out on his side. He didn't move, except to prop up on his left elbow.

Brydon asked if he was thirsty.

No.

Hungry?

No.

Brydon had brought along a can of 7Up. "Here, catch." He tossed the can with an easy lob at Warren, who made no effort at all, let it go by, off the island and into the mud.

That got Brydon's temper up, almost enough to go over and give Warren some of it. At Brydon's feet was the board he had brought along before. His notion of using it now as a bridge to Twelve was replaced by the thought that Warren was either mentally off and therefore perhaps better off, or else he was just a smartass and not worth the effort.

"If you get thirsty, you can yell," Brydon told him, leaving it an open question whether such yelling would do Warren any good.

Warren said something then that Brydon didn't get because it came out so sharply, like a spit. Brydon thought he misunderstood, what Warren said wasn't "Nigger lover," that didn't make sense.

Warren watched Brydon turn away, watched him all the

155

way back to Island Eight. Not until then did Warren let his grip relax on the Colt .45 automatic that he'd had concealed and pointed beneath the folds of his poncho.

On Island Eight Lois asked how her brother was.

"The same," Brydon told her.

"Maybe I should go talk to him."

"Maybe."

She was thoughtful, as though considering it, and it seemed to Brydon that she had decided to go to Warren. But without saying more she turned and went in the opposite direction, to her chosen place on Island Five.

"She's on something," Gloria Rand said. "Can't you tell?"

Brydon had long ago given up trying to figure out who was or wasn't on drugs. So many people, young and old, seemed to go around in a constant lazy float or too full of energy.

"I saw her take one," Gloria said.

"One what?"

"A yellow pill."

"You mean a capsule."

"No, a pill."

"Maybe just a vitamin or something."

"I think she's on uppers."

To end the subject, Brydon told her, "I'll look into it." He didn't intend to. If during this desperate, really down situation Lois was on a high, let her be.

Four o'clock.

They had been trapped here for nineteen hours.

Brydon went to the end of the island to check the mud-level marker. As he kneeled at the edge, he heard several raps from somewhere above — the ceiling? The roof? And there they were again, several more raps, muffled, indistinct. Could it be someone was trying to signal?

"Did you hear that?" Brydon asked everyone.

"What?"

"That rapping just then," Brydon said.

156

"I thought I heard something."

"So did I."

The hope of it had them all talking at once.

"Listen!" Brydon shouted.

They were quiet for a long while, heard nothing. Perhaps if they signaled in return. They beat on the island tops with the heels of their shoes and the ends of planks. At first excitedly, chaotically, and then, a more orderly, signal-like drumming.

They stopped and waited for an answer.

Nothing.

They signaled and listened again. And again.

After a while they gave up on it.

Brydon was positive he hadn't imagined it. He'd heard it, all right, but perhaps it had been merely a loose part of the structure knocking against itself, or even some rocks falling. Still, he wasn't entirely convinced it hadn't been a signal. Such a regular, deliberate sort of human-made sound. He believed it had come from the upper front of the building, off to the left. Anyway, for whatever reason, it hadn't continued.

He checked the mud-level marker. The rise was a steady half inch an hour. The mud was now only a little more than a foot below the island top.

He returned to Gloria, sat beside her. She helped herself to the cave of his arm. To keep his mind occupied he opened the carton of dog food. It contained three cellophane packets of something that convincingly resembled chunks of fresh beef. Flesh-red color, whitish fat edging and perfect marbling. Brydon thought about it being made to entice customers more than dogs. A dog wouldn't care if the stuff was green and blue as long as it had the right smell and flavor.

He tore open a packet, took out one of the chunks. It appeared wet, was dry.

Just for the hell of it, Brydon plopped it into his mouth. It tasted bland at first, then strong. Certainly it didn't taste anything like meat.

157

He read the ingredients listed on the side of the carton:

SUCROSE
SODIUM CASEINATE
CORN STARCH
PROPYLENE GLYCOL
DICALCIUM PHOSPHATE
ANIMAL FAT PRESERVED WITH BHA
BHT AND CITRIC ACID
IODIZED SALT
POTASSIUM SORBATE
ARTIFICIAL COLORING
ARTIFICIAL MULTIVITAMIN SUPPLEMENTS
ZINC OXIDE
CUPRIC OXIDE
MANGANOUS OXIDE
COBALT CARBONATE
FOLIC ACID
POTASSIUM IODIDE
THIAMINE MONONITRATE
WATER SUFFICIENT FOR PROCESSING

Why would any man want man's best friend to eat that? Cobalt carbonate sounded like something that would cause a combination of indigestion and radioactive poisoning. Maybe it would be better cooked. But then, considering the ingredients, if heated it would probably just melt.

Gloria Rand also tried a chunk, smiling like a conspirator. Her palate and stomach complained immediately, but she said, "I guess someone could survive on it."

"If it didn't kill him."

She laughed. The laugh came out as though it had been waiting there in the back of her throat, anxious to be released. Although brief, it seemed startlingly loud, out of place. It made her shiver, and she huddled closer to Brydon.

He lay back, taking her with him.

158

One of her legs overlapped his, possessively.

"Sleep," he suggested.

"I might be able to now. You'll—well, you'll watch over me, won't you?"

He assured her he would.

She closed her eyes and he felt her relax. Soon her breathing changed and he knew she had dozed off.

His eyes were tired, the sockets felt strained, drawn. But he didn't close his eyes because he might sleep and he didn't want to sleep. He wanted to see it if it came, think to the last moment.

He focused on the ceiling, the symmetry of the acoustical panels, a row of inset lights, and off to the left over the aisle one of the spherical black television fixtures. He knew what would be above the ceiling. Buildings of this sort were about the same. He could imagine the moment when some architect had decided on the dimensions of this supermarket, could picture him doing a rough draft, hitting on the feature of a higher-than-usual ceiling, and then carrying the feeling of expansiveness further by making structural allowances that permitted elimination of all interior upright beams.

Brydon cursed that unknown fellow and his inspiration.

Had some predestining force been at work—knowing it would come to this, when it would be absolutely necessary to reach that ceiling that was out of reach? Not that getting up there guaranteed anything, really, except perhaps a few more hours to live.

The will to survive.

Brydon had always thought of it as an instinct, but recently it had occurred to him that it wasn't. An infant human was helpless. It did not naturally think of its life as something desirable that it must, above all, preserve. Self-preservation was a realization and, honestly, not the first. It came after the first fear of death, after the first awareness, perhaps unconscious, that the body was vulnerable, destructible. So the will to survive became a reflex. More primary was terror.

159

Small children rarely cried in grief at a funeral. While millions wept, John-John was entertained by the many uniforms and the November trees on that hillside in Arlington. But the fear of death grabbed hold early and, insidiously, never let go.

People tried not to admit it. By praying to God in man-designated sacred places, by trying to accumulate worth, by waving flags of certain color arrangements, by fitting their sexual organs together for what seemed at least temporary transcendence.

Brydon recalled seeing somewhere, probably on television, a herd of water buffalo grazing, being shot at. No alarm as one by one, one next to another, the animals were dropped dead. No concern, none of that awful human fear and desperate reasoning that understandably led to the conclusion—the hope—of an afterlife.

Or in this situation, merely to escape, to be rescued. Brydon wanted it as much, maybe even more, than the others —whatever time he had coming.

Gloria, in her sleep, increased her embrace, pressed as much of herself as possible to Brydon. It seemed she was drawing what she needed from him, and he believed he felt that and it was good to be able to supply it. Then the feeling reversed, and it seemed he was taking from her—a recharging energy that dissolved much of his bitterness.

He lay absolutely still, figuring an architectural diagram and the geometric equations it required on the slate of his mind.

Gloria stirred.

Brydon turned his head to see if she was awake.

She was and was quick to take advantage of the easy proximity of his mouth. The kiss began too eager and a bit awkward, but became, with confidence, very tender.

He regretted that he had to lie to her.

He wished he could lie to himself.

160

After a while, he got up. Using the flashlight, he examined closely the surface of the island, its planking. He found eight-foot lengths consistently, except at the front end where several shorter planks had been used to finish off construction. He used the span of his spread hand, which he knew was ten inches exactly from tip of little finger to tip of thumb, to measure the length of those shorter planks. They were six feet. He measured again to make sure.

His mental calculations had been based on lengths of seven feet. The eight-foot planks would be too long, cumbersome. Would the six-foot ones be too short? Without any way of cutting evenly, as with a saw, he had to make do with whatever length there was. He figured it out again. Conclusion: six feet might be adequate, but just barely—if he was correct.

He got Spider and Peter to help pull up the six-foot planks, told them to be careful, they needed the planks intact.

"What for?" Spider asked.

"We're going to try for the ceiling," Brydon said.

"Don't you think we ought to wait to be rescued?" Peter said.

"Do you?"

"No."

"Let's go for the ceiling."

The idea hadn't just come to Brydon. It was one of the first things he'd thought of—and rejected because it was practically impossible. Thinking it out thoroughly hadn't made it any less so, but Brydon had decided it was as good a chance as anything else and the time had come to take it.

The activity on Island Eight attracted the other survivors there, except, of course, Warren.

Judith and Marion wanted to help.

Phil Kemp said he didn't think Brydon's idea would work, and he wouldn't waste any of his energy on it.

Brydon told Kemp he didn't need him or his comments.

Elliot Janick volunteered to do whatever he was told. Marsha avoided him. Each time Elliot tried to be near her she moved away.

Dan Mandel said he was willing to try anything.

Lois Stevens tried to stand still, and just watch.

Brydon stacked the shorter planks that had been gathered from this island and from others, to make sure they were all of equal length. Six feet. Two were a few inches too long, two more as much too short. Brydon discarded those. That left him eleven planks. He needed ten.

First, from a mark he made on the island surface, he measured off twenty feet, again using his hand span. That twenty would be the base. He divided it into thirds, making marks six feet, eight inches apart.

At each end of the base, perpendicular to it, he placed an eight-foot plank. He told Amy, Gloria and Judith to stand on one of the planks, Elliot, Marsha and Marion to stand on the other. Marsha exchanged places with Gloria. Brydon told them that from then on they must remain where they were. Their weight was vital. Those end planks had to stay put.

Next Brydon put the six-foot planks to use. He butted one tight against the perpendicular edge of an end plank, raised it diagonally until it seemed right. Meanwhile Spider placed another six-footer upright on the nearest third-way mark and lowered it diagonally until it met Brydon's plank at an equal angle. Spider held his plank at its base to keep it from sliding down.

The opposing weight, the lean, of the two planks kept them together at their apex.

With Peter's help, Brydon repeated that procedure exactly at the other end of the base. Then he added two more planks, simultaneously butting them at the bottom, one against Spider's plank, the other against Peter's.

So far, good.

What they had formed were three triangular supports of equal height. By adding two eight-foot boards across the peaks of the triangles, they had a tier five feet high—for the most part holding itself up, like a house of cards.

And like a house of cards it seemed a mere blow of breath would bring it down.

Brydon was pleased, somewhat excited, a spark of what he usually felt whenever he saw the materialization of a concept.

Kemp scoffed, shook his head and said: "What a piece of shit."

Brydon almost took time to punch his fat face.

The second tier was more difficult. They had to be just as exact and extra careful not to cause the whole thing to collapse. The main problem was what would serve as resistance at each end of the tier, as the perpendicular planks did the base.

Brydon could have used Kemp's cooperation at this point, but he didn't ask for it. Instead he decided to chance reducing the weight on the base. He had Elliot Janick step off. Peter and Elliot each took up an eight-foot plank. From opposite ends they lowered their planks onto the top of the first tier. Not perpendicular, but with the grain so to speak, so that the thickness of their planks provided a perpendicular resistance at each end. Brydon guided, measured and made sure they allowed just enough distance, thirteen feet, four inches between the two. He reminded Peter and Elliot that they would have to hold their positions. It seemed they would be able to, by resting the planks on their shoulders while maintaining their grips.

Now Brydon and Spider would construct the second tier upon the first by snugly butting planks and making a pair of supports of equal height in the same triangular manner as before. And topping them horizontally, apex to apex, with an eight-foot plank.

Finally, it was done.

A double-tiered scaffold ten feet high.

Without a single nail.

163

Not because Brydon wanted to prove anything. They simply had no way of driving nails through the boards firmly enough, and Brydon had decided it was better, at least psychologically, to know there were no nails rather than possibly depend on them too much.

As precarious as the scaffold appeared, Brydon was reasonably confident it would support the weight of a man. As a matter of fact, the more weight put upon it the stronger it would become. That was the structural system Brydon had put to use. Resistance and opposing pressures. If the scaffold collapsed it probably wouldn't be because of weight upon it but because it was not properly aligned or balanced. Well, they'd done, by eye, the best they could.

The island was six feet high. The scaffold was ten. That left seven from the top of the scaffold to the ceiling. A man could reach it easily.

Dan Mandel told Brydon: "I used to be a gymnast. Really. I was all conference for two years at Oregon State."

Brydon hadn't even considered that anyone other than himself should climb up there and try.

"My specialty was the horse and the parallel bars," Dan said. "I still work out now and then."

"Mostly then?"

"It's been a while," Dan admitted.

Brydon appreciated Dan's willingness to put himself on the line, told him that, told him: "Thanks anyway."

"I've got better balance than you," Dan contended.

He went to the next island, to the end of it, got a short running start, performed a couple of front flips and, for good measure, a hand stand. He even walked on his hands a ways. By no means were the flips snappy perfect, and Dan wavered some during the hand stand.

He looked to Brydon for approval.

Brydon decided anyone who wanted to do it that badly had a need to do it. And more to the point—however imperfect, Dan's demonstration had been impressive.

164

The idea was for Dan to get up there, use the gardening claw to remove one or more of the acoustical panels and climb up into the space above the ceiling. That accomplished, strips of clothing would be knotted together to make a rope that Dan would secure to a cross beam or whatever, so that other survivors could climb or be hoisted up.

Dan removed his shoes.

Spider squatted.

Dan stood on Spider's shoulders. Brydon helped Dan's balance while Spider came up slowly to a standing position. When Brydon let go, Dan was shaky, unsure, but soon he had the feel of it and was steady enough.

Spider moved to the scaffold, taking short steps, lifting his feet as little as possible so as not to jounce. He approached the scaffold from the side, at mid-point, got close up to it.

The top of the second tier was level with Dan's chin. He gripped the horizontal plank squarely, left and right. What he was about to do was something he'd done often in the gym—but years ago. He tensed his body, gradually took his weight off Spider's shoulders, pulled himself up by the arms to a vertical stiff-arm position. At once he transferred all his weight to his right hand. That allowed him to swing his left leg up and over, so he was then sitting astraddle the ten-inch-wide top plank.

The scaffold creaked, jammed itself against itself at every joint. It actually became a more solid structure.

Dan kept his concentration.

Brydon, watching him, now knew that he would surely have failed at it. Hell, by comparison Dan was a regular Olga Korbut.

Dan drew his legs up, placed his feet flat on the plank, one before the other, about seven inches apart. With arms out straight on each side for balance, in a single smooth motion he stood up.

It's going to work, Brydon thought.

Apparent success made Kemp decide it would be better for

him if he participated. He added his weight to one of the perpendicular planks at the base.

The ceiling was now within reach for Dan. Brydon was shining the flashlight upward, and Dan saw where the acoustical panels joined, not fitted as well as they appeared from below. Dan got the gardening claw in the seam between two of the panels and dug and pried at various points along the seam. He managed to shred away the edges of the panels a little, but that was all.

"Maybe I can punch a hole through it," he said.

To punch hard enough and keep balance would be difficult if not impossible, Brydon thought. He told Dan to keep at it with the gardening claw. "You'll find a loose spot." Brydon was hoping for something he ordinarily detested: poor workmanship—a limit of two hits allotted to each nail and good luck if that just happened to drive it home.

Dan jangled his arms to revitalize them.

He was reaching to the ceiling again.

At that moment the whole building interfered. Not a sway or a roll or a settling, but a sudden snapping pitch, just one.

The scaffold fell apart.

Dan leaped for the spherical television fixture that was hung from the ceiling off to his left over the aisle.

He would have been better off if he'd taken the fall straight down with the scaffold, but he grabbed hold of the stem of the fixture and, simianlike, swung his feet up, locked them around the stem.

It seemed he hung there a long while, much longer than thirty seconds.

The fixture itself was heavy. Not installed to hold an extra one hundred and sixty-one pounds.

It ripped away from the ceiling.

Nothing anyone could do.

Dan hit the mud still holding on to the heavy black sphere. He and it quickly sank from sight.

166

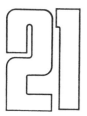

Since then, for an hour, Brydon had said nothing.

He'd just sat there, unmoved by Gloria's sympathetic words and touches. No consolation for him that the scaffold attempt had *nearly* succeeded. And he should have foreseen, taken into account, how a failure would affect the others.

When the scaffold collapsed, so did the hope they had built, the faith in rescue they had used for spiritual support. It was as though invisible fingers had been snapped before their eyes, snapped them out of their wishful reasoning, made them see reality all the way to the evident end.

They had felt special. So many had died in this catastrophe, but they were still alive. It seemed they had been chosen to survive by whatever force determined such things, or, to take the other way of looking at it, that they had been rejected by death. As it turned out, neither was the case. They were

167

merely the ones who would be taunted, tortured with a little additional time.

Should they pray?

Maybe, Brydon thought, they should offer supplications to this goddamned supermarket. Pardon the blasphemy, almighty check-out. He would, for minor atonement, make the sign of the dollar with his thumb on his forehead, a million million times. What tremendous values. Cash registers ringing beneath the mud, and over there was Kemp, wearing his money bags like a holy trapping.

Peter and Amy Javakian were on Island Four, lying side by side.

She said: "The air is getting close, isn't it?"

He didn't think so.

"I can't seem to get a deep breath. Are we running out of air?"

"No," he assured her, after assessing his own easy breathing. Anyway, it was too soon for the air to be depleted in such a large place, and besides, there was the chance that some was getting in through an opening they couldn't see.

He sat up.

"Where you going?"

"Just here." He kneeled above her head. His fingers found she was tense where her shoulders and neck joined. He massaged gently. She felt so delicate to him and yet substantial.

"I feel a tightness." She indicated the middle of her chest.

"Does it hurt?"

"Not a regular kind of hurt, more like a knot."

He kneaded the rounds of her shoulders. There was love in his hands.

She told him: "Know what I think it is, the knot?"

"What?"

"All the things I've left unsaid trying to get out at the same time."

168

He bent over and worshipped her with his most tender kiss.

"Are you forgiving me?" she asked, slightly ironic.

"No."

"You mean you won't?"

"Will you forgive me?"

"I can't blame you anymore."

"That's what I mean."

"But I was such a bitch, hassling you all the time."

"Not all the time."

"I never told you but when I was working in Sacramento I was awful lonely. That's the trouble with independence, it's lonely."

He remembered how much he'd missed her when she was in Sacramento, and all the other times apart. He also recalled when he last told her that, just the day before yesterday. She hadn't wanted to hear it, as though it revealed weakness. He wondered about the difference between then and now.

"Don't let me do all the talking," she said. "Anyway, at least say you love me."

He decided to believe in now.

"Please?" she asked.

He said it. It wasn't difficult. It was true.

While she absorbed his words, the baby in her changed its position. It seemed settled but then it shifted again. Finally it became calm. Restless, Amy thought, but immediately she realized that probably wasn't what the baby was feeling, that was only what she thought it was feeling. Even though connected to her, symbiotic, it was already having its own experiences.

"What are you thinking?" Peter asked.

"That in a way we never could have gotten completely together anyway."

He was very aware of the past tense. "Never?"

"Even if we spent every second of fifty years in the same room."

169

He understood. "That's a fact people have to live with."

"It's why I got the crazies," she said. "I was crashing against my aloneness and taking it out on you."

She had always felt it to some extent, naturally, but only over the past year had she tried to deal with it straight on. She could even remember the night, the moment, it had come forward in her mind, and instead of replacing it as usual with other less serious ruminations, she had opened it, fold after fold, as though it were an interesting package. She was exploring its contents before she realized she maybe should have left well enough . . . alone.

Aloneness.

What a maddening realization. All her life she had taken for granted that her common experiences were truly common, the same as those of others. Now she wasn't sure that her senses were not unique. And if they were hers alone, not sharable. . . .

The most ordinary things became embossed in her observation. Peter eating a peach. Peter painting with blue. Peter going barefoot.

Once at a nighttime outdoor concert, she got to thinking about all the different experiences the thousands of people were having as they listened to the same music. She imagined what a cacophony of responses lay beneath their collective attentiveness. An abstract din. It bothered her. It came between her and enjoyment. She developed a headache and went home.

"What's the matter, Amy?"

"I'm in an emotional valley."

A chronic case of aloneness was what she really had, that struck and spread to the nerve roots. Poets and such had died by their own hands from it. Of course she didn't suffer from it as intensely as that. Enough, though.

It was the reason, actually, why she hadn't had an abortion. She'd thought perhaps pregnancy might be the one way of overcoming aloneness, at least temporarily. She would be literally connected to another human being. Soon, and too late, she found her body was shared but not her feelings. No, unless she fooled herself, pregnancy wasn't the way to verify her existence.

Now, on Island Four, there had been silence enough for Peter to ask again what her thoughts were.

"I'm figuring out life," she said, matter-of-fact. She also managed a smile.

"When you do, let me in on it."

She hushed him. Her mind was going through a colloquy she'd started and stopped countless times before. Now it seemed more coherent. . . .

"Do you believe in God?"

"I believe in a creator."

"Why?"

"Because creativity is organization and nature is intricately organized, so it must have been created."

She didn't stop to consider whether or not that was logical.

"And we are part of nature?"

"Part of the arrangement."

"The creator had a free hand?"

"Certainly."

"Why, then, did the creator give us such a dilemma? Aloneness."

Her mind was racing now.

"There must have been a reason."

"Purpose."

"The creator could have made us differently, a more compatible design."

"Stick a finger in another person's ear to share an experience."

"Could have."

"What makes aloneness bearable?"

"Love."

"Doesn't cure it but makes it bearable?"

"Love."

171

"Perhaps, then, what the creator intended was to motivate us to love."

"Force us to love."

"Personal choice."

"Either love or be miserable."

It made sense.

Amy reached up, traced two fingertips along Peter's cheek, beneath his chin. A look of amazement on her face. She led his face down to hers.

"Open your mouth."

He did.

"Wide."

Into his mouth she said, "I love you."

And kept her words in with a kiss.

Across the way, only seven or eight feet away, Judith Ward and Marion Mercer sat facing one another. Connected by their hands. Judith had her hair pulled back severely, contained with a rubber band she'd found in one of her pockets. In the dim light her eyes appeared exaggerated, dark-socketed, and at times Marion thought the whites looked phosphorescent. It was eerie, and she thought perhaps it was Judith's fear showing or something in her anticipating death.

They had been quiet, had heard everything said by Amy and Peter. They had borrowed those words, emphasized them by squeezing each other's hands.

Knowing how easy it was to be heard, they whispered.

"What would we have done? Tell me."

"Gone away."

"Defied everyone?"

"Been together."

"Yes. We would have made it somehow."

"I wonder."

"I was getting ready to tell Fred."

"Were you?"

"I'd set a deadline for myself. Next Wednesday."

172

"Why then?"

"Just an arbitrary day."

"It surely would have been."

"Anyway. I couldn't have gone on being deceitful. It was hurting us."

"I know."

"Did you ever think that maybe we were using us to escape from other things?"

"Well, I guess that's something we'll never have the chance to disprove."

A silence.

"Judith?"

"Hmm?"

"I was happy until I met you."

"Oh?"

"Then I was happier."

"Darling . . ."

They leaned forward, placed their heads in the dip of each other's shoulders, Judith giving lover's kisses to Marion's neck. Anyone observing would have thought them merely a pair of distraught women exchanging consolations.

Marion whispered: "The things left unsaid, I also feel that."

"You do?"

"It's probably natural at a time like this."

"Actually, I think we communicated more than average."

"Average meaning normal?"

"Whatever. Even without words we said more."

"I agree."

"Because neither of us ever pretended to be a man."

"Once at Bullocks I came close to buying a boy's suit, tie and everything."

"Why?"

"To wear for you."

"I'm glad you didn't."

"I decided you would be."

173

"One of the things that made us special was our being female, our sameness."

"Likes attract."

"Yes, and that *was* beautiful."

Past tense. They both became painfully aware of it, soothed it away somewhat with their silence.

Judith said: "A lot of times when I made love to you I felt that you were me."

"Don't talk so loud."

Back to a whisper. "I was both doing and being done. It seemed as though I could feel what you were feeling."

"I know. It was like that for me when I made love to you. At certain times more than others, but always some. Like being melted, connected."

"Yes, in every way."

"Every possible way."

"Kiss me."

Judith did, a long kiss on the cheek. And although in its tenderness it conveyed all her affirmations of love, it appeared sisterly.

The inadequacy, the inequity of it was too much for Marion. "No!" she protested, unintentionally raising her voice. "Love is love."

That got attention from all directions.

Marion held Judith's head. Her mouth took Judith's mouth with passion.

Judith resisted momentarily, a reflex, but then she understood and contributed without shame.

Peter Javakian went over to Brydon. "I've got an idea," he said.

"What?"

"If we could get up to the office, from there it would be easy to go on up through the ceiling." He meant the glass-enclosed overhanging management office at the south end of the building.

Brydon had considered it. "The problem is getting up to the office."

"Let's take a look."

They went to Island One. Peter shined his flashlight through the window and into the office diagonally above, fifteen feet away. He pointed out how the office was built close up to the ceiling. He explained his idea and asked if Brydon thought it would work.

"Might." Brydon was still feeling the failure of the scaffold. He thought that might be the reason he couldn't believe in Peter's idea. Maybe, at that moment, it was just impossible for him to be receptive. He gazed up at the office, appeared thoughtful and then nodded. "Why don't you give it a try?"

Peter was encouraged. He hurried to get at it. First requirement was material to make a line. Denim was strong. Lois Stevens and Gloria Rand were wearing blue denim jeans. They cooperated, tore off the legs of their jeans. Peter ripped them into three-inch strips. He square-knotted the strips together, like the tail of a kite, twenty-five feet long.

To the end he tied the half-gallon can of liquid floor wax that had been salvaged. It was appropriately weighty, a compact five pounds. He tied the other end of the denim line around his right wrist, so he couldn't lose it. Holding the can of wax like a football, he stepped back and threw it up and across at the office window. It smacked hard against the glass pane, caused a cobweb pattern of cracks, but didn't break through.

Peter recovered the can by taking in the line hand over hand. On his third throw the glass shattered. Still, large hunks of it remained in the window frame. He continued throwing until he had broken away enough of the glass—an opening about ten feet wide by three feet high. Now he untied the can of wax, replaced it with one of the eight-foot planks. He double-bound and knotted the denim tight around the middle of the plank. Using both hands, he tried to toss the plank up through the window. The plank was unwieldy, weighed about twenty pounds, couldn't be thrown accurately.

Peter completely missed the window three times. On his fourth throw he hit the window frame. On his next the plank went up and in.

What he hoped was that the plank might work like a grappling hook, catch and wedge itself against the legs of a desk, behind file cabinets — anything substantial. Then he would be able to shinny up the denim line to the office, find electric wiring and cords that could be used to safely hoist the others up.

He pulled in the slack of the denim line, made it taut. Tried to feel whether or not the plank was caught on something. It seemed to be. He applied more tension, tugged. The board came flying out the window.

Peter flung the board up into the office again. Same result. He kept trying for nearly an hour, until he could barely lift his arms.

Spider also gave it a few tries.

So did Brydon.

It depended too much on luck, and they certainly weren't having any.

Captain Royden Dodd looked down at his bare toes and thought, *Old toes.*

The young Newport Beach police chopper pilot, Hackley, was in the dark bedroom screwing a new bulb in the lamp.

"My hometown is famous for a light bulb," Hackley said. "Livermore, California."

"Never been there."

"They've got a light bulb up there in the firehouse that's been burning for over seventy years."

"Regular bulb?"

"Hand blown, thick carbon filament, made to last. Just keeps on burning."

The light went on in the bedroom. Hackley came out with the bad bulb that he dropped in the wastebasket by the desk. He said: "Whenever it gets to me how lousy things are, that old Livermore bulb comes to mind."

177

"Maybe it's not the same one, maybe it's gotten to be such an attraction they keep replacing it on the sly."

"I don't think so," Hackley said.

"It's a possibility."

Hackley didn't want to think so. He turned off the idea by turning on the stereo, an FM rock station. It came out thumping loud. Hackley lowered it some for Dodd's sake.

They were in Hackley's apartment in Newport Beach. A three-room place counting the kitchen that was only separated from the living room by a barlike counter. The apartment was on the second floor overlooking the inevitable pool. Hackley lived alone, but from evidence such as a couple of string bikini tops and bottoms on the hook on the back of the bathroom door, excess lipstick on a crumpled tissue in a bedside ashtray, one brush but two kinds of toothpaste and a pair of foreign-made bikes hung on the entranceway wall like contemporary art, he wasn't alone much. No reason for him to be. Twenty-two, good rugged looks, a straightforward easiness about him that was immediately likable.

At the moment he was off duty, had on only a pair of well-bleached jeans. No one would ever have guessed he was a policeman. Too relaxed. There was a wound scar on the fleshy part of his back close to his right underarm. Like a large lopsided cleft, the skin there was pinched inward.

Dodd noticed the scar, guessed Vietnam and decided not to ask Hackley about it.

Hackley didn't ask Dodd if he wanted a refill, just took the J&B over and poured into the glass Dodd had in hand.

Dodd was as off duty as he ever was. He'd called headquarters, was told what was happening in the area, including a few things that had become almost routine since the rain: armed quarrels, a family murder, hit-and-runs. No telling what would happen next and no real way to prevent it. Dodd gave Hackley's number, told headquarters he would be calling in.

After his perilous slip down the slide, Dodd had had the choice of returning to headquarters or going home again. He looked and felt horrible, covered with mud. It would be too obvious to anyone at headquarters or to Helen what he'd been up to—disobeying orders. So he was glad when Hackley had suggested the apartment.

There Dodd had gotten out of his clothes—they must have weighed thirty pounds. He shoved them, shoes and all, into a plastic bag, having a flash of guilt because of how quickly Helen's loving care had gone to waste. He took his second shower of the day, had to dig the mud from his ears and was surprised to find that so much of it had somehow gotten packed into the crease of his buttocks.

Hackley had also supplied a robe and a drink.

Now Dodd appraised the robe. It was silk. He'd noticed an I. Magnin label.

"From a lady," Hackley said. "She ran a stop sign. Instead of her getting a ticket I got that."

Dodd didn't say anything, but his disapproval was obvious.

Hackley smiled. "My mother gave it to me."

That was better.

"What size shoe you take?" Hackley asked.

"Ten and a half."

Hackley brought out a pair of sneakers, a pair of jeans and a shirt.

Dodd's feet were slightly large for the sneakers and his middle was a couple of inches too middle-aged for the jeans. The shirt fit and he squeezed into the sneaks. Hackley solved the pants problem with a pair of blue denim overalls, the regular work kind with adjustable shoulder straps, which Dodd lengthened. Still, the overalls were short in the legs. Dodd would have to go with his bare ankles exposed. He glanced down at them. Pale and veiny, he thought.

Hackley made two phone calls. Tucked the phone between his shoulder and cheek and talked while dressing. His first call was to break a date. He didn't lie, although it would have

179

been easier to use the excuse that he was on duty. He just told the girl he couldn't see her that night and sounded sorry enough.

Dodd felt he was intruding, offered Hackley an out.

Hackley wouldn't take it, made his other call, started it with, "Hey, old buddy. . . ."

Dodd didn't hear the rest of that phone conversation because of the stereo and because Hackley took the phone by its long cord into the bedroom, not to get out of range, only to find a pair of old white moccasins among the disorder on the floor of the closet. He put them on. He was hanging up the phone when he came out. "All set," he said.

He provided Dodd with a lightweight hooded slicker, a sort of ski jacket. For himself, a trench coat and a regular white sailor's hat with the brim turned down all around.

They used Dodd's car, gassed it full at the first Union station.

"Can the two of us handle it?"

Dodd thought so.

"I mean, you don't have a bad back or a hernia or something?"

Dodd didn't bother to answer, young smartass.

"How much does one of those things weigh?"

"Don't know exactly."

"What's your guess?"

"Three, maybe four hundred."

"Maybe more," Hackley said. "We ought to find some help just in case."

Dodd agreed.

First, on Harbor Boulevard they rented an open trailer from a U-Haul place that lived up to its advertised pledge: OPEN 24 HOURS RAIN OR SHINE. The man in charge didn't help hitch up the trailer, just took the hundred deposit and watched from inside, keeping dry.

From there Dodd and Hackley cruised some of the side streets off Grand Avenue. They pulled over at a small stucco house that had been converted into a neighborhood grocery

180

store. Four men stood hunched with their backs close to the store front. It wasn't really a good place to stand because the rain poured off the overhang of the roof, hit the pavement and splattered the men. They didn't seem to mind getting soaked from the crotch down. Maybe because they were passing a paper bag with a bottle in it. They were Mexicans, migrant farm laborers, who usually lived from one day's pay to the next. The weather was particularly rough on them.

Hackley rolled down his window to call out, *"Hey, señors, vengan aqui, por favor."*

The men exchanged quizzical glances, shrugged and resumed their previous detachment.

"¿Hablan inglés?" Hackley asked.

No response.

Dodd leaned across and asked them: "Want to make twenty dollars?"

The four men rushed to the car, shoved one another roughly to be at the window. One said, "What I must do for twenty dollars? I don't steal."

Another said, "I steal."

Dodd liked that man's honesty, chose him. His name, he said, was Gilberto Fuentes. He got into the rear seat. One of the other men also climbed in.

"We only need one man," Dodd told him.

"Two for thirty," Gilberto said, "Good deal, señor, only fifteen each."

Dodd hesitated. They took that to mean he was considering.

"Him my brother," Giberto said. "We work together. Good stealers."

Dodd didn't believe the brother routine. Evidently they didn't expect him to, because when the car was under way the second man introduced himself as Paco Ramos. Dodd figured Gilberto's comradely generosity wasn't true either. The split would be twenty for Gilberto, ten for Paco, better than nothing in the rain.

Night traffic on the Newport Freeway was moderately

181

heavy. Everything looked slick, hazardous. Dodd thought maybe his tiredness was adding to the impression that any moment he would slip out of control. He kept to the right lane, under sixty.

The Mexicans hadn't asked where they were being taken or what exactly was expected of them. All they knew and cared about was a job for the money. Typically, they were saving their energy, slouched heads down, riding on the comfortable surface of sleep.

Making conversation, Hackley asked if Dodd knew anything about bio-rhythms.

"What's that?"

"We're all supposed to have three different cycles — physical, emotional and intellectual. The way they go up and down can be plotted on a graph for every day of your life—so you know in advance what you're in for."

Dodd grunted, thought how it would be knowing for sure tomorrow would be a bad day.

"When all three cycles are way down you should feel lousy and dumb."

"You believe that?"

"A girl I know does bio-rhythm charts. Did mine. Right now, I'm scheduled for a physical and emotional high and medium-low intelligence. Maybe there's something to it, because I'm sort of horny and in a good mood and, instead, look where I am."

Hackley was glad Dodd laughed. He'd nearly given up on the captain's sense of humor.

No talk for a while. One of Dodd's thoughts was about that silk robe he'd had on. He doubted I. Magnin had a branch store in or anyplace around Livermore.

They were approaching the Garden Grove interchange when the red and amber flashed through the rear window.

Dodd pulled the car over.

A highway patrol car parked behind. Two officers in it.

One got out and came to the window on Dodd's side. He kept a cautious distance, one hand on his revolver while the window was being lowered.

Dodd recognized the man, asked him, "What is it, the trailer?"

In the back seat Gilberto and Paco were up on edge, wary, taking it all in.

Dodd disliked the delay but it was his fault. He'd known, of course, trailers weren't allowed on the freeway, had wanted to save time. He flashed his identification and badge at the patrolman who didn't look at it until after he thought he recognized Dodd. He shined his flashlight head on to make sure.

"I didn't know it was you, Captain," he said.

"That's all right."

"I should have known the car. Anything I can do for you?"

Dodd told him he could get in out of the rain. When they were under way again, Dodd thought he should have told the man not to mention seeing him. What the hell, he probably wouldn't anyway, Dodd decided.

A quarter mile past the interchange was the Chapman Street turnoff. Dodd took it and headed east for two miles through El Modeno, where he picked up Route S25. After two and a half miles, that minor winding road ended, ran into another that wasn't paved. Dodd swung north for a short way, came to a flat, open area, pulled to the side and stopped.

Since the encounter with the patrolman on the freeway, Gilberto and Paco had been either apprehensively silent or whispering in Spanish. They had seen Dodd's badge, knew now they had admitted to stealing to a policeman of some sort. They kept excitedly advising one another to remain calm.

Hackley thought they might jump out and run for it, so he told them they had been recruited for an official job. Then the only thing that worried Gilberto and Paco was whether or not they would be paid in cash as soon as whatever had to be done was done. Hackley showed them some money to keep them in line.

The range of the car's headlights was cut down by the rain. Out there beyond the reach of the lights was the Lower Peters Canyon Reservoir, a triangular-shaped body of water with only about a mile of shore line.

Dodd had been at that spot a month before, before the rain, when he and Helen had taken an out-of-the-way pleasure drive. He had noticed then that the State Water Resources Department was putting in a new pipeline to serve the recent housing developments north of Tustin Boulevard. However, not a sign now of any such work. That was strange. If anything, all the days of rain should have halted the project.

Dodd clicked the headlights to bright. He steered the car around slowly. Through the silvery diffusion of falling drops the lights hit on something. Yellow. A heavy-duty ditch digger, what was called a payloader because of its combination digging – conveying system. Off to the left of that, a short distance beyond, was something blue, a shade between turquoise and robin's egg. It was a section of polyethylene pipe —plastic. Thirty-six inches in diameter, three-quarters of an inch thick. A number of ten-foot sections of it were strung out in a line ready to be put underground.

Hackley, Gilberto and Paco got out of the car. Dodd turned it around, backed the trailer near as possible to the pipe. He could feel the tires spinning some. Soaked, raw earth, it would be easy to get stuck.

Dodd cut the motor and got out.

Gilberto and Paco were standing there trying to get used to the idea that what they were to help steal officially way out there on this awful night was a worthless piece of pipe.

Dodd tried to heft it. It wouldn't budge.

Hackley told him, "Here comes your hernia."

The section of pipe weighed nearly eight hundred pounds. Good thing they'd hired both Gilberto and Paco.

Still, it was no easy task, wouldn't have been even on dry ground with solid footing. The mud was like grease. Twice they slipped completely, causing them to drop the section of pipe. They barely got out from under it in time. Finally, they had it up on the bed of the trailer. Dodd and Hackley tied it in place.

Dodd started the car, put it in gear and very gradually increased his foot pressure on the gas pedal. The car's rear wheels spun, whined and threw mud up. Hackley, Gilberto and Paco couldn't get footing enought to push. The wheels were digging their own hole. The car would soon be sunk to its chassis, useless.

"Hold it!" Hackley shouted.

He went over to the state-owned ditch digger, ripped off the tarpaulin used to cover its cabin. He spread the tarpaulin on the ground under the car, gathered and shoved the edge of it down between the rear tires and the mud.

They'd have only one try.

Dodd put the car in neutral, stomped the gas pedal all the way and threw the shift into low.

The wheels spun, grabbed the canvas, snapped the canvas, shot it and mud up behind. Just enough traction. The car and trailer lurched forward, fishtailed and continued on to the slick but better packed road.

Island Twelve.

Warren Stevens held up the front of his poncho with his chin. While he urinated. He had the Colt .45 automatic in his other hand. The stream of his urine hit upon the surface of the mud with a steady splat. He played with it, squeezed off the flow to cause a somewhat pleasant ache throughout his lower system. He released but allowed only a short spurt. Stopped and went again and again like that until he ran out.

It was something he often did—ever since he'd read about it in a pamphlet put out by the Army Medical Corps. Telling enlisted men what to do after sexual exposure.

ASSUME EVERY WOMAN IS CONTAMINATED

was a warning in bold type that Warren had no trouble remembering. The pamphlet also said that if a man who had

186

been exposed did not have a prophylaxis kit or couldn't get to an army pro station, his best emergency measure was to urinate immediately and squeeze it off, backing up the flow for a possible inner cleansing. Warren related the idea of squeezing off to squeezing off a shot, not that it was in any way the same, he told himself.

A bit sorry it was over, he closed his fly. He gazed across the islands, saw Brydon and Gloria. And Kemp. They were nearest. Where was Spider? Probably with Lois, wherever she was. Several times over the hours he had caught sight of Spider, had missed two or three good opportunities. Once he'd had the flat of Spider's back in the aim of the Colt and he was taking up the slack of the trigger when Spider moved aside. Warren didn't want to chance a shot at a moving target.

Like the bear.

The bear he had shot that had given his father something special about him to brag about. *Ursus horribilis,* nearly half a ton of killer animal coming head on a mile a minute.

Only Warren knew the truth.

The truth had been covered by layers of lies but it was still sharp in him—what had really happened.

That day of the bear, Warren had just come through thick brush where he'd picked up some burrs on the tops of his woolen stockings. At the edge of a small clearing he paused to remove the burrs. Not that they were bothering him. He was bored. The biggest game he'd seen all day were chipmunks.

At that moment a small, plump cloud passed before the sun causing an abrupt change in the daylight, causing Warren to glance up and see the animal at the opposite edge of the clearing no more than a hundred feet away. It took a while for it to register, for Warren to believe it was a bear, actually a wild, killable bear.

Warren was downwind.

The bear never saw him.

Typical of bears, it had poor eyesight, and besides, just

187

then it was trying to reach some high-growing berries. Up on its hind legs trying to get to the berries.

With a telescopic sight on the rifle, shooting the bear in the neck was like shooting point blank at a thick log. Even then Warren didn't have complete faith in the force of a 458 Magnum. He was afraid the bullet might pass clean through or perhaps penetrate no deeper than the bear's tough hide, only making the animal angry at him. Warren's stomach went hollow when the bear reared and appeared to be in a rage the moment before it fell over dead.

That was the truth of it.

Once Warren had come close to telling his father. During practice at the indoor target range they had at home. He actually did half tell him, hint around it several times, but each time his father changed the subject or put on a pair of those earphonelike target practicing protectors so he couldn't hear anything. It never occurred to Warren that his father already suspected. His father's maxim was that the truth wasn't true until he actually heard it.

The fifteen-hundred-dollar rifle. Now, in a way, Warren wished he'd never gotten it. His next wish was that he had it now. With the telescopic sight it would be a cinch at that distance to put one right between Spider's eyes. Easy as the bear. But better than the bear.

Warren's stomach growled and he was so thirsty he worked his tongue against the roof of his mouth and around his gums for saliva. His hunger argued in favor of joining the others; his thirst gave him hell for not accepting the 7UP from Brydon.

But no, he'd hold out. No matter what. Maybe later, when they all settled down again, he'd go on a raid. Cross over to steal eats and drinks from them and get back undetected. He was sure he could do it. They weren't as smart about such things as he was.

They were shitheads, did dumb things, got killed.

The scaffold, for instance. What a joke. He had watched

them put it together, known all along it was ridiculous. Being apart from them, excluding them, he was superior. He was in control. He allowed each step of the scaffold's construction—simply because it amused him. And when it was completed and Dan was up on it, he merely had to concentrate to make it collapse. As though his eyes beamed some kind of demolition ray.

Now, thirstier than ever. His stomach was grabbing at itself. His head was swimming some. Hot spots the size of eyes were burning into or out of his skull, his scalp bristling. It seemed he could feel where every hair grew from his head. Strength was pouring like warm wax from his legs.

He had the urge to drop, fall in a heap, give up and cry. Part of him inside was already crying. Tears running from behind his eyes, down his inside hollowness, choking his passages.

He sniffed dryly, coughed to expel nothing from his throat.

Another part of him told him to guts up. It supplied him with rage to fight thirst and hunger, to plug the leak of his legs and pump in some reserve strength.

But his tongue was dry, his lips tight and papery.

Around his neck on a cowhide loop was a .45-caliber bullet that he wore like a jewel, kept polished. Not a fake or a chargeless cartridge but a live usable .45. A girl once had flicked at it with her finger and laughed at how much she thought it looked like a penis, a hard miniature penis with a brass shaft and a gray head. It had cross slits in the tip where it was dumdummed.

Warren put the bullet in his mouth. Bedouins sucked on pebbles when they were lost on the desert, he remembered. He sucked on the bullet and soon, as though excited, the glands in his mouth responded with wetness. He played the tip of his tongue on the tip of the bullet, felt its cross slits.

Several weeks before, with nothing better to do, he'd made a whole carton of .45 bullets more lethal. Using one of his

189

hunting knives, he'd cut precisely deep enough slits one way and then the other on the tips of the bullets. Result was that all the bullets now in the Colt automatic and in the two spare clips he'd brought along were dumdums.

A slight, abrupt change of light. Warren spit out the bullet. He looked across the islands. For some reason they had both flashlights and all the candles on and now he could see them. There was Spider. Standing—how many islands away? Warren counted six. How far was that? He tried to figure the range by multiplying aisles and islands but was too impatient, his mind jumped around, offered several estimates and reassured him it was close enough.

Spider was stretching.

Lois was standing next to Spider.

Spider had his arms straight up over his head, as though surrendering.

What about Lois being hit?

Warren brought the pistol up, cocked the hammer. He put his arm straight out, stiff. The pistol weighed two and a half pounds. For steadiness, he held his right wrist. He sighted down the barrel, raised it a bit to get the little notch of the square rear sight in line with the fixed upright sight on the front, and then both in line with the center of Spider's chest.

Warren took up the trigger's slack. He breathed deeply, let it all out and held his breath.

Squeeze off.

Nothing happened.

The safety was on. He couldn't remember putting it on, was sure he hadn't. A dumb mistake. It made him angrier at everything. He released the safety and again, more quickly, went through the phases of taking aim.

Again, squeeze off.

Don't move, you stinking fried monkey, Warren mentally ordered Spider.

Explosion.

Louder than Warren had expected. And the recoil of the

190

pistol almost jumped it out of his grip. It seemed he had blown the lights out because now there was total darkness. No way for him to know whether or not he had scored a hit. He didn't believe he could have missed Spider, had had him dead on. It had been as easy as the bear, same as the bear, he told himself.

Except this time he couldn't see for sure. Maybe he'd missed. Oh, sweet Jesus, if he'd missed, Spider would be coming on, charging right at him that moment.

Warren fired blindly, rapidly, six shots. He ejected the empty clip, took a full one from his pocket, shoved it home and snapped back the housing to get the first bullet in the chamber. Ready again.

Black in the black. Where was that fucking black in the black? Probably sneaking forward, getting nearer. Warren could feel him, believed he could smell him getting nearer.

He fired the entire clip, seven shots, scattered them from left to right to better his chance of a hit. No squeezing off now. Too desperate for that. During the volley, he thought he'd heard someone cry out, but maybe it was only what he wanted to hear. He listened, kept perfectly still.

Silence. As accompaniment to the pitch black it was loud, a penetrating needle of noise that Warren's imagination soon increased to a thick, covering roar.

Used clip out.

Full clip in.

Seven more wild shots at anything in the dark.

Then, no more ammo. But perhaps he didn't need any. He listened again for any sound of life. Nothing. Maybe he'd killed Spider and all of them. Including Lois? He'd tell his father that Lois had jumped into the line of fire, was doped up when she sacrificed herself trying to protect her nigger lover. Warren believed his father would believe. Father cared for him more than he did Lois, lots more, for sure, and, although Lois's death would put a temporary crimp in things, it wouldn't stop father from eventually again boasting, hug-

191

ging him a single arm-around masculine hug from the side and saying in front of people, "This is a boy to be proud of."

Warren remained alert, kept listening for what seemed a long while before he breathed easier. He was about to sit down when he heard a movement off to his left. And another to his right.

They were coming.

More sounds of movement, more distinct, closer.

They were coming to get him.

Oh, sweet Jesus.

He remembered the bullet he was wearing on the leather loop around his neck. He dug at the knot that held it, regretted he'd soaked the knot in water to shrink it tight and harden it. He tore at the knot with his teeth and finally it came loose. The bullet fell out, escaped Warren's fingers. He got down on his knees, felt for it. They were coming. He had to find it. But maybe it had rolled off the edge. He swept all around with both hands. His right hand came on it.

Thank God.

Quickly, he jerked open the chamber of the automatic, inserted the bullet, snapped the chamber shut and cocked the hammer.

Wait, he told himself, wait until they were so close he couldn't possibly miss. That was what a smart hunter would do.

They, his mind repeated. That was it—the trouble. He was only one, had only one bullet. *They*, the bastards, weren't giving him a fair chance.

His panic spiraled, became terror that pressed from all sides, confusing. There was nowhere to run. He had to face it.

From the right a beam of light cut the darkness, sought, found Warren and stayed on him. And immediately another from the left. To Warren, the converging shafts of light were bright, solid arms of his enemy's reaching for him, holding him. He was helpless, immobilized for a long moment.

192

He brought the pistol up. Pressed the muzzle of it against the socket of his right eye and did not have even a final, rational thought before he pulled the trigger. . . .

Twenty-one shots before, the first Warren had fired had come so close Spider felt the brush of it on his cheek as it went by. The third shot of the second clip hit Kemp. He had tried to keep down flat, but the money bags prevented that. The bag in front was a large hump beneath his upper chest, causing his head to be up at an angle. The .45-caliber bullet exploded out of the barrel of the pistol at the velocity of 850 feet a second, so it took less than an eighth of a second for it to reach Kemp. It entered his neck one inch to the right of his Adam's apple. Because the bullet was dumdummed, as soon as it hit it spread open from its center, like a four-petaled flower blossoming. It tore through Kemp's windpipe to get to his left carotid artery. The artery was about as large around as his forefinger. The bullet ripped through, severed the artery and continued on through various sorts of tissue to make a hole the size of a silver dollar where it came out at the back of his neck.

Was death ever instantaneous?

It should have been for Kemp but he felt it. The searing smash of the bullet, its sudden crowding penetration. He was aware of choking as some of the blood from the artery flowed into his ruptured windpipe. Beat after beat, under pressure, his body pumped the life out of him. In under a minute.

The impact of the bullet was so great it had snapped Kemp up and flipped him. The money bags went flying. He ended in an ugly position, hanging half over the edge of the island.

When Warren killed himself, Brydon and Peter immediately changed the aim of their flashlights, so as not to keep such a grisly sight in view.

Next thought: was anyone hurt?

Judith Ward didn't realize she was. Her fright had her pressed so tightly to the hard surface of Island Five, she thought that was the cause of the pain along the upper, outer part of her right thigh. A sharp ache. Soon after the danger of

Warren, the pain changed, her thigh felt as though it had been scraped raw. She touched there and, although surprised, calmly told Marion, "I'm bleeding." Her skirt was already soaked.

She lay with her head resting in Marion's lap. Marion stroked her forehead, comforted her while Gloria Rand and Brydon tended the wound. A nasty graze, bleeding badly. The bullet had plowed flesh for eight inches, starting three inches below the hipbone. The location of the wound prevented using a tourniquet. The only possible way to stop the bleeding was to apply direct pressure.

Marion took off her white cotton blouse, tore it into strips. That didn't provide enough bandages, so Gloria also contributed her blouse. Gloria did the bandaging. Not too tight, Brydon reminded her. Circulation had to be slowed but not cut off.

"Can you feel your toes?" Brydon asked Judith.

"Yes."

From the way Judith said that single word Brydon knew she was in extreme pain. He told her, "If your toes start to tingle or get numb let us know right away."

Spider came over. He whispered something to Brydon. He had found Kemp. Brydon and Spider kept it to themselves, made nothing of it as they went alone to Kemp's body on Island Six. Brydon checked to be absolutely sure Kemp was dead. He decided it would be better for everyone to keep death out of sight. They shoved the body over the edge, lowered it head first into the mud that seemed hungry for it.

Brydon aimed his flashlight down to where Kemp's body had gone under. The light hit upon something on the surface of the mud, off a ways to the side.

The money bags.

They were flat and floating on the surface. Spider quickly pulled them up. They were heavier than he thought, weighed, he guessed, at least twenty pounds apiece. He unbuckled the flaps of the bags and looked in. Rubber-banded thicknesses of tens, twenties, fifties, hundreds.

Spider was awed.

It was enough to kill for.

Brydon read Spider's expression. He wondered if it were enough to want to live for. "I wouldn't keep the bags if I were you," he told Spider.

"Why the fuck not?"

"Without the bags it's only money—anybody's money."

"Anybody's?"

"Yours."

'You won't feel that way later, if we get out of here. You'll say I stole it."

"I won't."

Spider wanted to believe him. "You want a cut?"

"No."

"You're jiving me, man."

"I've already got enough to last the rest of my life."

The two men were eye to eye for a long moment, Spider looking for trust, Brydon trying to convey it.

Spider broke into a grin.

He removed the money from the bags, disposed of the bags by poking them under the mud with a plank. The rubber bands around the money were a quarter-inch wide, doubled around. Strong enough for Spider to use around the bottoms of his trousers, converting each trouser leg into a sack. He unzipped his fly and dropped the sheafs of bills to the left and right in equal quantities. As much as his trousers would allow before becoming too bulky, obvious. The rest of the money he placed inside the waistline of his trousers, distributing it evenly all around. He had to unbutton the front button and let his belt out two holes to accommodate it.

At nine o'clock that Saturday night, as though perversely celebrating the first twenty-four-hour anniversary of its destruction, the supermarket writhed again. More sharply this time, followed by violent buffeting.

The survivors were nearly shaken from the island tops, had only one another to hold on to. Gloria Rand certainly would have been lost had Brydon not grabbed and held her to him.

The structure didn't settle back to its previous near-level position. Now it remained tipped at a twelve-degree angle, front higher. The slant affected everyone's equilibrium, lessened what little sense of security they had. It reminded Amy Javakian of the slanted doghouse she had built.

Brydon checked the mud-level marker.

If the rate of rise was a half inch an hour, as it had been all along, it would now be up to the five-foot mark. He found it was two inches higher than that. Because the building had tipped and redistributed the mud?

Five minutes later Brydon checked again. In only that short while the mud level had gone up another inch and a half. He got down, kept close watch on the marker, could actually see the mud climbing. At that rate it would reach and start to overflow the islands in half an hour.

Brydon kept his alarm to himself. The others would notice soon enough. He went to Island One, played the flashlight across the way onto the metal stairs that led up to the office. Fifteen feet away. He had already considered attempting a bridge to the stairs. If they could get up to the office, as Peter had pointed out, they would have easy access to the ceiling. He had rejected the idea because it meant having to take the same fatal chance the insurance man, Emory Swanson, had taken. Two of the eight-foot planks would have to be joined to span the fifteen feet and support as much as two hundred pounds. There was just no way that could be done. It seemed so much simpler than the scaffold and yet it was even more of a longshot.

Well, the time had come for a longshot.

Brydon examined the stairs in detail. They were obviously unreliable, had come loose from the wall in two places and partly broken away where they connected to the metal ramp above. The stairs might be just hanging there ready to give way with the first step anyone put upon them.

He focused his attention on how, makeshift, to securely join a pair of planks. His memory chose that moment to interject what seemed an extraneous image: the money bags. Brydon let it pass. Within seconds the image was again offered. The money bags on the surface of the mud—heavy enough to sink but, instead, flat and floating.

Brydon suddenly realized what his unconscious was suggesting.

A preposterous idea. But then—He examined the unsound

stairs again and considered the problem of having to join two planks—perhaps it was no more preposterous than trying to walk on air.

He went quickly to Island Eight, to the pile of worthless things they had salvaged. Among them, the gardening claw he had retrieved when Dan dropped it at the last moment. He tucked it into his belt. He found the staple gun, felt the grit in its spring mechanism as he tried to work it. It was jammed with mud. He opened it and rinsed it thoroughly with club soda. One good thing: the stapler was almost fully loaded. He snapped it shut, gripped down on its handle. Still some gritting, but a staple shot out.

Next, he gathered up the plastic trash bags, both containers of those, along with the last three cans of diet soda and the box of No-Doz keep-awake tablets. He went to Island Five to Lois Stevens.

"Ever taken these?" he asked Lois, showing her the No-Doz.

Lois appeared perplexed, innocent. "No," she replied without even looking at the box.

"They're just No-Doz."

Lois smiled, as though someone had thrown something at her and missed. Her movements, especially those of her head and hands, were sharp. Brydon imagined tiny, nervous explosions going off inside her. No time, he had to be direct.

"What kind of pills are you taking?"

"I'm not."

"I'm asking for your help."

"All I've got is a prescription my doctor gave me to lose weight."

"Let me see it."

She wouldn't.

"Trust me."

She looked away, glanced once back at Brydon to assess him. Still looking off, she took a vial from her pocket, handed it to him.

The vial wasn't labeled. Brydon emptied some of its contents into his palm. Coated yellow pills.

"What are they?"

"Vitamin B," Lois said.

"Bullshit."

She shrugged, take it or leave it.

"We're all tired," he told her. "We've hardly slept or had much to eat and before we're done we may need more energy than any of us have left."

"I don't understand."

"It could help save us," he said emphatically. He needed her cooperation, couldn't give anyone a pill not knowing what it was. It might have the wrong effect.

Lois fidgeted. She let her head hang so her long straight hair concealed most of her face. "It's speed," she said. "Amphetamine."

"Exactly."

"Ambars, ten milligrams."

"How long do they keep you up?"

"Eight hours, they're spansules."

Brydon gave Lois a hug that surprised her.

Twenty minutes to go.

Brydon called everyone to Island Nine. He explained the situation. The rapid rise of the mud. Most of them were already more or less aware of it, solemnly awaited it.

"We have one last chance," Brydon said, and as he told them what he proposed, he couldn't help but think how absurd it sounded.

First they had to take off their clothes, so the mud couldn't soak in and handicap them with extra weight. It was impossible for them to be self-conscious. They undressed quickly and stood there like a group of naked primitives. Except Spider. He gave no excuse, merely said he'd try it as he was. No one urged or questioned him.

Brydon told them to lay face up a yard apart crossways on the island. Marion next to Judith, Peter next to Amy, Lois next to Spider, Marsha begrudgingly next to Elliot. Gloria awaited Brydon.

First, he attended to Judith Ward. She raised her legs, inserted them into one of the plastic trash bags that he held open. Dark green, hefty bags, thirty inches wide, forty-eight inches deep. Her legs in as deep as they could go. The bag pulled up to above her waist. She spread her legs to put tension on the bag. Brydon stapled the plastic together as close as possible along the inside of both her legs—from toes to crotch. He used a crushed flat soft-drink can as a base underneath so the stapler wouldn't drive into the wooden surface of the island. He gathered the top of the bag in folds at each side, made it close-fitting and stapled it.

Only partly done. He had to hurry.

Two more plastic bags for her arms. With her arms straight out Brydon shot a seam of staples through the plastic along the line of her arms, from her underarms to her fingertips. He joined those two bags front and back, made sure they were snug around her neck. Then he stretched them down to connect them with the first bag all around.

He stood for a full view of her. She was completely enclosed except for her head. The plastic between her legs was like the webbing of a duck's or frog's foot, and the stretch of plastic from her extended arms down to her sides was bat-like.

Brydon kneeled to her. Her eyes asked and he gave her some confidence from his nearly depleted inner source. "It'll be okay," he told her casually to make it sound true. She opened her mouth for one of the Ambars. He raised her head so she could wash it down with cherry soda.

One ready. Eight to go. He checked his watch, saw he'd taken too much time with Judith—but that was because she was the first. He became more efficient, faster at it as he went along, similarly suiting them in plastic, giving each ten milligrams of amphetamine. He got all nine of them ready with just two minutes to spare.

Two minutes for himself.

He used a few seconds to have a look at the mud. It was only about an inch below the edge now. He sat, shoved his feet into one of the plastic bags, made it taut and stapled it as he'd done for the others. But he couldn't do nearly as well for himself.

Gloria Rand saw his difficulty, wanted to help him. She couldn't reach. Her arms and hands weren't free. She tried to move, wiggle her way closer to him. He noticed and told her no. She kept trying until he ordered her sharply not to.

The bags for his arms were even more of a problem. Before getting into those he stapled them so they'd be connected behind down the center. He put the joined bags around his shoulders, inserted his left arm and lay back. He stapled along the line of that arm, confining it. From then on he had to work one-handed, do everything with only his right, and it was practically impossible for him to simultaneously stretch and gather in folds and overlap and hold the plastic so the two top bags could be attached to the bottom one. He just did manage to put in a couple of staples, connecting the plastic at his sides. The stapler began shooting blanks. All out.

He was by no means adequately enclosed. There was a critical opening underneath where the bags weren't joined top to bottom. He hadn't been able to staple the bag for his right arm at all. Or down the front or make a good snug fit around his neck. There were numerous openings the mud might take advantage of — invade and sink him. But he'd done as well as he could for himself. He placed the gardening claw on the flat of his chest, and the flashlight, turned on and aimed upward. He spread his legs, extended both arms just enough to create weblike tension on the plastic. Careful not to rip out the staples.

The mud was already overflowing, inching up.

Brydon first felt it cold as death on the back of his neck. He heard Gloria's breath catch as she had the same experience.

No one said anything.

The mud continued to rise.

Brydon felt it reach and enter his ears.

He realized then he was wrong. The mud was building up around them. If they stayed as they were it would soon cover them.

"Everyone!" he shouted. "Slowly roll over onto your left side. And keep your head up."

They did. He did.

And when the depth of the mud was six inches higher, nearly up even with Brydon's spine, he told them, "Now, slowly, very slowly, roll over onto your backs again, same position as before, arms out, legs spread."

They did. Brydon felt the mud squish and give when he rolled over. There was still the solidness of the island under him, but not as firm as before, cushioned now by mud. What Brydon hoped was some measure of mud would remain beneath them, the more the better, to act as a primer, buoy them enough to start them afloat. If they got enough initial support the mud might continue to lift them.

Was it asking too much?

Brydon silently said please.

The hardness of the island under him gradually became less distinct and soon he couldn't feel it at all.

They were rising.

Not a miracle—a matter of physics.

Nevertheless, Brydon was grateful to something more.

He asked the others to call out their names to signify they'd made it so far.

Everyone responded.

They had to keep their bodies rigid, their arms tensed straight out, their legs exerting pressure to the left and right. Otherwise the spread of plastic between their legs and from their arms to their sides would buckle, allowing mud to get above it. Even a small amount of mud would be dangerously heavy. It wouldn't take much to cause them to founder. That was what Brydon meant when he'd said they would need a

202

lot of energy. The continuous strain of keeping their muscles flexed to keep afloat.

By now the amphetamine was having its effect. To Brydon it seemed as though there were countless streams in his body and all of them were racing courses and everything inside him was rushing to finishing lines but never finishing. He felt much stronger, more alert than he knew he actually was.

They took life second by second, so the first two hours went by slowly. During that time the mud under them rose four feet, putting them ten feet over the floor of the place. Floating like mere objects, impotent. They breathed cautiously, didn't dare talk. Felt as though they were just above death, horizontally ready for it, kept from it by only a layer of something as tenuous as their will to survive. They fought off fear with distraction, projecting fantasies, optimistic prospects on the screens of their minds. . . .

Judith Ward imagined a conversation.

With husband Fred.

Him saying: "You thought I'd be angry."

"Aren't you?"

"It matters to me, naturally, but I'm not going to cry over it. Do you want to see me cry, is that it?"

"No."

"If anything I suppose I should doubt myself. You would, wouldn't you—if I came home, sat you down and told you I was making it with some guy."

"Marion isn't just someone."

"Anyway, I don't, not at all. Actually, I feel relieved."

"What are we going to do about Melanie?" Their daughter.

"You faked it with me all along?"

Don't answer.

"Must have been a bitch for you to come home spent and pretend to respond sexually to me. But women do have that edge, don't they?"

No need to answer.

"I'm not bitter," he said. "Really."

203

They were seated on the twin loveseat sofas in their den, opposite each other. The time was dusk, soft transitional light coming from the floor-to-ceiling sliding window doors.

Him saying: "I understand." With a slight smile. "It's our mistake, not just yours."

"Why not let it out? What you really feel. Don't ridicule me, Fred, please."

"I'm not ridiculing. In a way I'm happy for you."

"Honestly?"

"You've learned about yourself. Few people ever do."

"I know what I am."

"So will everyone—"

"I don't give a damn."

"Not true. Face it."

"What about Melanie?"

They were in their backyard on their white outdoor chaises. Mid-afternoon. Fred stripped to the waist. Both wearing wraparound aviator-type sunglasses that didn't block out her view of the black hair growing on his back.

Him saying: "You can have the house."

"It's not paid for."

"I'll go back east, take that better job."

"I realize I shouldn't count on you for any financial support."

"Sure you can, whenever I can."

"Promise?"

"Not legally."

"You hate me, don't you?"

"Be happy, Judith, for Christ's sake. It's your choice, be happy."

"What about Melanie?"

"I would think the last thing you and Marion would want is a lot of responsibility." . . .

They were at the table in the nook having breakfast as though it were only another day. Fred in size C polyester pajamas that couldn't be wrinkled, his teeth crunching unbuttered toast according to his diet.

204

Him saying: "You can have custody."

"You mean it?"

"I'll have someone draw up the papers so I can sign them before I leave."

"You're very kind, Fred. Always were."

"Any court in the country would award her to me in a minute. You know that, don't you?"

"Yes."

"But for your sake and hers . . . well, she'll be better off with you. She's closer to you; she's more you than me."

"Yes."

"I'll send a couple of hundred dollars a month. More when I'm making more. Fair enough?"

"Yes."

"I want to be fair."

"Thank you, Fred."

"Besides, a while back I read that they're beginning to believe being like you and Marion is a genetic thing, not something you develop but something that gets passed on, you know, like a tendency toward high blood pressure or heart disease. . . ."

Marion Mercer pictured an all-year house.

An ideal composite of those of her New England childhood. Set on enough of its own land for the confidence of privacy. Walled all around by piled rocks, not a high wall, but such hard, heavy evidence of strength it intimidated any trespassers.

Along the drive lilac bushes bowed sweet welcomes, softly brushed their blossoms across windshields. Enormous old amiable maples on the front slope — three, perhaps four maples. The house with a raised porch, a porch swing, pillows on the front steps. Two half-finished glasses of a fresh lime drink left for a moment on the porch rail.

Perhaps the house in need of paint. Yes, patiently asking for paint.

A late spring day.

205

Putting on their most expendable clothes. Buckets of white, rollers, brushes, everything necessary. Up on tall ladders and doing normally what a man would do, except not destroying a huge head-shaped yellow jackets' nest discovered under a high eave. Respecting that gray, papery stronghold and its inhabitants that swooped and circled around them, threatening, but as though in repayment for mercy shown, not striking.

The overlapping boards of the house soaking up the paint, while their overlapping loves, hers for Judith and Judith's for her, soaked up one another with their eyes. Brush on the white—innocent as their hands that loved to glide and glided to love all parts of each other, pure as that. Then the house, theirs, completely painted, proud of itself.

Contentment.

Any evening.

Dinner on a table on the porch. And afterward, side to side on the steps, hand-holding, sharing the sense of greater intimacy that came when darkness combined with their isolation. Together. Listening to the sounds of night creatures, venturing, calling out to mates. Perhaps a dog, a collie or retriever, at their feet. Its ears and head suddenly up, aroused by a far-off fragment of a bark. The dog leaving them for adventures, disappearing into the darkness. Returning with its lower legs and the fur of its underbody wet from the dampness of tall grass.

Home rule: they could kiss whenever they wanted. Nobody hurt.

Peter Javakian foresaw a delivery room.

Hospital white, intensely lighted, an odor reassuringly antiseptic. How many nurses? Three—to attend to his Amy who was on the table.

Amy's hair entirely contained, out of sight, in a white headpiece, a white gown from her chin down, and a white sheet propped tentlike over her lower half, prevented her from realizing how awkwardly she was exposed.

Amy's face seemed so tiny amidst all the white. Her eyes on the two doctors at the foot of the table. She closed her eyes, and when she opened them was looking straight up at him.

He was allowed there. As much as possible—really impossible—to share the experience. He felt he was more responsible than a part of it, responsible for the pain that alternately ashened and reddened her face. He wished his love for her could serve as an anesthetic. In the moments between the pains she seemed amazed at herself, the incredible, natural thing she was doing. One nurse wiped the perspiration from her forehead and from above her lip, but more beads immediately appeared.

He felt helpless.

Everyone, except Amy, wearing a white mask covering their mouth and nose.

The routine competency of the nurses, skill of the doctors. Very little talk. One of the doctors, the one in charge, winked at him to put him at ease. It didn't.

Amy screamed.

She connected to him only by her hand, not by her pain. He felt so impotent.

"Bear down," the doctor in charge told her.

Her face went red.

Her mouth opened wide, stretched open, so much it seemed her lips would tear at the corners. From almost directly above Peter could see into her mouth, the pink pillow of her tongue, the slicker, more crimson membranes of the back of her throat, from which came another, longer scream.

The doctor in charge motioned him to the foot of the table, to stand back out of the way but where he could see everything.

There was some blood running from the lower juncture of Amy's vagina, which was distended and parted. It seemed unfamiliar. Impossible that it had ever been a source of pleasure.

Amy's stomach was like a mound of risen dough, that pale.

Its skin so tight it was almost transparent. The doctor in charge kneaded her stomach expertly with both hands.

"Here we go," said the doctor in charge.

"That's a good mother," said the other.

Amy's vagina expanded its fleshy perimeter, changed shape into an elasticlike ring to accommodate the top of the new human head.

All the head emerged.

Neck and shoulders.

And the rest of it came easier, eagerly it seemed, almost spurted out.

It was a boy, he thought, from what he could see. But the doctor in charge said, "It's a beautiful girl." He always used that adjective.

It would be sometime later, at least a day or two. The child in Amy's arms. No embrace more possessive. He, Peter, there to watch a feeding. The child given Amy's nipples, that dripped the sweetest kind of milk, love in it.

Amy Javakian thought of a future morning.

In Peter's studio, an extension of where they lived.

A spacious room with the skeleton of its framework left exposed for warmth and a skylight of numerous panes.

Sibelius on the stereo.

Sunlight to guarantee the truth of the colors squeezed from tubes by Peter.

Peter there, her love. Before the challenge of a huge fresh stretch of canvas. That moment a contemplative moment within his need to paint. His eyes, fixed on the white infinity, searched for the endless beginning. His face was pulled toward his mouth and his eyes, tightly, as though in pain, as though he were looking directly into the sun or trying to make out some distant object on a bare, bright horizon.

For the longest while he found nothing. But then he must have hit on something. His concentration reflected off the blank expanse, back to him, causing an opening in the creative part of him. At first a mere pinpoint, a distant single star in the sky of his unconscious, then quickly it dilated and he was able to reach down in, grab hold and bear it out.

She saw, she thought, squeezes of color on a palette. But no. More paint than that needed for such a major canvas. Buckets of it.

Green.

Peter dipped the wide, bristling head of a brush into green and gave it to the canvas. In all creativity, she realized, there had never been two brush strokes exactly alike.

The green went on. He continued with a different color, others, working rapidly, caught up in it. Images crowded out of him, the next pushing the next. A rare sort of labor. A birthing.

Every so often, without stopping work, unable to, really, he used the sleeve of his shirt to wipe perspiration from his forehead and upper lip.

Finally, suddenly, the painting was done.

And they named it together.

Lois Stevens pictured herself transformed into a different kind of creature.

A puma.

From her nose to the end of her tail she was as long as a tall man. With a fawny coat, light grayish brown, luxuriously thick, that only she could rub the wrong way. Ears and tail tipped puce to black, as though she had dipped them into dyes. The fur on her belly white and softest.

She was a roamer, a lethal vagabond.

Born, one of a litter of two, on a ledge beneath an overhang in the Crazy Mountains of Montana. For most of her life she had wandered from range to range, never staying more than a night or two anywhere—from the Flat Tops of Wyoming, the San Raphael Swell of Utah, to Sweetwater Park in the Sierra Nevadas. An independent with no destination.

She traveled the greater distances at night, her eyes peripherally set like polished citrines, naturally capable of night sight, and her blonde whiskers, out left and right, equalled exactly the width of her body to measure and warn her when the going got too narrow.

She lay now on a huge domelike boulder, typical of the dry terrain there on the western shoulder of the Sierras. She nearly matched the hue of the boulder, knew that and found security in it. Resting in the sun, blinking, sweeping her tail back and forth to entertain her edgy disposition. Cleaning her fur with long licks.

Finally, she settled into a nap. But was bothered by a blue fly that peskily lighted on her ear, tickling. She twitched it off. The fly, or perhaps another, circled and lighted on her again. She was almost irritated enough to scratch. The fly flew away, probably frightened.

Noises then, from below in the canyon less than seventy yards away.

A hunter.

According to his senses he believed he was being silent.

Lois, the puma, watched the older man picking his way, following her tracks. It amused her. She stood, so she was profile against the sky, asking for attention.

He saw her, brought his rifle up, got it butted snugly into the socket of his shoulder but did not have time to aim before she leaped from sight.

She led him on, purposely padded over soft, sandy places to leave impressions for him. Several times he lost her and she had to snarl for him to reestablish direction. After a while it became boring for her, too easy. She circled around from rock to rock to be at his back. There he was, thirty feet away, confused about which way to hunt.

She crouched, head low, ran her tongue over her teeth, extended and retracted her twenty claws, while deciding whether or not she loved or disliked him enough to spring.

210

Spider Leaks had his fuck-you money.

Now he thought what he was going to do with it, not *if*, but *when* he got out of the mud.

For sure he wasn't going to start flashing green all over the place right away. He'd stash it, keep scuffling straight as usual, so his parole officer had nothing to get on him for. Wouldn't be easy, having all that bread and not showing it. Maybe every once in a while, like on a Saturday night, he'd treat himself to a hundred to spend. But that would be the limit. No matter how good a deal came along he'd cool it for three, maybe four months.

Then he'd put in to have his parole transferred to New York. No reason why his parole officer shouldn't go along with that. No suspicions. Spider had an aunt and a bunch of cousins welfaring it back east. He'd leave California looking trashy and hit town looking to take care of business.

A white El Dorado with automatic twin antennas, not a mile or a scratch on it, his. Glad rags, like those he'd seen Clyde, Walt Frazier, wearing in a magazine article. He'd ask around and find out who Clyde's tailor was. He'd also get himself a three- or four-room crib in one of those big apartment buildings, thirty stories above the dirt. Chrome and mirrors and lots of upholstery that looked like real fur and stereo speakers everywhere, even in the bathroom, both bathrooms.

Chicks. He'd have two main ones. Two of the foxiest, a tall black and a tall blonde, so he could mix them up. They'd wait on him every minute, do anything he wanted, let him do anything he wanted. Fight over him.

Soon as he had it all together he'd shag ass to radio station KBLS for a job. KBLS, New York, the soul station. He'd look so good they'd have to believe he could do it good. He knew how. All those years in slam he'd practiced disc jockeying in his mind and sometimes aloud. And since he'd been out he'd kept at it at home, using a pair of grapefruit crates up on end

211

for turntables and the empty socket of a gooseneck lamp bent to his mouth for a microphone, while he turned the volume of his radio up or down according to his own verbal cues, as though he were actually on. They'd dig him at KBLS, sign him up right away, long-term unbreakable contract. He'd play Barry White and James Brown punctuated by his own appropriately cool phrases, and before long he'd be as famous as Frankie Crocker. He'd never heard Crocker, but from what he'd heard of him from back-east blacks that man was what Spider wanted to be.

Spider Leaks.

It just didn't sound as good as Frankie Crocker.

Maybe, Spider thought, he ought to change his last name, so no one could make any more of those pissing jokes.

Elliot Janick distracted himself with a moral accounting.

Entering rights and wrongs on a mental ledger.

He only concerned himself with what he'd done professionally. Otherwise, his thoughts became jammed, too much to handle.

He sorted through the years, the deals, starting way back. Strange how clear and chronologically correct those events, important and minor, were presented by his memory. He refused to fool himself, called a right a right and a wrong a wrong. But too soon the ledger was way out of balance, and he was deep in the red.

That wasn't going to get him anywhere but bankrupt. He had to be easier on himself. There were two sides to every life.

Maybe, instead of all this self-accusing mishmash, if he could settle things with just one, face up to just one sort of representative offense, that would take care of the rest. . . .

Walter Nyland came to mind.

Elliot pushed him aside. Not Nyland, he told himself.

But Nyland returned. He'd been chosen and there was no use trying to get away from him.

Nyland was an author who had written his first novel at age

forty. He'd quit a steady career to take that late longshot. The first novel came pouring out. It was acceptable but a psychological catharsis with too many of Nyland's own problems in it to be a critical or popular success. Nyland went at his second less sure of himself and with more respect for the craft. Somehow he tapped an extremely perceptive source in himself and the result was *Love Knots*, a story about a marital infidelity that managed to keep on the fine line between artistic frankness and sensationalism.

One of the assistant editors at Nyland's publisher was a woman named Janet Hamlyn. Ambitious, underpaid, more of a clotheshorse than a workhorse, she was one of the links in motion picture producer Elliot Janick's chain of inside connections. He had women in similar positions at every major New York publishing house. Not on his steady payroll but part of a reward system. When a promising manuscript came in, they immediately made duplicates that they sent to Janick.

That way he got first look, first chance at all the better material, and if, as a result, a deal was made by him, the editor involved received a nice chunk of cash that she didn't have to report as income.

Janet Hamlyn passed a copy of Nyland's *Love Knots* manuscript on to Janick, who read it and realized it had all the ingredients of a best seller and a big grosser at the box office. Janick had the jump on all the other producers. He personally got to Nyland, who was hungry for recognition. Nyland ate up the famous filmmaker's attention and flattery. Talent should be appreciated, and how much he wished he'd been blessed with such ability, Janick told him among other things. No mention of wanting to buy *Love Knots*.

Next, on a public bench opposite the Sherry Netherland Hotel, Janick put Nyland's agent in his pocket by promising to buy at least two other properties of lesser quality the agent had been trying to peddle. Plus fifty thousand cash on the side.

Janick made his firm offer on *Love Knots*.

213

Forty thousand and a small percentage of the producer's net.

The agent recommended Nyland take it. Nyland signed where he was told and didn't learn until much later that he could have gotten as much as four hundred thousand. The book went on to be on the lists, a bestseller. Nyland made a considerable amount from the paperback sale and a book club but the bigger money would have been from the movie rights.

Mainly it was Janick who screwed him.

Nyland knew but didn't have a fact to stand on.

Love Knots, as it turned out, was Nyland's only important book. Some said it was the only one he had in him. Actually, being suckered by Janick brought so much disillusion and rage it blocked him, got in the way of any other feelings he tried to put down on paper.

As a film, *Love Knots* earned sixty million, was the picture of the year and took over eighteenth position on the all-time box-office grossing list.

One night years later Janick happened to run into Nyland at the La Scala Restaurant in Beverly Hills. Nyland couldn't really afford the dinner he'd just signed for. Aside, to hell with pride, he asked Janick for a screenwriting assignment. Janick, with a big smile and no hesitation said, "Why not?" and told Nyland to call him the next afternoon at the studio, knowing he was leaving for London in the early morning.

The next week Nyland was dead from downers and booze and ingrown anger.

Now there he was on the screen of Elliot's mind, waiting to be answered to. Elliot tried to diminish the hard edges with contrition. Nyland stared out, stiff, damning.

"It was a deal," Elliot explained. "All's fair in making a deal."

Nyland appeared to soften.

Elliot grabbed the opening. "Forgive me."

"I forgive you," Nyland said, exactly as Elliot wanted, a sincere pronouncement.

The trouble was Elliot didn't believe him.

Marsha Hilbert saw herself with a new strong man. Better looking, younger, certainly more masterful than Elliot.

Her new one had a jaw that set, clamped like a lock, and eyes that reached out dark and hard as stones to punish her for the slightest infraction. He wouldn't let her get away with anything, no matter how much she tried. He was poor but with taste, one of those who knew and wanted the best if only he could afford it. He adapted immediately to having her money.

There she was, in something gray and relaxing by Ungaro. A little loose sable around her neck.

He in proud, dominant black serge with a subtle stripe.

They'd be in Zurich together, beating Elliot to the bank by an hour, withdrawing every cent. Without a hitch because she had it memorized like a line in a part: One, three, nine, eight, zero, nine. Zephyr.

Worth, she was sure, millions.

They'd wait in the car across the street from the bank for Elliot to arrive. They'd watch him go in and, when he came out, she'd call him over so she could wave the Swiss bank's cashier's check at him. She'd fold it slowly, deliberately and, with beautiful insouciance, tuck it into the breast pocket of her new love's suit.

Up would go the car's electric window as she zoomed away, watching Elliot become smaller in the sideview mirror.

Gloria Rand thought how certain she was that she and Brydon would never do anything ordinary.

They wouldn't, for example, ever go to an obvious, over-trampled place like Hawaii or Bermuda. Two weeks on a barge, nomadizing on the canals of Holland would be their style.

A comfortable, Dutch-clean barge hired privately by them. No more expensive than staying at a hotel, renting a car and all that. Much more romantic. Cheese and wine on deck at twilight. Friendly windmills turning into entertainingly ominous silhouettes. Them making long, good love, falling asleep overlapped, and then waking to a flood of pastel tulips as far as they could see.

Lots of such times.

Years and years of such times.

How true he'd be. Compulsively loyal. Never even a turn of the head for young legs or the walking pump of a young derriere. He'd tell her she was far more attractive than any other woman or girl, in every department, and mean it. Better yet, demonstrate it.

All ways.

Next she had them in Provence—the beautiful old religious city of Avignon, where they vowed and worshipped one another and placed alms in the form of loving pleasure upon their plates. Walking the banks of the Rhone. Napping beneath almond and fig and olive trees.

She went on and on and on with her romantic itinerary.

Frank Brydon spent some of the time on thoughts of that Navajo healer he'd heard about.

In his mind he went to Taos, New Mexico, inquired about her. The mere mention of her name, Sky Touching Woman, made other Indians suddenly silent. Brydon took that to mean respect and was encouraged by it.

He finally located Sky Touching Woman ten miles out on the wasteland—in a crude adobe hut. It seemed consistent that she should be apart from everyone. Brydon tried to disregard the Ford pickup truck parked around back.

He entered the hut but had to stoop because the doorway was so low. She was sitting on the earth floor off to one side, profile to him. With a handwoven robe around her, although it was a warm day. She might be immune to such mundane conditions, he thought.

She was about fifty, squat, plump-breasted. Her face was flat as it should be, time-lined. Eyes with dark pupils, yellowed whites, an appropriate vacantness to them.

She didn't greet him, remained unmoved, as though she

had expected him. Was there the chance that someone, one of those he'd asked, had told her he was coming? He had to put himself into her line of sight. Still she said nothing. He told her his name, his problem. In the corner off to her left was a regular brown paper shopping bag on its side, its contents partially spilled out: two cans of Chef Boy-ar-dee spaghetti and an economy-size bag of potato chips. She had to eat, he told himself.

She spoke for the first time. A single word.

He undressed as instructed and understood from her gesture that he was to lie down on the rug that was spread before her. She raised her head, looked briefly skyward and then down to him, not at his face but his chest. She repeated that motion several times, more and more rapidly, until it became a sort of delirious nod. He decided it might be her way of trying to connect him spiritually with her source of supernatural power.

She stopped doing that a bit too abruptly and reached for an object by her side. A carved piece of hardwood with a series of toothlike notches. A rasp. She held it above him, ran another piece of wood over it, back and forth, creating a hard scrubbing sound. He took that, possibly, to be the cleansing of him prior to the operation.

When she was done with that, she said, "Did you bring your gratitude?"

It bothered him that she didn't wait until it was over. Also her using the word gratitude. He reached for his trousers, took a twenty from a pocket and, as a second thought, another twenty for good measure. She shoved the bills down inside her high-top, rubber-soled work shoes.

A black cross was painted on his chest. Black stuff made from a tree that had been struck by lightning, she explained, more talkative now for some reason.

She shook her right hand as she would if it held a rattle, and she moaned some.

He had the impression that she was merely going through

217

the motions now, getting through it as quickly as she could. She made grabbing gestures at his chest, as though digging into him, getting hold of something and pulling it out. Several times. She grimaced. She wiped her hands with her hands, snapped them sharply as if ridding them of some substance, then applied a couple of squirts of Vaseline Intensive Care hand lotion that she worked in.

On the overnight drive home he was sure it had been a waste of precious time. At least he hadn't been taken for much. From what he'd experienced he couldn't see how Sky Touching Woman had gained such a far-reaching reputation. Oh well, the world was full of gullible, desperate people who would rather believe in the powers of someone like Sky Touching Woman than admit to being beyond help.

The next day he went in to see Doctor Bruno. He made no mention of his trip to the healer, felt a fool for it.

X rays were taken. Just routine.

Bruno studied them, alone, for a long while. He ordered another whole series.

Same thing.

Definitely.

The cancer was not diminished.

It was gone.

At midnight the ten survivors were on top of twelve feet of mud. By 2:00 A.M. it was eighteen feet.

Only five more feet to the ceiling.

"Everyone all right?" Brydon asked.

Down the line they said they were, except the last, Judith Ward.

"I can't feel my right leg," she said. From the bullet wound, torn muscles and nerves.

"Don't let yourself go," Brydon told her sternly.

"Oh, my God." Marion shook.

"It's numb," Judith said. "I don't have any control over it."

"Try, keep trying."

"I am."

"Pretend you feel it."

"That's what I've been doing."

"The leg is there. You know it is. Make yourself feel it."

"I think it's sinking."

"Oh, please, no," Marion said.

"Only a little while longer," Brydon told her. He wished he was over there next to Judith instead of farthest from her. At least maybe then he could help her in some way.

"My other leg!" Judith was hysterical. "It's being pulled under."

"No!" Marion protested, a wail.

"Fight it," Brydon shouted.

Judith's wounded leg was almost completely submerged. Mud had gotten above the plastic, pound after pound of it until it put so much weight upon her she couldn't hold up. It caused her back to arch. Her legs bent at the knees. She strained, asked her body for more strength than it had. Her lower half sank gradually.

"I'm going under!" she screamed.

She felt as though she were standing upright and would be able to remain that way.

Marion could no longer restrain herself. She broke position to reach for Judith. As she turned onto her side, she sacrificed the tension on the plastic that had kept her afloat.

Judith slapped out, desperately, caught hold of Marion's arm. They clutched, pulled, tried to get to one another, but the mud resisted.

Screaming, Judith went under first.

Then Marion—because she couldn't let go.

Nearest was Amy Javakian. She trembled, couldn't stop trembling. Her breath came in shallow catches. She was on the edge of losing control.

Not only Amy. What had happened to Judith and Marion

219

might set off a chain reaction of panic, Brydon realized, and they would start reaching to one another for support and all be lost.

Brydon told them to keep calm, to concentrate on the ceiling.

Somehow they did.

Within the next half hour the mud lifted them another two feet. Three more to go. The ceiling was just out of reach.

The flashlight that lay on Brydon's chest now made a more intense circle of light on the white acoustical-tile paneling above. Brydon could easily make out the perforated pattern of the tile, and he saw that it was installed in three-by-five sections, held in place by narrow white aluminum strips, a normal installation.

Any moment he would be able to reach the ceiling. He told himself not to be overanxious, to wait until he was surely close up. They had been floating precariously on the surface of the mud for six hours. Another ten or fifteen minutes could be endured.

Brydon fixed his gaze on the dotlike perforations of the paneling, using them to gauge progress.

A quarter-hour went by.

The dots seemed the same size as before. Perhaps, Brydon thought, his weary eyes were tricking him.

After another half hour there could be no doubt.

They were suspended, held up just inches short. The mud, their sadistic enemy, had stopped rising.

At 10:30 that night Captain Dodd and Stan Hackley were headed south on Trobuco Road in East Irvine. A half mile past Sand Canyon Avenue they stopped at the main entrance to the El Toro Marine Corps Air Station.

One of the sentries came out of the permanent glass-sided booth. He had on a white helmet, white leggings and a blue poncho that glowed whenever light hit it. He also wore glasses that got spattered with rain, so he had to lower his head and look over them when he looked into the car from the driver's window.

Hackley showed his identification.

The sentry didn't ask Dodd for anything. "Straight ahead, second stop, take a right. First brick building you come to."

"Got it," Hackley said.

The metal barrier was raised, allowing Dodd to drive in—a bit too fast, because there were two unavoidable eight-inch bumps built up on the roadway to prevent speeding. Dodd didn't see them. The car and the trailer jolted and the pipe in the trailer bounced around.

Hackley stretched, rotated his neck that had just been snapped. "Ever been here before?"

"Obviously not," Dodd said. "Where'd you get all your pull?"

"It's not pull, it's leverage."

"We'll see." Dodd still doubted Hackley could deliver what he'd claimed.

The streets of the air station were deserted. There were hardly any lights on. The rain, for one reason. Also, it was Saturday night and, except for the minimum number of men to satisfy peacetime standby requirements, everyone was on weekend liberty.

Dodd located the brick building, parked in front. They went in. There was a corporal seated behind a desk behind a four-foot-high partition. He wasn't doing anything, not typing or writing or reading or smoking or listening to the radio or anything, just sitting there alone. He had a hat on and no tie. A stenciled sign taped to the partition read:

WAIT YOUR TURN

"Yes, sir?" the corporal said. He was wearing a sidearm.

"Lieutenant Santiano," Hackley said.

"He's sleeping."

"Try him."

"Who are you?"

"Tell him Stan."

The corporal didn't jump to it. He appraised Hackley and Dodd. They didn't look important. Muddy overalls and jeans, sneakers and moccasins. "Maybe it's something I can handle."

222

"Call Santiano," Hackley insisted with a tinge of *or else.*

The corporal didn't like that. He stood abruptly. The vertical wrinkles between his eyes became more pronounced; his mouth tightened as though getting ready to spit. He seemed on the verge of vaulting over the partition to have a go at Hackley. However, when he was sure both Hackley and Dodd had gotten that impression, he picked up the phone. He guarded the mouthpiece, mumbled into it, put the phone back on the receiver and said, polite, almost as kissass as he'd be to a major's daughter, "Take the corridor to your left, sir. All the way down. You can't miss it."

The corridor was not well lighted. Government gray-painted walls, scrubbable enamel, asbestos tile underfoot. Closed doors all the way to the only one that was open.

In there was a narrow room mainly furnished with a gray vinyl-covered couch, two armchairs and, shoved against one wall, a wide metal table with an electric coffee maker on it. A twenty-four-inch color television, an older model, was on a shelf higher than everything.

Lieutenant Santiano had his shoes off, shirt unbuttoned four down. Slouched in one of the chairs with his legs crossed and feet up on an arm of the sofa. Although he didn't rise when Hackley and Dodd entered, it was obvious he was a large man, big boned. He probably could have played pro football but was now in his late twenties.

Santiano put his hand out, palm up. Hackley slapped it and introduced Dodd, who got a regular handshake. Santiano offered coffee. Hackley didn't want any. Dodd helped himself. Santiano was smoking a cigar. Hackley asked if he had another and was told it was the last. The ashtray contained several well-chewed stubs, evidence that the night had been dull and lonely. Santiano pulled officer-of-the-day duty one weekend every month. It seemed to him ridiculous that his presence should be both in such demand and unnecessary. To pass the time he'd been watching a war movie starring Dana Andrews, who was supported by a type-casted platoon.

There were Dana and his guys firing on the run, using a tank for cover as they charged. One man got hit, spun, threw his arms and legs around and otherwise did his best performance of getting killed in action.

"He was one of the good good guys," Santiano remarked.

It was difficult to disregard the television. The vertical hold was off so the picture often flopped over for attention.

"Know where they shot that movie?" Santiano asked and answered, "Catalina, on the seaward side. They used to make practically all of them over there. I know a guy they hired a couple of times as technical advisor. All he had to do was sit on his ass for five hundred a week and see that everthing looked real, which, if you think of it, is important, because counting both world wars, Korea and Nam, at least maybe half the guys in this country have an idea what it's really like."

"Dodd here is a captain in the highway patrol," Hackley said.

"Looks it," Santiano said.

Dodd didn't know how to take that. He let it pass.

Santiano puffed up a cloud and through it asked Hackley, "What's the favor?"

"I want to borrow a buzzard."

"You're crazy."

Hackley said he was serious.

"What the hell for?" Santiano asked.

"I want to haul some bales of shit up from Baja. How's that?"

Santiano knew better. He got up, went to the window, took a peek out through the metal slats of the venetian blind. "Fucking rain. If it wasn't raining at least I could take a nice walk. This morning one of the mess cooks, actually a baker, went berserk with a cleaver. He wanted to bake pies but because of the weather all the sugar was stuck together. In fifty-pound sacks, like rocks."

Dodd asked to use the phone. While Hackley and Santiano discussed the weather, Dodd checked in at headquarters and then called Helen. She sounded tense. He told her where he was and not to worry. She didn't tell him she loved him, the way she usually did before she hung up. Dodd decided she was tired. He sure as hell was.

Hackley brought Santiano back to it. "What about it, Harry?"

"Don't you have a chopper over in Newport?"

"Too light. We need one that can take a load."

"Shit, Stan, you can't just walk into a government installation like this and borrow a buzzard."

"Why not?"

Santiano shrugged. "I'll get busted."

"Fix it so there's no chance."

According to Santiano's expression that wasn't possible.

"We also need a couple of men," Hackley said.

'What kind?'

"Ground-crew guys, good fast ones, like armament fitters."

"Those I could let you have easy. Lots of guys in the brig for trying to beat each other to death. Has to be the weather."

"They'll get paid. Fifty each."

"Do they have to go up?"

"No."

"I couldn't let them go up."

"I promise."

"You're really putting me on the crapper, Stan, you know that?"

"Yeah."

"Well, I can't let you have a buzzard."

"We'll have it back in the morning, by noon at the latest. Nobody will ever know."

"Unless you crack it up or something."

"Me?"

"I can't, Stan. No way."

After some silence Hackley told him, "You owe me, Harry."

It came out level, easy, but there was considerable behind it. It went back to a paddy in Pen-Lem close to the Cambo-

225

dian border. More fire power than expected from the enemy. Mortars and rifles. Santiano and his patrol were about to be wiped out. Hackley, in a buzzard, came in over the treetops. The enemy threw everything they had at him. Hackley put himself on the line, put the helicopter down, was a big sitting target soaking up hits while Santiano and his men climbed aboard to be lifted to safety. If it hadn't been for Hackley . . .

Since then the only thing Hackley had asked in return was that Santiano buy for him at the Marine Commissary, where things such as Scotch were cheaper. Hackley didn't like pressuring with such a debt. He apologized to Santiano.

Santiano looked away. "I owe it to you."

To ease the situation somewhat, Hackley told him, "If you do this favor for me we'll call it even once and for all."

"Never."

"You won't do it?"

Santiano grinned, "We'll never be even."

Hangar 11-R was way out of the way on the extreme northern corner of the far side of the base.

It was a huge reserve hangar presently used to store helicopters that had been brought back from Vietnam. They were HSL-1s, the kind Hackley called "buzzards." Stowed as close together as possible, they looked like a swarm of grotesque, giant insects at rest. Not a one had been moved or even touched in nearly two years. They were just left sitting there, millions of dollars' worth of aircraft, waiting for some military committee to decide whether they should be sold to private concerns, needy countries or perhaps just scrapped.

Probably one wouldn't ever be missed, certainly wouldn't for only a few hours.

The hangar was so crowded there wasn't room for Dodd to drive the car and trailer in. He backed up to the hangar door.

Hackley went in among the buzzards to look them over. He decided he might as well choose one of those in the row nearest the door. Be easier to get at and get out. He settled on one, examined it inside and all around, paying special attention to the rotor connections, which, he was glad to find, were well protected by layers of grease. He noticed numerous flak and bullet holes along the fuselage. It was jungle camouflaged except in one place on its starboard, where it was named in red paint:

RAQUEL BABY

Obviously out of devotion rather than any likeness.

At 11:30 two men showed up at the hangar door.

"I'm Poss," one said.

"Ruzkowski," said the other. "Lieutenant Santiano sent us."

Poss's left eye along the brow bone and below was red, blue and black, almost swollen closed. Dodd asked who gave it to him. "He did," Poss indicated Ruzkowski, who was the larger of the two by two-thirds of a head.

"For this," Ruzkowski contended. His lip was split and puffed.

Hackley told them, "We can't afford any fighting."

"We're buddies," Poss assured.

Ruzkowski verified that by smiling painfully and nudging Poss's shoulder with his fist.

"How long will it take to get this buzzard going?" Hackley asked.

"Just turning, you mean?"

"I mean for flight."

"Not a complete breakdown."

"No."

"Well, to look her over and, let's say there's nothing much wrong, to gas her up and everything shouldn't take more than two, three hours," Poss said.

"Know how to weld?"

"Sure," Ruzkowski said.

"No bullshit?"

"Why bullshit?"

"Okay, you're hired. But if you fuck off or fight, it's back to brig double-time and no pay," Hackley told them.

"Santiano said fifty each."

"Right."

"Can we see the money?" Poss asked.

Hackley deferred to Dodd, who only had eighty cash. Hackley put up the other twenty.

First Dodd explained what he wanted to do with the pipe. Poss didn't seem to be paying attention, but immediately afterward he used an ordinary lead pencil on the concrete floor to diagram precisely the kind of rig Dodd had in mind. Actually, Poss improved on it, showed how it would work even better with a simple pulley system that could be controlled from inside the buzzard.

They went to work. Dodd wanted to be of help but, after trying for a while, it seemed he was only getting in the way. He stood aside and watched. It amused and amazed him that every so often either Poss or Ruzkowski or both would go out and return with such things as new parts, welding equipment, special tools. They knew where to "requisition" anything, even at that unlikely hour. Once Ruzkowski brought back a portable radio so they had rock music to set a working tempo to.

The engines and rotors were of first concern. No use building a special rig onto a buzzard that couldn't fly. Around 1:00 A.M. they put in some fuel and tried starting the forward engine. It coughed sickly, sputtered, misfired, but Ruzkowski kept at it and soon had it running smooth enough. Then the rear engine. They were at work on it when the headlights of a car beamed through the partially open sliding hangar doors.

That would probably be one of the base's senior officers, a captain or major somebody come to see what the hell was going on, Dodd thought. His personal project, his, had gotten Lieutenant Santiano and these enlisted men in serious trouble. He tried to think quickly of some explanation that might get them off the hook, but nothing came — and that seemed proof of how quixotic the whole thing was. As for himself, it was going to be embarrassing all the way up and down the line, especially up.

A figure appeared in the doorway. Wearing a beige trench coat with the right sleeve hanging empty.

Helen.

Why the hell was she here?

Dodd went to her, gave her a brief, public sort of hug that she coolly received, letting him know she was annoyed. He introduced her to Hackley, Poss and Ruzkowski. She was more pleasant to them. They continued their work, while Dodd and Helen went to a corner of the hangar, sat on a pair of high stools by a workbench. Facing one another.

After a long, steady look at him, she asked, "What is it you're doing, Roy?"

It was too complicated to explain now. He promised to tell her about it, all of it, later.

That didn't satisfy her. Usually she didn't want to know what he was into because it would be too nerve-racking.

"It has something to do with that mud slide, doesn't it?"

"Yes"

"Commander Everett called."

"Called you?"

"He's worried about you, about your . . . well, the way he put it was . . . your mental state."

Dodd thought Everett probably knew every move he'd made up to now. But, if so, why hadn't Everett intervened? Maybe Everett was letting him hang himself. Maybe he owed someone a push up to area captain. Soon as he thought it, Dodd knew it wasn't true.

"What else did Bill have to say?"

"Just that it wasn't like you to disobey orders."

"I have before."

"Maybe you've been lucky up to now."

He grunted. "And maybe my luck won't change."

She tried being direct. "Come home with me."

His eyes told her he wanted to. He said, "I can't."

"Why, for God's sake?"

"Because unless I see this thing through, I'm going to be the damnedest loneliest man alive—"

"With me?"

"Even with you."

Helen had intended to be firm with him. Through the night and on the way there she had worked herself up to the point of wanting literally, single-handedly, to throw him in the car and haul him back home. But now, looking at him, believing she understood what he felt, she had to soften.

"Well, I couldn't sleep anyway," she said.

They kissed and silently promised one another more loving than that when time got back to normal.

"By the way," she told him, "your lemon tree fell over."

"What do you mean, 'fell over'?"

"Late this afternoon I noticed it lying on the ground. I guess it just gave up at the roots."

It didn't mean anything, Dodd told himself. "I'll plant another," he said, but he seemed worried.

Helen stood, smiled her best for him, took his hand. "Come on. Show me what you're doing with that weird-looking plane. Maybe I can help."

She already had.

The mud had still not risen more than a fraction of an inch in the past hour. The ceiling was still just out of reach.

Judging from his own condition, Brydon knew the others must be beyond their physical limit. It was incredible that they had endured this long. Over six hours of rigid, cataleptic exertion, riding the surface of the mud.

Now, the help of the amphetamine was beginning to wear off. Brydon could feel exhaustion starting to take over every muscle. A trembling sensation inside, increasing. He doubted he could hold up another half hour, definitely not an hour. Any minute he expected to hear Amy cry out as she gave up. Or any of the others.

If only he could reach the ceiling.

But, so what if he could?

They'd still be trapped. It still wouldn't give them a way out. The mud that had lifted them there would follow them up, eventually fill the place, overwhelm them. Except for the difference of a little time, more frustration and anguish, they might as well have it happen now. Death.

God, how he hated this mud. More intensely than he'd ever hated anything. It was so goddamned relentless, evil, the way it ate up the time of their lives, devoured their future feelings, tastes, sights, touchings, every delicious moment, even the reassurance of pain.

The mud seemed to take exception to Brydon's thoughts. As though deciding to prolong their agony, taking perverse delight in giving hope in order to take it away, the mud suddenly began to rise again. Several inches in just a few minutes, finally putting the ceiling within range. Easy range.

Brydon told the others not to reach for it, to not yet relinquish the stretches of the plastic from their arms to their sides that kept them afloat. Then, not heeding his own warning, in a single swift motion Brydon tore loose the plastic and punched upward, hard, with both hands. Knocking one of the three-by-five acoustical panels up and out of the way. Immediately, before he could sink, he tossed the flashlight and the gardening claw through the opening and made a grab at anything up there. He got hold of a cross beam and, as he pulled himself up, the plastic bag dropped from around his legs.

Up there was a clearance of about six feet. Brydon hurried, lifted away other panels, helped Gloria up, then Elliot and Marsha and soon they were all up there, all eight, naked, except for Spider.

Brydon retrieved the flashlight and the gardening claw.

That area between the ceiling and the roof. They had imagined it would somewhat resemble a regular attic, but the atmosphere was industrial and unfamiliar to them. Even Brydon with his architectural experience found it unusual, particularly the size of the steel beams, the bar joists that ran front to back across the top of the building. They were immense. One hundred twenty feet long, six feet high, three

232

inches thick. Twenty-eight of them, parallel, spaced ten feet apart. The major bones of the skeleton, they were the structural factor that had allowed the supermarket's uninterrupted spaciousness.

The faces of the beams were diagonally latticed, to accommodate air-conditioning ducts, electrical conduits and various pipe lines. Openings large enough for even a large man to climb through. So, although the beams divided the area into separate, long straight sections, all of it was accessible. There were extending angles on the upper and lower edges of each beam, like the serifs on a tall, extremely condensed capital letter I. The upper for the laying on of the roof. The lower allowed wooden stringers to be run from one beam to the next, and also offered a four-inch ledge that could, with caution, be walked along.

Brydon advised they stay where they were for the time being, not to go wandering off. He estimated their present position was near mid-point at the front of the building. Spider had brought along the stubs of two candles, which he lighted and stuck upright in their own melt.

Those tiny tongues of flame drew the survivors and helped hold them together.

Peter and Brydon, with flashlights, went to search for any place where the roof might have been torn open. They hurried separate ways, down the length of one section, up the next. There wouldn't be time to investigate the entire area.

Meanwhile, waiting, the other survivors felt more hopeful now. At least they weren't surrounded by mud as before. Because it wasn't in sight it seemed as though they were beyond its reach. Freedom was surely just above, and the only remaining obstacle was the roof. Not so much, they thought, compared to what they'd already been through.

"I think we're going to make it," Amy said.

"I'm going to make it," Elliot Janick realized aloud. He looked over to Marsha, who was standing on top of an air-conditioning duct. He made his way along the ledge of a beam.

When she saw him coming, her first thought was to retreat, but something she sensed kept her in place, and when he was close, confronting her, she knew he had reestablished himself. At once her body began to respond, a surge of wanting.

"I'm sorry," she whispered.

"What?"

"I'm sorry," she repeated, just above a whisper.

"What?"

"I'm sorry," she said, normal level.

"What?" he demanded.

"I'm sorry," she cried out.

He slapped her, so sharply her head spun. She immediately brought her head back around to face him, chin up. He took a step back to improve his range, a more solid stance for a backhand blow. She was ready for it, as though waiting for a kiss. His hand was up, his arm diagonally across his face, but only the top of his toes found the edge of the metal duct.

He toppled backward.

He was much too heavy for the ceiling panels. He crashed through them, into the mud just below.

Screams.

Elliot grabbed out, hit only upon another panel that also gave way. He was sinking fast. Spider tried to reach for him. Perhaps if he'd not been so frantic he could have found Spider's outstretched hand and been hauled to safety. Instead, he flailed wildly. Those last moments were longer, more terrifying for Elliot than for any of the others who had been lost. Because the flat of the panels momentarily buoyed him.

He was screaming, struggling furiously, looking up to Marsha as he went under.

When Brydon and Peter heard the screams they cut short their search, returned quickly to the others.

Marsha was doubled up, cringing, hugging herself as though in terrible pain.

Gloria tried to console her, although to her way of thinking it seemed strange, a waste, that a victim should feel such remorse.

Again, the survivors, only seven now, had been frightened back to reality. Brydon and Peter underlined that by reporting they had not found a way out. Not a sign of hope. To the contrary. Both had noticed a heavy flow of mud down through the roof along part of the rear wall. Brydon believed it best they remove themselves as far from that as possible.

They climbed through the openings in the beams, traversed section after section, bruising their knees, scraping their shins on the steel. Wood and metal hurt their bare feet. Finally they reached the second section from the end. If Brydon was correct there was their best bet. The front left corner of the building. It fitted Brydon's theory about the position of the market. Also—a more practical reason—it was from here, Brydon believed, those sounds had originated—those signal-like rappings they'd heard yesterday.

At once Brydon went to work on the sheetrock surface above, using the gardening claw. His first efforts hardly made a scratch, but he kept digging at it and it began to give, crumble. He made a hole large enough to get two fingers into. The sheetrock was five-eighths thickness. He tore at it, and, when he'd adequately increased the size of the hole, Peter and Spider helped break away the plasterlike substance until the hole was about eighteen inches in diameter.

Above that, insulation. A six-inch layer of Fiberglas. Not really an obstacle. Like dull yellow cotton candy. Spider and Peter quickly ripped it down.

They were making good progress.

The mud seemed to resent it.

Tilt.

It caught them unaware. Not a mere quaver or shift but a sudden convulsive heave. No time for them to brace or balance. It jolted them and threw them upward, sent them slamming against the beams, colliding with one another, clutching at anything they got their hands on.

Amy Javakian was thrown down on the ceiling panels, the same sort that had collapsed under Elliot Janick. She was foundering, about to sink. Brydon was nearest. With one arm wrapped around the lattice opening of a beam he reached for Amy, had to grip whatever he could of her, was lucky to even get her by the hair. He held on until Peter could take her wrist. They pulled her to safety.

When the heaving subsided the building was left at a steeper pitch. About thirty degrees. Half of that ceiling-to-roof area was under mud. Theirs was the high side. If they had chosen the rear they would have been dead.

Now they had to hang on, resist the tilt to keep in place. All the more difficult to work on making the hole in the roof. Brydon went back at it. With the Fiberglas insulation eliminated, a single layer of woven wire, light gauge, the kind commonly called chicken wire, was revealed. In view above that was a thickness of poured gypsum impregnated with white gravel. That would be the last, the top layer of the roof.

But what would be beyond that?

It depended on whether or not the entire supermarket was buried. It depended on whether or not Brydon was right about this spot.

If wrong there wouldn't be any second chance.

The mud was now coming up fast, rapidly filling the place. They had another fifteen to twenty minutes. Perhaps not even that, because the air was getting poor. All at once their breathing was shallower, their hearts were beating faster, they had less strength.

Brydon hurried.

He inserted the prongs of the gardening claw through the wire mesh, gave it a yank. The wire merely stretched. He pulled harder but the wire refused to break. He swore at it and tried a different approach. This time only one prong of the gardening claw through a single loop of the wire, which he twisted. The wire tightened. More twist. The wire snapped. He repeated that process at various places and, when next he pulled down hard, a patch of the wire came free, and he was then able to undo more of the wire and bend it aside.

Brydon's arm ached, burned from so much reaching up. Peter and Spider offered to take over.

Brydon glanced down. The mud was up to their feet. At the rate it was rising he'd never get through the roof in time. He clawed at it. The gypsum was solid. He kept trying.

Meanwhile Spider and Peter tore free several rafters, three-by-sixes, which they shoved through the openings in the huge steel beams. They laid the rafters across from beam to beam about three feet up, creating a platform. Everyone climbed up onto it. Now, only three feet of clearance to the roof. They had to crouch.

Which made it harder for Brydon. He couldn't get as much force into his digging. He slashed at the gypsum time and time again. Mere scratches were all that showed for his effort. It was impossible; it was their only chance. He kept at it. A small chunk came loose. A start. He slashed and clawed. Several more chunks fell and, finally, a large one.

He had broken through. About a six-inch hole.

Mud poured down, streamed down through the hole.

No doubt now.

There was mud above them. They were buried.

The buzzard named RAQUEL BABY lifted off at El Toro.

Within five minutes it was over the San Joaquin Hills, then the ocean, where it made a banking turn so sharp its frame strained and creaked.

On the starboard side of its fuselage was a special rig, a davitlike arrangement with loops of nylon line serving as a sling to carry the ten-foot section of thirty-six-inch polyethylene pipe.

Hackley brought the buzzard in close to the slide area.

Dodd searched for that ledgelike spot he'd fallen from the

day before, but the face of the slide had changed. The mud had slipped, run down, covered over the letter E that would have been a sure marker.

"Were we this high up yesterday?" Dodd asked.

"Just about," Hackley told him.

"I think we were a little lower."

Hackley backed the buzzard off and came in twenty feet down the slope. Still there was no visible hint of where the supermarket lay.

They made three passes back and forth across the face of the slide. It all appeared the same, except at one spot where there was a slight hump around a sort of bubble.

Could be, Dodd thought. Or it could be just a random air pocket. Taking a calculated chance was better than doing nothing, he decided.

Hackley maneuvered the buzzard closer, hovered it over that spot.

The way the rig was built, the forward lines could be released first and the pipe lowered into a vertical position. Dodd's plan was to jam the pipe down through the roof of the supermarket—*if* he could locate it. If necessary he'd use the downward force of the helicopter to drive the pipe through the roof. Then he'd climb down through the pipe and in. Hackley had insisted he tie a safety line around his waist like a mountain climber.

Dodd released the pipe.

It swung into a vertical position and was lowered to that bubbling hump in the mud. The pipe penetrated quickly under its own weight, nearly eight hundred pounds. Dodd watched it disappearing. Half of it, six feet, seven feet of it. Before he could react the entire pipe had sunk from sight.

"Pull up!" Dodd shouted.

Hackley throttled the buzzard. The nylon lines connected to the pipe snapped straight with strain.

It seemed the pipe should slip out easily, but it was as

though something beneath the mud had a powerful locking hold on it, refused to let go.

Hackley gave the buzzard more throttle.

Surely the lines would break or the rigging would tear loose from the fuselage. How good a welding job had Poss and Ruzkowski done?

More throttle, more strain.

If they lost the pipe they were through.

Dodd saw the blue circumference of it emerge. First just the mouth of it. He held his breath while the pipe was extracted slowly, foot by foot. Then, when most of it was out, the rest came all at once, like a plug pulled, and the buzzard recoiled suddenly from its own power, whipped upward.

Hackley fought to compensate for that and finally got the buzzard under control. He banked it wide out over the ocean. The pipe was dangling from it.

"Same altitude?"

"Yes," Dodd told him.

Hackley brought the buzzard in for another attempt.

Dodd again studied the slide. He saw a jutting, like a corner, almost the same as the one yesterday. It seemed right. He pointed it out to Hackley, who proceeded to put the buzzard directly above it.

And then Dodd's eyes caught upon something else, about twenty feet farther to the right and up a ways.

An indentation in the mud, not very large, a sort of cleft, as though something underneath was sucking at it.

Something underneath?

It was unlike anything else on the slope.

He decided on it.

Hackley adjusted.

The pipe, in a vertical position, was lowered precisely on target—the indentation. The pipe penetrated quickly, and, as Dodd watched it sinking, he had a second second thought. Maybe he'd chosen wrong again, before it was too late they should pull up and try elsewhere. . . . He was about to tell Hackley to do just that when the pipe, about six feet of it already under, stopped.

It remained straight up.

It must have settled on something.

Down inside, the seven survivors crouched. The mud poured in through the hole in the roof. It was like being in the bottom part of an hourglass with time running out. What little space remained was filling fast. The mud was nearly up to the platform. Not enough air. They breathed in rapid gasps, their hearts pounding. The more they breathed, the less they could breathe.

Lois closed her eyes.

Marsha hugged herself.

Spider hung his head and gritted.

Amy and Peter stared at each other.

Gloria pressed against Brydon, who felt done, finally, with nothing more to give.

But he was the first to notice the sudden decrease in the flow of mud from above. He didn't mention it because he didn't believe it and there was no use wasting breath. But he saw the flow was definitely less, reduced to a dribble.

And then directly below the hole, on the surface of the mud, appeared a circle of light.

Brydon crawled over to the hole, looked up.

He saw outside.

Air was pouring in.

He and the others tore at the gypsum, made the hole larger.

Peter climbed through first, through the hole and into the pipe. Made his way up the pipe in a crouched, horizontal position, keeping pressure with his shoulders and feet against the inside surface. He inched his way upward to the mouth of the pipe.

He was a complete surprise to Hackley and to Dodd, who

was standing on the landing skids about to lower himself into the pipe. It was as though a dead man had risen from the earth. Appropriate that he should be naked.

Dodd threw Peter a nylon rope ladder, which he fed down the opening. Peter helped Amy out.

Then the others came. Up, out and into the belly of the buzzard.

Lois Stevens. She was crying.

Marsha Hilbert hesitated, blinked, touched her hair, as though striking a pose.

Gloria Rand kept looking back for Brydon.

Spider had difficulty because his clothes were so heavily caked with mud. Odd the way his trousers were bound at the bottoms, and bulging. Of course, he wasn't aware the man giving him a hand was a police captain.

Brydon was last. He was standing knee deep in mud when he stepped onto the ladder to go up the pipe.

Outside, the rain had stopped.

The clouds were disbanding.

With all aboard, the buzzard lifted itself away, a joyous, side-slipping swoop over the beach.

Brydon glanced down.

It was Sunday morning.

Two girls in bikinis already lay stretched out on bright towels, starting to bake once again in the good California sunshine.